Without Faith:
Book Two of the
Sienna St. James Series

Without Faith:
Book Two of the
Sienna St. James Series

Leslie J. Sherrod

URBAN CHRISTIAN

www.urbanchristianonline.com

Urban Books, LLC
97 N18th Street
Wyandanch, NY 11798

Without Faith: Book Two of the Sienna St. James
Series Copyright © 2013 Leslie J. Sherrod

ISBN 13: 978-1-60162-770-4
ISBN 10: 1-60162-770-X

First Printing October 2013
Printed in the United States of America

10 9 8 7 6 5 4 3 2 1

Distributed by Kensington Corp.
Submit Wholesale Orders to:
Kensington Publishing Corp.
C/O Penguin Group (USA) Inc.
Attention: Order Processing
405 Murray Hill Parkway
East Rutherford, NJ 07073-2316
Phone: 1-800-526-0275
Fax: 1-800-227-9604

Without Faith:
Book Two of the
Sienna St. James Series

Leslie J. Sherrod

Fear doesn't stand a chance against me . . .
My faith can move mountains.

Every word of God is pure: He is a shield unto them that put their trust in Him.
—Proverbs 30:5

Acknowledgments

When I wrote poems in high school and short stories during college, I never imagined that I would complete an entire novel one day. With the release of this one, the second in the Sienna St. James series, I will officially have four completed novels under my belt . . . and counting. I am eternally grateful to God for allowing me to live out one of my life's dreams. Thank you, Jesus, for the opportunity to serve you in this way! I do not take the opportunity to share these stories with readers lightly, and I am thankful for the many people who have supported me with this continuing goal.

Special thanks to my husband, Brian, who never stops encouraging me to write, and who backs up his words with his artwork. Special thanks, also, to my parents J. Adrian and Maxine Datcher, who encouraged me to seek Christ at an early age and gave me the foundation I needed to grow and walk in His calling. My children give me inspiration every day and all of my extended family members give me strength. I thank God for each of you!

Thank you, Carla Jackson, for being a major cheerleader as I lit the midnight oil and pushed myself to write while balancing a full-time job, family life, and more things than my memory can hold. Samara Stone: you have been a godsend and a true encourager. Thank you for seeing how writing and social work intersect for me and for giving me new ideas and clearer vision

Acknowledgments

to manage both. Thank you Yolonda Tonette Sanders, MaRita Teague, Mata Elliott, and Tiffany L. Warren for your support, prayers, and feedback. Big shout out to Ms. Maxine Bigby Cunningham; you are a true and fearless testament to "power walking." Angela Graham and Charese Robinson, I am blessed by your friendships. My Rhode Island cousin, Debbie, you'll never know how timely your "texts of encouragement" are. My beautiful aunts, all of you, are also special blessings; my uncles, too.

I am grateful for the staff of my publisher, Urban Christian, for all you do. Thank you, Joylynn Jossel-Ross for your continued encouragement. You are a joy to work with and your passion and pursuit of excellence in Christian fiction ministry is obvious. Special thanks to my agent, Sha-Shana Crichton. I sincerely appreciate all you do.

I get some of the biggest support from my church family, The Upper Room Worship Center. Thank you for your encouragement, your prayers, and checking to make sure that I am meeting my deadlines. Big thanks also to my extended church family at Mt. Pleasant Ministries for your support over the years. Sis. Tonyai Cato, thank you for giving me opportunities to write.

Finally, and most importantly, I thank you—yes, YOU—for picking up this book, flipping through the pages, and deciding to settle down and join Sienna in her latest adventure. I am forever grateful for the readers, book clubs, book promoters (including Tyora Moody of Tywebbin Creations and Lashaunda Hoffman of SORMAG), and all who have in some way supported me, encouraged me, or taught me something new. Thanks, y'all!

Chapter 1

"We've had five marriages and three children between the two of us. That's why, this time, we need to make it work."

The woman in the tailored black suit and high heels spoke as the man sitting beside her nodded. He wore a tweed brown sports coat paired with dark blue jeans, and a cologne that would intoxicate any living, breathing woman from ages eighteen to eighty-one.

The two held hands.

What were their names again? I stole a peek at the notepad in my lap.

Jenellis Walker and Brayden Moore.

"So, you want to make this work," I echoed, crossing my legs and putting on my most sincere I-really-care-and-I-am-here-to-help-you look despite the fact that the clock was ticking closer to 1:00 p.m. Roman's flight left in three hours.

Clinical social work 101.

Empathy. Even when it was inconvenient.

The man, Brayden, who'd been quiet the entire walk from the waiting area to the loveseat sitting in front of me, exhaled and settled back into his seat. With a square-shaped head, slight shadow of a beard, and a knotty afro that on another man would have looked sloppy, but on him looked wildly refined, he was the perfect blend of cocoa-flavored fine and sexy. Jenellis, for her part, was all curves, tasteful bling, and high-quality weave.

Even without the obvious money between them, they still would have looked like a beautiful power couple on the cover of an *Ebony* or *Jet* magazine.

"Thank you, uh, Ms. St. James." Brayden glanced for the third time at the framed diploma that hung over my plush armchair. "Thank you for signing up to save us."

I didn't know that I'd signed up to save anything, but as I was the one with the notepad, the degree, and the business cards that said I was a psychotherapist. I guess I, at the moment, was the chosen one.

"What's going on?" I cleared my throat, trying my best to look like I knew what I was doing. Jenellis wore what looked like a huge quadruple-carat rock on her left ring finger. With all that money going on in that loveseat, I could not help but wonder if they should be the ones saving me.

The two looked at each other and I knew already from my brief foray into the world of therapy that a long story was about to follow.

My son had better be finished packing.

I tried not to let my eyes drift back to the mantel clock that sat next to a Tiffany lamp I found at a yard sale.

When I graduated with my master's in social work, I had not planned to become a therapist. I had specialized in child welfare and had done most of my work with foster children. However, after a girl named Dayonna Diamond had me driving around the city of Baltimore—shoot, the state of Maryland, it seemed—looking for a sister named Hope that nobody else said existed, I knew I'd had enough.

Apparently, so did my old supervisor, my life mentor, Ava Diggs. The day she announced her retirement following Dayonna's case was the day I came up with my present plan. Ava had wanted me to take the reins over from her, but I quickly directed them to my former officemate, the control-hungry diva Sheena Booth. I'd had enough of the system and the sorrows within it to not want to become the captain of a sinking ship.

I'd stayed as long as I could under Sheena's leadership, swallowing my pride to follow the girl child's directions; but I started working toward my private practice immediately. It had taken two years but The Whole Soul Center was now finally up and running, full time and fully on me.

Nobody had told me how difficult it would be to build up my own practice. As close as I was cutting it to my son's flight, I was even closer to bankruptcy.

I could not afford to turn away Jenellis and Brayden when they'd called asking for immediate help just under an hour ago. They had offered to come as cash customers—no insurance forms or protocol to worry with. And I figured I could spare an hour for them, especially if they turned out to be regulars.

I was having second thoughts.

The two still looked at each other, a silent conversation occurring between them.

"What brings you in today?" I pried again.

"We're getting married." Jenellis finally broke their silence.

That's it? I wanted to say. Plenty of people had been there, done that. I mean, even I had made a visit to the altar, uttering a "'til death do us part" promise that I wholly meant and wholly failed.

Actually, I had not failed. I just had not seen my husband in sixteen years, and was uncertain about whether death had done us part.

It's complicated.

The last time something RiChard St. James came up in my life, it almost cost my sanity and my son's safety.

I shut my eyes quickly to the searing pain that wanted to well up in me at the memory of the empty urn and the gaudy ring that sent me on a wild goose chase nearly two years ago. I'd put the pain aside since then, determined to show an absent man and a proud me that I could carry on my life without him.

Without any man.

"When's the big day?" I blinked, blocking out the host of emotions that wanted to break through me like a water dam. Plus, I was still waiting for why these people had me about to miss sending off my only begotten at the BWI Thurgood Marshall Airport.

"Our wedding is two weeks from now." Jenellis tried to smile. The way she looked, I could not help but wonder if we were talking about a wedding or a funeral.

"And we just got engaged two weeks ago." Brayden cleared his throat and wrapped his large hands tighter over Jenellis's delicate, manicured ones.

Why the big rush? I caught myself from saying it out loud. They had to be pushing their mid-forties, so I doubted that a hush-hush baby was the reason for their run to the altar.

As if reading my mind, Jenellis piped in, "We wanted our wedding reception to be at the La Chambre Rouge and that weekend was the only date they had available for the next eighteen months."

Brayden had more to add. "They had a last-minute cancellation and Jenellis and I offered the highest bid out of eight other couples."

"Oh, I see." I nodded like I even knew what the La Chambre Rouge was. I jotted a quick note on my pad to Google it later. Brayden seemed pleased that I was scribbling something down.

I was thinking of another question to ask to move the conversation forward when a loud ring interrupted me.

"I'm sorry," Brayden mumbled, pulling out a phone. He started to press a button but his finger froze in midair as he focused on the number flashing on the screen. He turned to Jenellis.

"It's her." His voice was slightly above a whisper.

"Ms. St. James, we're going to have to go." Jenellis never looked his way. "But we want to come back, if that is okay. Can we reschedule for later this week?"

"Friday," I said a little too eagerly. "I mean, I have time on Friday morning. Is ten a.m. okay?"

The couple did not seem to notice my relief at their leaving. They were already headed to the door.

"Yes, we'll see you then." Brayden barely looked at me as he rushed out the suite door, Jenellis right behind.

I stepped back into my office and peered from my second-floor window to the parking lot below. After one bad experience during my first full week at my center, I rarely left immediately after my clients.

There are some crazy folk out there and I don't need not nary one of them knowing the make or model of my car. But that's another story for another day.

It was a little after one now. I needed to get home. I held my breath as the handsome couple stood talking in the parking lot a few moments, then exhaled as Brayden finally turned to a large black Escalade and hopped in. Jenellis pointed her keys toward a red Lexus coupe and the headlights flashed.

I dialed my son Roman's cell phone as I gathered my coat, workbag, and purse, set the alarm, and locked the front door of my beloved office suite.

No surprises. He did not answer.

"I'm on my way," was the message I left on his voice mail as I opted for the steps instead of the elevator in the outdated three-story office building. Though I'd done my best to make my personal suite look impressive, I had no control over the grounds of the best space I could afford to lease in the nondescript building in Rosedale. The hallway carpet was gray and frayed in some spots, and the main lobby forever smelled like chlorine, although to my knowledge there were no swimming pools anywhere near the premises.

It was going to take a lot more than one cash-paying couple to make it in my new adventure, I considered as I reached for my car door.

"Ms. St. James." The voice from behind startled me.

"Oh." I jumped a little. Jenellis Walker stood eye to eye with me.

"I need you to do me a favor." The sultry quality of her voice reminded me of one of my great-aunt's old Billie Holiday records.

"A favor?" I was off balance and wanting to get home, but I had enough sense to know that siding up with one party is dangerous ground in couples therapy. "I'm sorry, Ms. Walker, but before you continue, I think we should wait to discuss whatever your concern is openly in our Friday session."

"You don't understand." She blinked with false lashes. "Brayden can't know about this."

Her eyes and tone were expressionless, but my resolve was unmistakable and firm. "I would prefer not to begin our work together with secrets and picking sides. It does not help with anything, especially if you are planning to join in marital union in less than a month."

"I understand your concerns, Ms. St. James, but I need you to hear mine."

I resisted the urge to check my watch. "What is it?" It wasn't the question I needed to ask, but I had to get home.

I saw a smile in Jenellis's eyes and we both knew that she had won our first battle. "Brayden will tell you more about why the two of us need your services when we come back on Friday, but I have my own personal reasons for seeking your assistance." She lowered her voice, and moved her head closer to mine. "I need you to fish through Brayden's past."

"Excuse me?"

"I need to know more about him, not his childhood or family or any of that psychobabble stuff. I just want to know about his past relationships. Romantic relationships, marriages, and otherwise."

"Um, for some reason, I got the impression that the two of you had already talked about your former loves and disclosed whatever needed to come out onto the table." I felt totally off script.

"Yes, yes." Now she was the one rushing. "I know about his three ex-wives and most of his girlfriends, but I'm not looking for names and dates. I only want to know one thing about him."

In spite of myself, I raised an eyebrow. "Are you questioning his fidelity?"

Jenellis sighed and rolled her eyes impatiently. "No, no. I mean, let me correct myself. I couldn't care less about his fidelity. I'm the last person who should be questioning the faithfulness of anyone." She stared at me so unabashedly, I felt shame for her.

"What I need to find out, Ms. St. James," she said, her voice lowered again, "is simply this: whether Brayden was abusive to any women in his prior relationships. I have a high tolerance for a lot of things. Some issues that other women fall apart over are but small matters of foolishness to me. But abuse of any nature I do not tolerate."

"You've had experience with this." I had meant to make my words more of a question than a statement, but Jenellis smiled wickedly at my observation.

"Let's just say that my first husband was not a kind man, but I am stronger because of it."

I considered her declaration for a moment as I reached again for my car door. "Ms. Walker, I am a therapist, not a private detective. Now I can help facilitate an open dialogue between the two of you where you can explore some of these concerns. But if you are wanting to get more detailed information about his past behavior with other women, without his knowledge, then I am not the right professional. Indeed, I'm not sure that I even feel comfortable providing services to the two of you with such a lopsided beginning."

Jenellis stared at me a few moments, her expression unreadable again. "Okay," she finally breathed out, "you win. We'll go about things your way. Explore. Talk it out. But I do know that the law states that if you as a therapist find out that someone is dangerous you are required to inform the targeted party."

"That's only if there is a stated or implied homicidal threat."

"Yes, that's right." Jenellis nodded her head and turned away.

I guess that meant good-bye. At the moment I did not care. I was supposed to be driving my son to the airport in twenty minutes. As I was about to sit down in the driver's seat, I realized that I could not shake a question that was nagging me.

"Ms. Walker," I called after her. She turned around and faced me again. "Whatever happened to your first husband? Did he face consequences for whatever he did to you?"

She paused, looking over to a distant memory to the left of me. Then she looked me right in the eyes. "Ms. St. James, my first husband is dead. Of natural causes," she quickly added.

"Oh," was all I could say as I finally found my driver's seat. Jenellis marched over to her Lexus, got in, shut the door, and sat there with the engine idling.

My engine was on and I was off.

Lord, I could not help but wonder as I turned off the small lot, *what have I gotten myself pulled into with this couple?*

A familiar feeling, and not a pleasant one, sunk slowly into my stomach.

Dread.

Chapter 2

"Please tell me you are all ready to go." My heart sank the moment I stepped into the foyer of my home and saw Roman's bare foot propped up onto my new coffee table, a noisy video game wrapped in his hands, and a suspiciously small—and only half-filled—duffel bag sitting on the floor next to his other bare foot.

"Huh?" He didn't even bother to look up from whatever game he was playing.

"Huh? Is that your way of saying hello now?" I shook my head, wanting to kick myself for believing that Roman was capable of packing appropriately for a week-and-a-half trip across the country. He'd turned sixteen earlier in the month, and although he was maintaining a B+ average in trigonometry and working steadfastly at his part-time job at a store in White Marsh Mall, I swear I felt like I was still dealing with a six-year-old sometimes.

"Roman." I plucked the video console from his hands. "We have to leave for the airport in no more than ten minutes. Where is your luggage?"

"Officer Sanderson has it," he mumbled as he stretched and stood. Potato chip crumbs fell from his lap.

"Leon has your bags?" I resisted the urge to pat my hair to make sure it was in place as I scanned my living and dining rooms. I kept a full length mirror against the far wall, but I knew that the image in it would not be comforting.

I had not gotten a relaxer in a couple of months as I was considering wearing my hair all-natural and chemical free, but now my hair looked like something between a shoulder-length bob and a chia plant as I struggled to imitate the hair care videos I'd found online. My eyebrows needed to be arched, and I'd yet to start my New Year's resolution to lose the extra pounds I'd picked up since I'd turned thirty what felt like many years ago.

It was March. So much for my New Year "new me" quest.

I had my eyes, though. Almond-shaped and captivating and emphasized with extra coats of eye liner and mascara, I knew that my eyes were the defining feature of my face and capable of making all my other physical flaws forgivable. At least that is what Leon hinted to me at times.

"Is . . . Leon here?" I managed to breathe out, hoping that my son did not hear my heart's sudden hard pounding.

"You didn't get my message? Oh, I forgot to leave it." Roman yawned. "Officer Sanderson called about an hour ago and I asked him if he could take me since you hadn't come home from work yet."

I didn't know what bothered me more: the fact that my son really had thought I wouldn't be there for him or that he had become so dependent on Leon lately.

I remembered when Roman could not stand the idea of the good-hearted officer sitting at my mother's Sunday dinner table with us.

I remembered when I could not stand the idea of Leon period.

A lot had changed over the past couple of years. But I'd been holding my ground, and Leon respected that.

"Roman, I was coming." I reached up to wrap my arms around his now-towering frame. "You know I would not let you go all the way to Arizona without a proper sendoff."

"Ma, it was not like that. I know you're working hard. I was trying to help you so you wouldn't have to worry about me. I'm being responsible." He tried to shrug off my hug, but it was a weak attempt. He played it cool enough to let me know he didn't *need* my hug, but he still *wanted* one.

At the end of the day, my son would always be my baby.

Responsible. The word echoed in me and I could not help but feel pride at who he was growing to be, video games, potato chips, bare feet, and all.

"Your luggage," I remembered. "And where's Leon?"

"He went to pick up Skee-Gee and Tridell. They were catching the bus here and Officer Sanderson thought it would be better time-wise to pick them up from the bus stop. He should be back here any second."

"And you didn't go with him to pick them up?"

"I had to say bye to you first, Ma."

I wanted to smile at his words, but something else was nagging me. "Tridell is going on this mission trip?" My eyebrow rose. I meant no harm, but Tridell Jenkins was not someone I would think would volunteer his spring break for such a work-intensive cause.

When Randy Howard, the youth minister at our church, first brought up the idea of the teens and young adults spending spring break volunteering on a Native American reservation near Flagstaff, Arizona, my son was the first to raise his hand in support.

I'd like to think that Roman had gotten his caring heart and wanderlust from me and his father. RiChard St. James had spent Roman's entire life trotting the globe, trying to rectify wrongs and social injustices in his own renegade way.

I loved and hated him for it.

I'd initially dropped out of college to follow RiChard, but the journey got too confusing. It took me almost a decade to get back on a tolerable path.

My nephew Skee-Gee was being forced to go on the trip to Arizona by his mother, my little sister, Yvette, who, before the church had raised enough money to cover all the expenses, was ready to sign over her entire state check for him to be gone for a week. Maybe forced was too strong a word. The mentoring Officer Sanderson had been providing for both Roman and Skee-Gee over the past two years seemed to be having a small, subtle effect on my nephew. I'd actually gotten a birthday card from him in January.

But Tridell Jenkins was another story. The nineteen-year-old nephew of our pastor was the type of young man who kept his fingernails squared and clean, his wardrobe seasonally coordinated and his eyeglasses designer. He seemed too pretty to want to roll up his sleeves and sweat in the desert to help renovate houses on the reservation.

"He said it would look good on his resume," Roman answered.

"Mmmm." I shrugged. "Okay, that makes sense."

I started to ask him another question but a loud knock at the door made me forget what else I wanted to know.

"Sienna."

Wildflowers blowing in a spring breeze. That's what my heart felt like when I opened the door and saw Leon Sanderson standing there in full uniform. The way he said my name . . . Jesus, have mercy.

His eyes lingered on mine for a second before he stepped into the foyer and gave his full attention to my son. "So you are bringing that bag, too, young soldier?" he quizzed at the sight of Roman stuffing his video game into the small duffel bag that had been sitting next to the sofa.

"It's my carry-on," Roman mumbled as he zipped it up loudly.

Leon shook his head and looked back at me. "Your son has enough luggage to clothe a small village. The baggage fees alone are going to eat up all the spending money he's been saving up from that little part-time job he has. Skee-Gee and Tridell could barely fit in the car."

"Gotta look good for the Native American ladies." Roman patted one of his biceps. In addition to mentoring, Leon had Roman and Skee-Gee on a health and fitness kick. The baby fat that had lined my son's body for years had given way to a solid, sculpted frame thanks to his regular workouts on Leon's equipment.

It was scary watching my son grow up.

He looked more and more like his father.

"Well, I guess we're ready to go." I grabbed my purse and keys. Leon and Roman looked at each other, then looked at me.

"Sienna, honestly, with the amount of luggage from these three young men—especially your son—there's not enough room in the car for you to come. I know this is a hard moment for you, but you might need to get your good-byes in right now."

"Ma, I'm in good hands," Roman quickly added before my face completely collapsed. This was not how I imagined this trip would begin.

"But this is Roman's first time going on an airplane," I lied, ignoring the guilt and searing pain that came with the memory of flying across the country with him as a newborn, chasing down his father, my husband, in Southern California.

The last time either one of us saw him face-to-face.

"Ma, I'm a big boy. I can handle it." A dark glimmer, which I imagined matched my own, washed over his face. I guess I was embarrassing him.

"Okay, big boy. Be good out there. I love you." I reached to hug him, and he kissed my forehead.

That was another thing about him being sixteen. He'd grown a full head taller than me.

"Love you too, Ma," he threw back at me as he bounded down the steps after Leon.

I watched as the two traded jokes and barbs all the way to Leon's Altima, mostly about how much stuff Roman was bringing.

"Bye, Aunt See." Skee-Gee rolled down a back window and yelled from it. I could see Tridell Jenkins sitting next to him, checking the waves in his hair in a small hand-held mirror. He glanced over at me and offered a single nod.

As the engine roared to life, foot-stomping, body-swaying, spirit-moving music blared from Leon's stereo, the latest from Tye Tribbett. Leon looked back at me from his seat at the wheel and gave me a reassuring wink. I tried to smile back, but was unprepared for the wellspring of emotions that were running through me. I missed my son already. He'd never been gone this long from me.

Roman finished adjusting some bags in the trunk and then walked to the passenger side door. Just before he disappeared into the luggage-stuffed interior, he looked back up at me.

"Bye, Ma," he mouthed.

And then they were gone.

Chapter 3

I could not remember the last time I'd had an afternoon to myself at home. I had been working so hard to stay afloat that the idea of a few hours of free time felt foreign to me. Sitting in the family room of the new townhome I'd bought right after Ava announced her retirement nearly two years ago, I realized that I'd had rare moments to actually enjoy the home that had been the symbol of my disconnection from all things RiChard St. James.

I lived in my small rancher in Woodlawn for nearly fourteen years, wishing, waiting, hoping, praying for my husband to call, to mail a letter, something, anything. And he sent just enough to keep me imprisoned in that rancher, afraid to move, afraid to leave, afraid of missing his sporadic communication. I'd told myself for years that it was for Roman's benefit, but I knew better now.

I unlocked the front door of my new home in Rosedale—on the other side of town—exactly two months after dealing with Dayonna Diamond and my search for Hope. When I unlocked that door that first time it was as if I was unlocking my own prison cell. The bars rolled back. The chains fell off.

I was free.

At least that's what I'd felt like.

And I did not want to get entangled again as I sorted through the meanings of my newfound independence.

Leon understood. Though he made it clear that he would wait for me to find the answers I needed about RiChard, I knew he would be waiting for a while.

I did not want any more answers about the man who'd abandoned me to go off and save the world.

Wanting answers made me feel imprisoned again.

And what purpose would the answers serve anyway?

I did not like this train of thought so I put a quick end to it. "I'm going to enjoy the rest of my day," I decided out loud.

My new home had every upgrade imaginable: granite countertops; stainless steel appliances; garden bath; finished rec room. I'd even splurged and had a deck built that faced the nature preserve the new townhome community bordered.

Of course the price tag that came with such amenities meant that I worked all hours of the day and evening (and most weekends) to make the ends meet. Did I say meet? It was more like the ends were coming in the same vicinity of each other.

As I ran water into my whirlpool tub and poured in a generous dose of seaside-scented bath beads, I tried to block out the nagging idea of calling in some clients for impromptu sessions back at the office. Lord knows I could use every bit of those dollars.

But I also needed time to relax.

So that's what I did for the next four hours. I caught up on a novel while resting on the terry-covered bath pillow in my tub. I found the foot spa Roman had given me for Christmas, used it for twenty whole minutes and then gave myself a bright pink pedicure. I fixed myself some coconut shrimp and my mother's creamed cornbread, lit a candle, poured some sparkling cider, and listened to Caribbean music on a local radio station as I dined at a table set with my real dishes. I even indulged myself with two leftover slices of fudge brownies that Leon had baked for Sunday dinner at my mom's that week.

But as the music turned into political talk show debates and the dishes in my sink began to pile up, I suddenly decided that I was tired of relaxing and I only wanted to get in my bed.

It was six-thirty, three hours after Roman's flight had taken off. There had been no phone calls from either him or Leon.

I clicked on the television to drown out the thoughts of worry that were threatening my sense of peace as I collapsed into my bed. I did not want to listen to the evening news, and the comedy reruns sounded like meaningless banter to me. So I turned on a local cable network just in time to catch an episode of a regional dating game show.

"She looks a hot mess." I shook my head at the twenty-something woman with the fake everything grinning at the camera. She wore a dress that even she was trying to pull down to her thighs or up to her cleavage, whichever way you looked at it.

Yes, it was that short and nasty.

"I'm looking for a brother who can treat me with class before I give him some—"

I clicked the mute button before she finished her sentence. I already knew where this girl, this show, this world was going.

Nothing was sacred anymore. Not even self-respect.

I was about to click the whole thing off when something caught my eye—or rather someone. The camera had swept the panel of three bachelors and the one at the far end looked vaguely familiar.

"Huh?" I moved closer to the television and blasted the volume. "Go back to the last one."

As if the camera had heard me, the screen zoomed to the man on the end. He was introducing himself.

"My name is Kwan and I am a business owner from Laurel. I've got the triple threat: the bucks, the brain, and the bang, baby. Pick me and you won't know what hit you."

The line was corny and the name didn't match, but that was Brayden Moore for sure, Jenellis Walker's fiancé. The two had been sitting in my office only hours ago so I had no doubt about my memories of his fine face.

"What is he doing on *The Soul Mate Show* if he's getting married in two weeks?" Maybe this was a rerun of an old episode, I considered. Or maybe the show had been taped before Jenellis and Brayden had gotten engaged two weeks ago. *But they still would have been in some type of relationship before then,* I assumed. I pressed the menu button on my remote to bring background information about the show onto the television screen.

It was taped five days ago.

I turned the volume up as the plastic-filled contestant—she called herself "Silver"—had narrowed down the panel to Brayden/Kwan and another man who had an egg-shaped head and beady eyes, but boasted that he played minor league baseball.

"I'm a home run, lady!" he said after almost every sentence.

"My last question is this," Silver smacked into the microphone. "If you were a lollipop, what flavor would you be and why?"

What the heck kind of question was that? I frowned. And what answer would be the right one to help choose a potential soul mate?

"I would be grape because that's the flavor of the energy drink I'm about to be a sponsor of for five thousand dollars." The baseball player's beady eyes glistened as Silver giggled.

"Oooooh. And you, Kwan?" She turned toward him.

"Chocolate." His voice was deep and smooth. His diction spoke to a quality education. His swagger hinted at the streets.

I had not noticed any of this when he and Jenellis were in my office.

"Oooooh." Silver giggled again. "And may I ask why chocolate?"

For an answer, Brayden/Kwan slowly licked his lips and the audience clapped and cheered their approval.

I didn't get it. Any of it. Why would an engaged man scheduled to be married in a matter of weeks appear on a television dating show, flirting and carrying on like that?

I couldn't care less about his fidelity. I'm the last person who should be questioning the faithfulness of anyone. The words of Jenellis came to mind. I could still hear in my mind what she said, but really, what woman about to go down the aisle would truly be okay with the spectacle I was witnessing on television? *I have a high tolerance for a lot of things. Some issues that other women fall apart over are but small matters of foolishness to me.* Maybe Jenellis really would not care. At any rate, was it my responsibility to bring this up in our next session? She wanted to know more about him, but not about his faithfulness. She made it pretty clear that she only wanted to find out if he had a propensity toward violence.

"It's a hard decision." Silver was fluttering her fake eyelashes, her lips pulled down in an over-the-top pout. "But I think I know who I'm going with. Kwan, with your triple threat, you are my *soul mate.*"

I watched in disbelief as the man I knew as Brayden strutted over to Silver, pulled her deep into his arms, and planted a heavy kiss on her plumped lips.

"Bang," he whispered into the mic and the audience roared their approval again.

I sat there stunned and disgusted. And confused.

I was about to switch off the television but the host of the show, a man who was the color of tar and who had a face that somehow reminded me of a turtle, was announcing the grand prize for Silver and "Kwan."

"You lucky *soul mates,* prepare yourselves for the ultimate dream date fantasy. Silver and Kwan, you are going to be wined and dined in over-the-top luxury at the one and only La Chambre Rouge."

As a quick photo montage of fancy gardens and candlelit dinner scenes blurred across the screen, I tried to remember why that name sounded so familiar.

"La Chambre Rouge," I repeated the name. Then it came to me.

"We wanted our wedding reception to be at the La Chambre Rouge and that weekend was the only date they had available for the next eighteen months."

I'd scribbled the name of the venue down on my notepad during my brief session with Jenellis and Brayden, with the intention of looking it up later.

My laptop was stashed away in my workbag, which was all the way downstairs. Even if I got it out and researched this place, what difference would it make? I had no idea how I was going to broach this issue with the couple—or even if I should. If Jenellis really meant what she had said, that she did not care about Brayden's faithfulness, was it my place to be concerned about him smooching all over another woman on a televised dating show?

But what was the deal with the La Chambre Rouge connection? From what I'd heard today, Brayden/ Kwan—whoever he was—had both a fantasy date and wedding reception with two different women lined up there in the coming weeks.

But it wasn't my business, and I did not have to deal with the two of them until Friday. I turned off the television and decided to call it an early night.

I was about to attempt to go to sleep when the sweetest sound filled my room. My cell phone chirped, letting me know my baby boy had texted me.

I'm here, Ma, unpacked and settled. No worries.
Love ya.

Sitting on the edge of my bed, closing my eyes, I imagined Roman at his campground, undoubtedly gulping down the bag of chips he didn't know I knew he snuck into his carry-on. I let that image help calm my nerves and bring sense back to me after watching the nonsense that had blared on my TV.

I fell asleep, but even in my dreams, I could not shake the feeling that I'd missed something important, something terribly wrong.

Chapter 4

"Wake up, Sienna." His beautiful voice whispered in my ear.

I reached over to turn off my alarm, but then realized that the buzzing had been my cell phone, which I had somehow managed to get to my ear.

I was not dreaming, nor was I sleeping. Leon was on the phone and I'd answered it.

"Wake up, Sienna," he said again.

"Oh." I sat up and turned the volume up so I could hear him more clearly. "I'm sorry, Leon. I was just waking up and thought the phone was my alarm clock."

"No, I should be the one apologizing, Sienna. I know I'm calling early, but I wanted to catch you before you got too far into your day."

"Well, you've caught me." That statement had meanings on many different levels. I hated talking to people when I was half asleep. I always seemed to find a way to embarrass myself.

Leon chuckled. "Look, are you free tonight? I'm not asking for a date or anything like that. I know where you stand. I . . . I just need to talk to you and the sooner the better."

He'd started his request with a chuckle, but there was an edge to his tone that I could not decipher.

"What time? Where?" I had finally gotten out of the bed and was headed to my closet. My first client was at seven-thirty—a long-time client who met me before going to her job every Thursday morning. I was at the point in my practice of accommodating any client's schedule.

"Uh, I was thinking we could go to the Harbor's Edge Inn. I could pick you up at six?"

"Oh, you don't have to get me. I can meet you there and spare you the extra drive to Rosedale."

There was a long pause.

"Okay, Sienna." He sighed. "I'll see you then." He hung up with no other words.

"Weird." I clicked the phone off and began going about the business of my day, getting dressed, skipping breakfast, starting with my clients. It was my usual Thursday routine, but nothing felt normal about it. And not just because my son wasn't there and Leon sounded, well, different. Something was agitating me but I could not put my finger on it.

I checked the tropical island–themed calendar that hung next to my refrigerator. No, it wasn't PMS. I had about another good week before I could start blaming my hormones for my "off" moods.

The unease followed me through my morning appointments and only grew as the day wore on me. It took all I had to listen through my seven-thirty's sobs over not finding the right dress for her upcoming class reunion; my eight-thirty's fears of "finding herself" only to find out she was completely like her mother; and my nine-thirty's obsession with pasta that was ending his marriage. When my ten-thirty did not show up and my eleven-thirty abruptly cancelled, I knew I needed to do something to settle myself before I saw another client or we would be crying together, and I wouldn't even be able to explain why.

I got in my car and headed to the only place I knew to go.

***

She was out tending the colorful buds that framed her near–century old Cape Cod in East Towson when I pulled up in front of her home. Even before I got out of my car, I could already see the smile on her face as her bare hands pressed gently on the rich mulch around her Easter lilies, hyacinths, and irises.

As a revered social worker and non-profit director, Ava Diggs had kept a stern face, letting all know that beneath those warm eyes was a no-nonsense professional who would fight to the end for what was right for her charges. Now, as a retiree and a full-time gardener, the only fight on her face was whether her smile could outdo the glory of the flowers she nurtured.

"My Sienna is here before lunch. Something must be up," she whispered to the colorful blossoms as she pulled herself up to a stand.

I swear those flowers whispered their secrets back to her the way they bobbed up and down in the almost-there breeze.

"Hi, Ava." I grinned, knowing she would see right through the plastered smile on my face but would play along until I was ready to voice what I was unsure of myself. "I should have called to tell you I was coming over for lunch."

"Oh, honey, you know you are always welcome, breakfast, lunch, dinner, or midnight snack."

We were stepping into the dark hardwood foyer of her meticulous home. Although it was only mid-March and only in the mid-forties, a floor fan oscillated in the nearby sitting room, adding a soothing hum to the already calming interior as we headed to her kitchen.

"I just put a spinach and mushroom frittata in the oven. Should be ready now, if you want some. Have a seat." She pointed to a white-washed wooden chair.

Ava had one of those kitchens that looked like it had been transplanted out of a storybook, a perfect blend of cottage and modern. I envied the charm and comfort that she'd flawlessly pulled off with no help from any designer.

She served the frittata with a fresh fruit salad, a testament to her new eating habits and lifestyle changes. In the two years since her retirement, she'd lost over fifty pounds and counting. When I didn't show up unannounced for lunch, we'd plan times to walk around Lake Montebello, chatting and laughing the entire time.

"Are these real eggs?" I did my best not to frown as I chewed on the rubbery substance.

Ava chuckled. "It's some kind of egg substitute I found on a Web site and had delivered to me yesterday."

"After years of avoiding all things digital, you've finally gotten online." I did not hide the pain on my face as I swallowed. "But I think you need another lesson on Internet safety. Be careful what you click on."

We both let out a generous laugh as even Ava pushed her plate aside. Then she put her elbows on the table and rested her chin on her knuckles.

"What's going on, Sienna?"

I closed my eyes, shrugged my shoulders, opened my eyes again. "I don't know. I can't put my finger on it. Roman's gone—which is fine; my practice is struggling; Leon . . ."

"Still trying to find your place in the world, huh?" Ava shook her head.

"What do you mean?"

"Sienna, for as long as I've known you, seems like you've always been looking for something, searching for something, waiting for something to finally validate you. When you bought your new home and started your practice, though I knew you would face challenges, I thought you'd finally begin to feel settled in your life. But the bigger the accomplishments you achieve, the more you seem to grow restless. Now, I'm not sure if your move to Rosedale was to get settled or to get away from something—or someone." She raised an eyebrow. "You moved to the complete opposite side of town from the one man I've ever known you to have half an interest in. And I find it very interesting that that this man, Leon, made it to your shortlist of what's currently bothering you right now."

Ava knew nothing about RiChard St. James. Indeed, she'd never, not once, quizzed me about Roman's father. It was almost as if she believed that my only child had magically appeared to me one day, brought by a stork or a bird or a bee. No man involved.

"You think I'm feeling out of sorts because of Leon?"

Now Ava was the one shrugging. "Well, the only male who's been a part of your life hasn't even been gone for twenty-four hours, and you're already feeling lost. I know that you are eager to see your son grow, so I don't think you missing Roman is what's getting to you. I think that without him here, however, you're subconsciously aware that you are missing something out of your life. And that missing piece is something that even your job can't fill."

"So long story short, you think I need a man." I playfully rolled my eyes at her. "I would expect this conversation from my mother. Not you. Anyway, I probably need to head back to my office. My one o'clock should actually show up." I could not believe that I no longer felt like talking to Ava. I did not like the road she'd taken with me. Didn't like where it could lead.

"Here, honey. Take the rest of this fruit salad with you. I'd feel bad if you came all the way here for lunch and left hungry." She chuckled again at the one bite I'd taken of the frittata.

If I had an appetite, I certainly did not feel it. And I certainly was not going to tell Ava that my stomach felt too agitated to eat. I took the plastic container of fresh pineapples, cantaloupe, apple slices, and grapes she wrapped up and passed to me and then I headed back to my car.

I needed to stop running over here every time I did not feel right. At some point I needed to act like a grown woman and not a lost cause. Ava was my mentor, my friend.

Not my therapist.

I was turning onto a ramp to get back on 695 toward Rosedale when a bright red Lexus that had been trailing behind me for a while suddenly zoomed past me, cutting me off. I had to swerve to avoid a collision.

"Goodness gracious, what was that about?" I watched as the shiny red coupe sped away and disappeared into the long trail of speeding cars ahead of me.

Jenellis Walker had left my office in a car like that yesterday, I remembered. *Was she following me?* It was a fleeting thought, but one that made me feel silly. Maybe Ava was right. Maybe I did need a man.

I seemed to be going off the deep end left to my own devices.

Chapter 5

They were waiting for me in the parking lot when I pulled back up to my office building. I had just cut off my engine when I noticed the black Escalade parked a couple rows ahead of me. As soon as I got out of my car, there was no mistaking the handsome duo walking toward me.

Jenellis and Brayden.

There was no sign of a red Lexus anywhere. I felt silly for even thinking moments earlier that I was being followed.

Why would that be happening anyway?

"Ms. St. James," Brayden's bass voice sounded before they had even reached me. Despite their casual walk toward me, I could not help but pick up a sense of urgency oozing from them.

But then again, my instincts and judgment seemed to be failing me lately.

"I know you weren't expecting to see us again until tomorrow morning, but we really need to talk to you. Right now."

"It's important," Jenellis piped in.

Brayden/Kwan.

I remembered the spectacle I had seen on television last night and wondered if Jenellis had seen—or heard about it—too.

Maybe that's why they were here.

I wondered if I really wanted to get involved in their foolishness. I checked my watch. It was a little after twelve-thirty and I knew my one o'clock was a faithful attendee. "I really don't have much time right now. Another client is coming, so—"

Brayden reached into an interior pocket in his coat and pulled out a wad of crisp twenties, tens, and what seemed to be all other dollar denominations put out by the U.S. Mint. "We will pay you double your rate, in cash, three sessions up front." Jenellis eyed the money with the same intensity that I did.

I could actually smell the freshness of the bills. Lord, money never smelled so good. Intoxicating. Even still, I had to pull it together. I was a professional. A broke professional, but a professional nonetheless.

"I don't need double the amount. That would be unethical for me to accept." I smiled, hoping they would not be offended by my gentle resolve.

"Then accept this as full payment for six sessions."

I contemplated the offer, their urgency, the craziness I knew was coming. I considered my desperation to keep the lights on, the lease up to date, and my mortgage paid.

"I only have twenty minutes. This will count as a half session. We'll work the other half in another time." I took the money out of his hand and restrained myself from counting it right then and there.

Jenellis smiled wickedly. "She plays by the rules," she whispered to Brayden as if I could not hear her as we entered the building and headed to my office suite. "That's why I like her. That's why she has to be the one."

"We'll see," was his reply.

I wanted to shake the feeling that I had walked into some type of set-up, that I had emphatically lost whatever upper hand I'd held as the professional and was now at the whims and mercy of this couple I did not pretend to understand. I wanted to tell myself that the dread that had started growing in my stomach when I first met them yesterday—the dread that had only intensified the moment I saw the money—was merely my imagination. I wanted to believe that my instincts were in a failed state, thrown off by the confusing emotions I felt, emotions I could not name.

But I knew I was kidding myself if I accepted any other fact than that this couple was trouble someway, somehow.

And yet, here I was, inviting them back into my office, offering them my customary bottles of water, grabbing my handy notepad. We resumed the same seats we'd had yesterday.

"Again, thanks for taking us," Brayden started as Jenellis blinked up at him. "Our story is complicated, not really something that lends itself to a twenty-minute time frame, so we'll simply get to the point of why we are here and fill in the extra details later."

"Okay. What's going on?" How many times had I already asked this couple the same question? They looked at each other, and I knew immediately that whatever was coming next would be a lie.

"As we told you"—Brayden leaned forward as he spoke—"we're getting married in a matter of weeks. After years of both of us searching for true love with the wrong people, we both know that we've finally found it. In each other." Jenellis had been stroking her slender fingers on his forearm. She paused momentarily, but if Brayden noticed, it did not stop him from continuing. "When we marry, we are determined to become 'one' in the full sense of the word as it's used in the Bible."

"You have a church background?" Maybe I should not have asked that question out loud, but I could not hide my surprise at the biblical reference. Something about Brayden and Jenellis did not scream "holy union" to me.

"Something like that." Jenellis chuckled. Brayden did not look humored.

"Anyway," he continued, "in our quest to become one, we've hit some, let's say, bumps in the road from both of our pasts that's threatening to destroy our oneness before we even get to the altar."

"Old flames have a way of reappearing at the most inopportune times." I nodded.

"No, Ms. St. James." Brayden shook his head. "I'm not talking about old relationships. I'm talking business. Dollars and cents. We're having a hard time merging our money and because we know that disagreements over finances are a major marriage killer, we want to address this now."

"It's not so much money that's the issue," I interjected, "it's usually *communication* that's the underlying problem. If you don't know how to really communicate with each other, that deficiency comes out when it's time to deal with hot-button issues like money, and sex, and the other usual culprits named as marriage enders. Not knowing how to effectively communicate expectations and desires is usually at the core of all these matters."

"Well, that's just it. Jenellis won't tell me where she got all her millions from."

"And he"—Jenellis's words were pointed—"won't tell me where he got his."

Millions. The word was not lost on me. *Focus, Sienna, focus.*

"Okay." I nodded. "Before we get to the communication piece, let's look at the foundation on which effective communication is built. Trust. What's keeping both of you from openly disclosing parts of your lives to each other? Is it fear of being judged or rejected, betrayed or used? Can you trust each other with your secrets?" I held my breath, knowing that my final question was a loaded one on many levels and for different reasons for both of them.

"Ms. St. James"—Brayden leaned forward even more—"can I ask you a question?"

Before I could think of a reasonable response to his query, he continued. "What does money mean to you?"

"What I feel and think about money is not the issue." I was not going to be shot down that easily. "I'm here to help the two of you figure it out between yourselves."

"But what you think does matter to me. Jenellis is certain that you are the person we should be talking to, but I'll be honest. I'm not convinced. *I* need to know how *you* feel about money. The fact that you were practically panting when I showed you a handful of twenties a few moments ago tells me something, but not everything. Tell me." His voice was barely above a whisper as he leaned even closer to me. "What does money mean to you? Fear? Trust? Those were your words."

"Okay." I took the wad of bills from out of my work bag. Their brand of trouble was not worth it. "I apologize, but I'm not going to be able to work with the two of you. I am not sure what it is that you want, either one of you"—I eyed Jenellis—"but I can give you a list of other therapists in the area who you can contact and interview to find the best fit for your needs. I'm sorry, I'm not the one." I held the money back out to them, but neither one of them reached for it.

"You passed." Brayden smiled and sat back.

"What is going on here?" The money was still extended in my hand. "You told me that you had an urgent matter. That is why I agreed to see you. We're out of time now, but I still do not see what the emergency is."

"Twenty-four hours."

Both Jenellis and I looked at Brayden with confusion.

"Twenty-four hours," he repeated. "By this time tomorrow, both of you will understand why we are so pressed for time."

"I wish you would just tell me," Jenellis hissed at him before turning her attention to me. "For the past two weeks, all Brayden has been saying to me is that by this Friday, I'll know all there is to know about him. I can't stand the secrets. He wants me to trust him. I'm trying to, but in so doing, I need him to trust me too."

"Twenty-four hours. It will all make sense." Brayden never looked at her, his eyes only bore into mine. "I'm going to leave the money with you for now, Ms. St. James. If by tomorrow evening, you are still intent on not helping me and my fiancée, I will come and get every last bill back from you. Thanks for your time. Let's go, Jenellis." He stood and headed toward the door.

I saw Jenellis's hesitation, but she walked out right beside him.

"Wait." I followed them, the money still in my hands. "I'm not keeping this. You're going to have to take it back."

But they were already about to pass through the waiting area, and did not even turn around to speak to or acknowledge me.

"Mr. Moore and Ms. Walker," I demanded, marching right behind them. "Wait a minute." My one o'clock client, a twenty-something Asian woman with a severe anxiety problem, was sitting on a couch fumbling through a magazine as I practically ran after them.

"Ms. St. James," she gasped, her hands starting to shake. "Is everything okay?"

Jenellis and Brayden were gone. The money was still in my hand. My client was on the verge of a panic attack.

"Yes, Li, everything is okay." I followed her eyes to the stack of bills in my hand. Smiling, I slipped them into the back of my notepad. "You can come in my office now."

I kept a smile on my face to help ease her nerves and she managed a small smile as well. I was doing well keeping up the façade as we settled into our seats—until I noticed that there was a small sheet of paper peeking from behind the sofa pillow where Jenellis had been sitting.

Somehow, Li and I made it through the session, me going through the motions of listening and encouraging; her appearing to be getting her weekly dose of help. The moment Li left, I reached for the torn scrap and read exactly what I had expected to see.

Please find out if this man is violent. I don't know who else to turn to without there being major consequences.

"See you next week, Li." I followed my client out, the paper a mashed ball in my hand. My two o'clock, a middle-aged woman with an anger management problem and my final appointment for the day, was waiting.

"It's about time you got out here." She looked up at the wall clock to emphasize my three-minute lateness.

"I'm getting real tired of having to wait for you every week."

"Okay, Ms. Sherry, let's get started." I smiled. I had to put up a front for at least one more hour.

Chapter 6

"You should try the salmon. I know how much you like seafood." Leon's bald head almost glistened in the glow of candlelight at the Harbor's Edge Inn. The color of dark chocolate with undertones of copper, Leon's strength surpassed his sculpted frame. Strength exuded in the slight tilt of his head, whispered in the tenor of his voice, the gentle smile of his eyes.

Why couldn't I simply let this man love me and I love him?

"Mmmm. Yes." I smiled. "I have heard about the salmon here." I felt like hiding behind the menu. I did not want Leon to see the bad nerves that had taken root, grown a stem, and pushed out buds in me ever since Brayden and Jenellis had left my office.

The stack of bills was still tucked away in the back of my notepad. I hadn't even bothered counting it yet, but I knew that whatever the final sum was the cost of trouble. *What am I supposed to do?*

"Here's your appetizer." A middle-aged woman with graying blond hair and a black apron put a steaming plate of maple-broiled scallops between us.

"Thanks." Leon smiled up at her. I did not miss her blush. The man's smile could trap any woman. He used to wear a gold cap on one of his teeth, but after he chose to let go of the painful history behind it, his pearly whites had a golden quality all their own.

When he looked back at me, his smile was gone.

"Sienna, I know we haven't finished ordering yet, but I need to at least let you know why it was so urgent we talk."

"Okay," I squeezed out, trying to remember all of a sudden how to breathe. Leon had stopped looking at me, was studying the etched leaf pattern of his salad fork. Time ticked by and to alleviate the agitation that was threatening to swallow me because of his silence, I escaped into my comfort zone.

"Whatever this is about is difficult for you to share." With my therapist hat on, I had the courage to look him directly in the eyes when he finally looked back up at me. Focusing on his feelings kept me from feeling my own.

Leon was not going for it. "Look, Sienna, I'm not one of your clients. I'm . . . I—"

"Are you ready to order?" The waitress was back, all smiles at Leon.

He looked at me and shrugged. "I guess that's what we need to do next. I'm not that hungry, so, Sienna, please get whatever you want. This appetizer will fill me."

"What would you like, hon?" The words were friendly, but the waitress was looking at me disapprovingly, as if Leon's poor appetite was my fault.

"I'll try your grilled salmon entrée."

"Mmm, hmm." She scribbled on her pad and took off, but not before frowning at me and smiling at Leon again.

"And I'll try this again." Leon sighed. "Look, Sienna, our friendship has really grown over the past two years. You know that—"

My cell phone chimed. I did not recognize the number.

"I'm sorry, Leon. I forgot to silence it. Let me do that now." I slid it to vibrate and pushed it to the side of the table.

"No problem." Leon was ready to begin again. "Um, like I was saying—"

My cell phone buzzed, sending the silverware that lined our table into a vibrating chorus. It was a different number. Still did not recognize it.

"I'm so sorry. I probably need to shut the whole thing down. I tend to keep it on in case a client calls, but I'll deal with it later." Brayden and Jenellis crossed my mind. As much as Leon was scaring me, the thought of them frightened me more. I hoped to goodness that was not them trying to call me. I reached out to turn my phone completely off, but then a new number, and one that I recognized, jumped on the touch screen.

Yvette Davis, my younger sister. Leon saw the name too.

"Go ahead and answer. I know how your sister gets." He sat back in his seat, staring off into space as he stirred his iced tea with a straw.

"Hello, Yvette?"

"Sienna, why haven't you been answering your phone?" she yelled in my ear.

"Um, hello, how are you, um, is that too much to ask?" I rolled my eyes. My sister was always in the middle of some drama.

"I don't have time for your sarcasm any more than you seem to have time to pick up your phone."

"You just called me. I just answered." I looked up at Leon to offer him a smile, but he was busy flipping through the menu.

"Your home phone? You haven't been answering that."

"Obviously I'm not home, Yvette. Did it ever cross your mind that I might actually be out somewhere and can't talk to you?"

"Well, I gave them your cell phone number and you obviously didn't answer it either or you wouldn't be talking to me."

"Them? Yvette, really, I don't have time for this. What are you talking about? What is going on? Who is 'them'?"

"Reverend Howard and Tridell's mother."

My heart skipped a beat. "What? What happened?"

"They gone!"

Her words didn't make sense. "What? What happened?" I asked again.

"Your son, my son, and that prissy Tridell Jenkins—along with Reverend Howard's rental car, might I add—are all gone from that desert campground you talked me into sending my child to!"

Chapter 7

"Gone!" I hollered into the phone. An elderly couple at the table next to us gave me a look of displeasure. Leon's eyes were wide as he leaned closer to me.

"You heard me!" Yvette hollered back in my ear. "You got my son out there missing halfway across the country."

"Yvette, you know good and well I did not do anything to your son. He makes his own choices, just like *you* chose to send him on the trip on *your* own accord—even before I signed the permission forms for Roman." This direction in conversation was not what I needed. I needed answers, not Yvette's perpetual blame-game drama and her act that Skee-Gee was the perfect child, the innocent one. For anything, a year Roman's senior in age, and a decade his senior in street knowledge, I knew one thing for certain: wherever they were, it was Skee-Gee's doing—or that darn Tridell Jenkins. "I'm not doing this with you right now, Yvette. I need to know what is going on. Where is my son?"

Leon was at full attention on the other side of the table. "What's wrong, Sienna?"

I held up a finger, shaking my head at him. "I can't . . . I don't know what's going on. Yvette, where is my son?"

"That's what I'm trying to tell you. They gone, Sienna. Roman, Tridell, and Sylvester took off in Minister Howard's rental car, and don't nobody know where they are right now."

"Okay," I said, hanging up the phone. There was no point in trying to continue a conversation with her. I dialed Roman's number and his voice mail came on immediately, letting me know his cell phone was turned off.

"Roman," I shouted as if he could somehow still hear me, "you need to call me as soon as you get this message. I'm not playing with you. Call me!" I hung up and put my head down.

"Sienna, let's . . . let's just go." Leon's voice was gentle, soothing in my ear. I realized right then that he was rubbing my shoulder. His touch had been so natural, I hadn't even noticed it was there. Awareness of this subtlety made me stiffen up my shoulder under his fingers. He felt the tension and backed away, but his tone stayed soft.

"I know from your words that something is going on with Roman. Let's get you home and we'll figure out what to do." He left a fifty on the table though we had not yet eaten. As we headed toward the parking lot, I recalled that we had driven in separate cars. I wished right then that I had taken Leon up on his offer of picking me up for our non-date. How was I to ever drive while not knowing where my son was?

Our non-date.

Leon had wanted to meet for a reason, I remembered.

"Leon, I'm sorry about—"

"Not right now, Sienna. We'll talk, but this is not the time. We've got to find Roman first. And we will."

Roman was AWOL on the other side of the country, and yet Leon, who was standing right beside me, felt even further away.

I was losing all the men in my life.

I knew it.

Felt it.

But I still did not want to believe.

Chapter 8

My wedding ring from RiChard had been a simple one: a white, ivory-like rugged circle he said was crafted in the tradition of some indigenous village he visited during one of his many trips to South America. He put it on my finger as we stood in the marriage ceremony room at the Baltimore County Courthouse. There were no witnesses present as my parents were infuriated that I was taking this step, and his parents, he said, were "in their own worlds" in other parts of the world.

I found out later that the ring that symbolized our hasty commitment was actually made out of bone: a piece of a vertebra from a small rodent-like mammal that ran through the floors of the rainforest, feasting on even smaller animals. This crude bit of jewelry was in stark contrast from the lion's head ring, the heavy golden orb with eyes made out of rubies and sapphires and a mane edged with diamonds. The lion's head ring had belonged to the son of an African chief whom RiChard had befriended when both were studying abroad in Europe.

Kisu.

RiChard was gifted with the heavy ornament after he avenged Kisu's murder during a political rally effort he planned in KwaZulu-Natal in South Africa.

That was years ago.

The last trip I took with him.

To my parents' dismay, I'd given up my full ride to college to follow him on his social justice mission around the world. What could I say? I was eighteen and in love, as I thought it to be, and that bull carried me for a while.

But something in me changed when I saw the blood on his hands.

He said he'd killed a man for killing Kisu.

I couldn't put my finger on it then, but I practically ran from his side, packed my bags, got on the first plane out of there, and landed in my mother's living room, not knowing I was pregnant with RiChard's son.

Random gifts through the years, inconsistent phone calls.

Roman.

The only three proofs that a man named RiChard St. James had loved me.

I guess.

"Sienna, did you try the church number again?" My mother's sharp voice cut through my thoughts. She was a highly respected principal at what was once a struggling Baltimore City elementary school, and although we were all sitting in the basement of my parents' Randallstown home, she was in full authoritarian mode.

"Mom, I've called the church secretary, Pastor McKinney's wife, Elder Nance, and Sister Henry, who heads up the church's crisis line. Like I said before, nobody has any additional information. We only need to let the authorities do their job."

"Authorities?" My sister yelled from the dark brown leather loveseat across the room. "I thought we all agreed to let Minister Howard handle this."

"Minister Howard doesn't even want the rental car company to know the boys took the car, although I'm sure the company would be able to track down the car's GPS."

"Minister Howard is trying to avoid getting the authorities involved, remember?" Yvette snapped back. "The boys left on their own accord, so it's not like they're in some kind of trouble, kidnapped, or something like that. They'll resurface when they're ready. We just need to wait it out, that's all."

Yvette glared at me and I glared at her, knowing that the only reason she did not want the police involved was because then it would have to be reported to Skee-Gee's probation officer. I'd listened to her beg and plead on the phone with Minister Howard that very point, and for some crazy reason he went along, agreeing with her that the boys were up to a harmless adventure and would surface soon.

I started to say something about her beloved son, the eldest of her five children, but I did not have the energy.

Years ago, watching RiChard disappear down a path with Kisu for the last time, I'd had a sick feeling in my stomach, like my insides would cave in and disintegrate into acid.

I had the same feeling now.

RiChard.

The lion's head ring.

I had been thinking about him and that. And now I remembered why.

"Yup, if someone calls demanding a ransom," my father was saying for the umpteenth time, "I'll cash in my highest value cards and signed baseballs and that should do it."

"There will be no ransom because there's been no kidnapping!" Yvette sighed and huffed and puffed.

My father, Alvin Davis, a truck driver for a bakery in Little Italy, had the most extensive sports memorabilia collection this side of the Mississippi, or so it seemed. A local newspaper had once featured him surrounded by the baseball bats, boxing gloves, jerseys, and other pricey artifacts that made up his cache; but few people had ever laid eyes on the smallest, yet most expensive treasures he kept locked in the basement safe.

"Even still, I'm sure I have something that would be enough to save three boys caught in mischief." He kept eyeing the corner of the basement where the safe was, hidden cleverly behind a small fridge in the wet bar of the wood-paneled den.

The lion's head ring.

I'd pushed the massive jewel into that same safe nearly two years ago. I needed to get it out before it was noticed by my dad or anyone else. I did not want any questions.

I'd never gotten the answers I wanted two years ago when the ring had shown up in an urn mailed to me from the other side of the world.

The urn, I would later find out, had actually been mailed by Kisu.

Who clearly had not been murdered like RiChard claimed.

The letter. The e-mail. The picture. The unconscious Kisu lying on a hotel floor, found by authorities in Portugal two years ago. The questions I'd left unanswered. The answers I did not want to know.

I swallowed hard and squeezed my eyes shut while another piece of my stomach collapsed into the acid pit.

"Sienna, it will be okay." Leon's fingertips brushed over the back of my hand. "I'm sure Roman will show up real soon. He's a good kid."

We were all crowded in my parents' Randallstown basement: Leon, Yvette, my parents, and a woman named Sadie Spriggs, the self-appointed church comforter who showed up at all homes of the newly departed and recently ill with a box of tissues, a hymn book, and a tambourine.

Her presence was not comforting to me at all.

And not just because she was studying me and Leon with her mouth moving and no words coming out.

"I have some friends on the force who may have some helpful connections if it comes down to it." Leon's voice was a whisper, for Yvette's benefit I knew. He glanced uneasily at my sister, who was staring angrily at us. Good thing he was not in uniform. Then again, the way she was glaring at us, maybe he needed to be.

Yvette, her son, and their bad history with police.

And her son was with mine.

I swallowed hard as the acid in my stomach seemed to be turning into a hot, roiling boil.

"If you want connections, why not talk to Brother Tyson? Doesn't he still work for channel 55?" Sadie Spriggs's suggestion surprised me. Aside from the fact that I thought she was sitting out of earshot from us, I was not sure how I felt about her offering advice. Prayers, hymns—those I was used to hearing come from the elder, turban-wearing church mother; but suggestions and directions seemed out of the normal realm of her ministry scope. Besides, a media spectacle didn't seem like what was needed.

My sister, for obvious reasons, immediately agreed with my unexpressed thought.

"The media?" Yvette gasped. "No, we don't need any extra attention right now. Let's just wait until the boys finish their fun and then they'll call home."

Mother Sadie had her left eye squinted and her mouth was moving silently again as she looked back and forth between me and Yvette.

"Okay, I'm going back upstairs." I stood up, ready to get away from all of it, all of them.

The lion's head ring.

I sat back down, knowing that I was going to have to figure out a way to get that ring out of my father's safe before he started rummaging through it as a heroic gesture. I say gesture because everyone in the room knew that Alvin Davis wasn't selling any of his beloved baseball cards or other prized possessions, didn't matter what kind of trouble his grandsons were in.

"Sienna," Leon began, his hand, I suddenly noticed, locked over mine. "I think, I think—" His cell phone interrupted him with a soft wind-chime ring. I didn't recognize the ringtone. I'd been around him long enough to know the falling-rain ring had been his late grandmother who raised him; the bullhorn was his current supervisor; the drumroll was his best friend, Benny. And I had managed to squeeze out of him that a robin sang when I called.

But wind chimes? I had no idea.

"I . . . I have to go. I'm sorry." Leon glanced at the screen of his phone and mumbled something else, but I could not make it out. "I'm sorry," he mumbled again, shutting the ring off without answering. "I'll check in with you soon. Keep me posted."

He was leaving so quickly, I was halfway up the basement steps behind him before I realized that I was following him out. "Leon, wait."

"I really need to go."

Is he trying not to look at me?

"I know. I only wanted to thank you. For everything." We were standing on my parents' front steps, right under the porch light where a circus of moths was circulating. Leon stopped and turned around to face me.

"You know I am here for you." He spoke soft and low. I had to move closer to hear him.

Any thoughts I'd had about him trying to avoid eye contact with me were dissipated as his eyes pierced mine. We were inches apart, the closest I could ever remember being to him. And the longest we'd ever been that close.

"Roman will be okay." His voice could have been fingers massaging my neck, loosening the knots and kinks that were tightening it. That's how warm and amazing and comforting the sound of his voice was to me at that moment. He took a step closer to me, as if there really was more room to fill between us. His face was now inches from mine, our eyes still locked, the smell of his cologne intoxicating.

I became aware of the rise and fall of my chest, the breaths I was taking, the quickening pace of my heart.

This feeling.

So foreign and yet so familiar.

RiChard.

A literal pain flashed through me from the base of my skull to the tops of my knees. My eyes dropped. I backed away.

"I need to go back inside." I studied the words on my parents' welcome mat. ENTER WITH LOVE. EXIT WITH CARE. "That's kind of a weird welcome mat message." I chuckled.

Leon was not laughing. In fact, he wasn't even standing where he had been. I watched him look up at the unusually bright moon before the wind-chime ring of his cell phone interrupted whatever thought he was having, whatever moment I was trying to avoid.

"I have to go. Call me if you hear anything."

Down the steps. Car door slam. Engine roaring. Gone.

I had not felt that emotionally and physically close to a man like that for sixteen years. And RiChard found a way to ruin it for me.

Now it was just me, the bright moon, the flutter of moths overhead, and the lingering scent of Leon's cologne.

What is wrong with me?

I didn't have time to answer that question. I had my son to think about. My son and that lion's head ring I wanted to recover before it was discovered.

"Good, you're back." Sadie Spriggs nodded as I descended into the basement once more. "I told you he still worked for channel 55." She was pointing to the television that someone had turned on in my absence. The eleven o'clock news was on.

"Yes." I nodded back. "I knew that Brother Tyson . . ." The rest of the sentence became lodged in my throat as I tried to make sense out of what was flashing on the television screen.

Oh my, Jesus, what is going on? I prayed in horror, not believing my eyes.

Chapter 9

Brother Lazarus Tyson, or Laz as we called him, had been a news anchor for channel 55 for several years. A graduate of Morehouse College, he had previously worked for networks in Atlanta, then in Houston, and, right before returning to Baltimore, New Orleans. His brave, risky coverage and on-air political rants during Hurricane Katrina had earned him the nickname "Brass Laz." The rants had also marked him as a potential troublemaker for news stations. With no other networks across the nation willing to take a chance with his unscripted and unapologetic live commentaries, he'd been forced to accept the only job opened to him, back in the newsroom of the Baltimore-based network where he had interned as a teen.

He was a mystery at our church. The heavily opinionated and brazen journalist barely said a word to anyone on Sundays. Sitting in the back row, he came late and left early, usually walking right out the door after walking around the sanctuary to drop his customary fifty dollar bill in the offering plate each service.

But all of that was irrelevant to me at the moment.

"Turn that up," I demanded as I marched over to the flat-screen TV my father had hung over his overly used wet bar.

"This is Lazarus Tyson reporting live from the Baltimore City Police headquarters. Back to you in the studio, John."

"Wait a minute, what . . . what did he say about the girl whose picture was just up on the screen?"

My parents and Yvette were arguing about some money she owed them. Sister Spriggs was rocking back and forth in her chair, humming, watching them all go at it.

No one even heard my question, so I was certain they had not been paying attention to the news story that had gone off seconds earlier. I picked up the remote, wondering if my father had paid the extra money with his cable subscription to have the ability to rewind and record.

He had.

I pressed the rewind button to see the entire clip of Laz's story.

"Police are asking your help tonight with the reported kidnapping of a young woman in the neighborhood of Fells Point." Laz spoke somberly into the live camera shot, his signature brown trench coat whipping in the nighttime breeze, his brown fedora barely holding on to the side of his head. I held my breath, waiting for the snapshot that had grabbed my attention moments earlier to flash on the screen again.

"Witnesses describe a horrifying scene of an African American woman who looked to be in her early to mid-twenties come screaming out of an alley, begging and pleading for help," Laz continued. "She appeared to be bleeding and residents of this quiet neighborhood immediately contacted police, who are reporting that at least ten 911 phone calls were made from community members between 9:06 p.m. and 9:08 p.m. However, by the time police arrived at 9:10 p.m., there were no signs of her.

"At least two witnesses are reporting that immediately after she came running out of the alley, a dark-colored minivan came from behind her, nearly hitting her. A passenger exited the van, grabbed her, and threw her into the back of it, at which time the van sped away. Police at this time do not have a name or any other information about the victim, and are also not clear on the make and model of the vehicle. All that has been released is this still from a security camera that caught a few seconds of the victim when she was within its view."

I held my breath and pressed the pause button as a grainy photo filled the screen. The long weave, overdone boob job, and deep cocoa brown skin left no question. It was her.

Silver.

The woman who'd been on *The Soul Mate Show* locking lips with Brayden/Kwan/whatever his name was.

I shut my eyes, rubbed my forehead. Too much was happening for a Thursday night. When I opened my eyes, I pressed play and watched as the camera zoomed in on the photo, close enough to see the genuine fear filling Silver's eyes, the slight parting of her lips in terror and the butterfly tattoo on her neck.

Wait a minute.

A butterfly tattoo on her neck?

I pressed pause again. I did not remember the woman on *The Soul Mate Show* having any tattoos, especially one as large and elaborate as the still showed. I had been tired last night when I watched the episode of the local dating show, but for as much as I studied the overdone fakeness of Silver, I think I would have noticed a large butterfly on the side of her neck.

That can't be Silver.

A part of me felt relieved, though I wasn't sure why. A woman was still in danger.

But I had no other responsibility toward her than to pray. I mean, what else could I do for a stranger?

I pressed play and let the story finish playing. Laz reappeared on the screen. "Despite the additional tax and community dollars going toward keeping this trendy, upscale neighborhood near the Inner Harbor safe—money, I must add, that has not been equally invested in other areas that experience far higher crime rates and need more of a police presence—a young woman has gone missing violently and against her will. Police are asking that if you have any information at all that can help either identify this young woman or provide information about the crime committed against her, to immediately contact Metro Crime Stoppers. Tips can be submitted anonymously. This is Lazarus Tyson reporting live from the Baltimore City Police headquarters. Back to you in the studio, John."

I sat dazed, and, yes, confused, as the news turned to a story about a controversial new home development in an agricultural zone.

"Is everything okay, Sister St. James?"

Sadie Spriggs was staring at me, her mouth uncharacteristically still. I had not noticed that she'd stopped humming. Her alto voice had been a comforting white noise against the backdrop of my mother's stern demands and my sister's nonstop accusations. My father had retreated from the fight. I had not noticed him leaving the room.

The safe.

He kept it in the basement. I prayed a silent prayer for the unidentified woman kidnapped in Fells Point, and then prayed that my father hadn't rummaged through his safe where his most prized, smaller sports treasures were kept. *Along with the lion's head ring I hid.*

"I'm okay. I'm just . . ." Really, what was I supposed to say?

"Father!" Sadie's sudden shout startled me. Her eyelids fluttered shut and she raised a hand in the air. "Help this family during this difficult time, Lord Jesus. Bring the baby boys back home safe. Comfort the mothers, calm the grandmother, bring healing and peace that only you can bring to all these burdened relationships. In Jesus the Christ's name I pray, Ayyyy-man."

And then the tambourine began to rattle and the hums from a few minutes ago turned into full-blown singing. My mother and Yvette had no choice but to shut up under the metallic pounding, foot-stomping, whimpers, and shouting of the ancient woman. Honestly, I think they stopped fighting for the simple fact that they couldn't hear each other's yells over the spirit-filled commotion.

I realized then that Sadie Spriggs clearly understood her function and role in family catastrophes—and she lived up to them well.

Heavy footsteps in the kitchen told me that my father had retired upstairs for the night. From the impromptu prayer service initiated by Mother Sadie and the unfinished argument left to simmer between my mother and Yvette, I knew I had time to fish for the ring in the safe later. I'd come back tomorrow when the basement should be empty and I would not have to provide any explanations to anyone about anything.

"Hold to His hands, to God's unchanging hands." Sadie's tambourine was in full-fledged Sunday morning mode as she belted out the hymn. Her eyes were closed and tears streamed down her face. When she opened them again, she nodded at me. I smiled and nodded back, accepting her unspoken directive of dismissal.

She had work to do with my mom and sister, and her tambourine was only warming up.

I stood and made my escape.

Yvette glared at me as I dashed up the steps, leaving behind her and my mother for what promised to be a near all-night music and prayer affair.

There was never any stopping Mother Sadie once the Spirit moved her to action.

I had my own deliverance to work through.

Chapter 10

Roman was five years old the day I put every single picture I had of RiChard through a shredder. My son had just received another package from his absent father and was running through our old rancher wearing the Bolivian ceremonial mask that was his newest treasure from the man who traveled the world to save it, but never came home to see us.

Ever.

I remember the day vividly. I had turned in a paper for a sociology class, taken an economic exam for which I didn't have time to study, and used the last cent of my student loans for the semester buying a hot dog, baked beans, and potato salad dinner for Roman.

After losing my full scholarship to chase RiChard's dreams around the globe, and returning with nothing to show for our "love" but a bulging belly with a baby kicking inside, I was determined to finish the college education I had abandoned at age eighteen. Of course, doing so as a single mother, with my own mother willing to see me fall flat on my face only to prove her point, made college enrollment and completion difficult. It took me years of taking classes and working, full time, part time, and alternating between both times to first get my bachelor's and then my master's degrees. Ava Diggs was my sole cheerleader and the only reason I did not quit during the final stretch of grad school.

But on that day, the day Roman was having his own Carnival festival in my living room and my shredder was on full blast, I was nowhere near my master's degree. I was only about halfway through my undergraduate journey, facing foreclosure for the second time, counting nickels and quarters to fill my gas tank, and living off of ramen noodles and celery sticks so that my son could have three balanced meals a day.

And the man who fathered Roman but never held him, who had never sent a dollar bill to support him, who had never asked for a photo, or mentioned plans to come see him during his sporadic calls, was the parent that Roman was praising as he jumped around the room.

"Look what my daddy got me!" he shrieked over and over, as if the handcrafted mask were food, water, shelter, and sustenance—the things I was providing—no, sacrificing for—to ensure his health and well-being. "Look what my daddy got me!"

I felt sick to my stomach hearing Roman's cheers and gleeful shouts, knowing that I was going to have to dip into his Christmas present fund to pay the gas and electric bills. I felt sicker still when I recalled that the Christmas fund had already been depleted the month before to keep our water from being shut off.

I could not stop Roman's cheers. Despite my nausea, I could not turn my five-year-old son against his father. So I did what I could do. I erased every picture, letter, memento of RiChard from my presence by letting my shredder devour each one to pieces.

But my son's cheers did not stop until two years ago.

The arrival of the lion's head ring had changed everything. Even, especially, the way Roman thought of his father. Roman did not know the full story behind the prized jewelry piece. All he knew was that his father was not there for him, and, I guess, that was enough.

***

Why had I even thought I would go to sleep? It was four o'clock in the morning and any rest I'd had came in fitful tosses and turns. I'd sleep a little and then start dreaming about Roman, then wake up and start worrying about him. Or I'd sleep a little and then that terrified girl who looked like Silver would haunt my dreams. Like a blender set on grate, my thoughts and dreams were whirling around in uneven pieces, and thinking about old photos that were no longer in my possession did not help.

The grainy photo on the news had shown a woman with a butterfly tattoo; however, Silver did not have one. *Or maybe she used makeup to cover it up depending on what kind of first impression she was trying to make on that dating show.*

The thought had not occurred to me before, but now that it did, I realized that it was totally plausible, and that the kidnapped woman really could be Silver.

"I'm not going to get much more sleep anyway," I told myself as I reached for my laptop and pulled up the Metro Crimes Stopper Web site. I could be 100 percent wrong about that woman being Silver. *But what if I am right?* I was sure that a loved one, a family member, or friend would identify her to the police; but I was also sure that my conscience would not rest if I didn't pass along my suspicions. The Web site allowed anonymous tip submissions, so I had nothing to lose.

I typed in the fact that the victim looked similar to a contestant who called herself Silver on a dating game show that aired earlier in the week. For good measure, I even pulled up the episode on my television using my cable company's On Demand feature and provided the episode number in my tip. True to my memory, Silver did not have a tattoo, but that did not mean she had not covered it up with makeup. I mentioned that in my comment, though I was sure the investigators could come to their own conclusions, that is, if they even bothered to look at my tip.

After pressing Submit Tip on the Web page, I lay back down in my bed, though I did not expect to sleep. How could I? I needed my son home, and to even close my eyes without him down the hall in his bedroom felt unnatural.

But worrying is exhausting.

I did not realize that I had fallen into another fitful sleep until a loud pounding set me upright with a start.

Someone was banging on my front door.

Chapter 11

My alarm clock read 6:23 a.m. but the heavy pounds on my door told me that someone had a matter that could not wait until sunrise.

"Hold on, I'm coming," I shouted, half asleep and barely aware that I was wearing my old granny robe and bright orange head scarf. Not exactly the look I usually go for when answering my front door.

"I said I was coming!" I hollered, getting rather irritated by the continued knocks on the door. "Goodness gracious," I mumbled to myself as I finally grabbed the knob and swung it open.

"Sister St. James, I'm sorry for all the knocking. I know it's early, but I wanted to make sure that you heard me. I didn't have your phone number to call in advance."

He was not wearing his brown trench coat or fedora, but it was him nonetheless.

Laz Tyson.

"Brother Tyson?" I wiped the sleep from my eyes and tried to remember if I'd wiped away the dried drool stain that always ran from the corner of my mouth to my chin whenever I woke up. I did not know if a camera was about to appear behind him and I knew I looked a hot mess.

"Can I come in?" Laz seemed oblivious to my appearance and instead was looking past me, checking out the artwork hanging in my foyer.

"Is that a Faith Ringgold or a Romare Bearden?" he asked as I stepped aside to let him in.

"Uh, actually, neither. It's a Sienna St. James." I grinned, joining his gaze at the poster-sized multimedia-framed collage I'd hung in my entryway. I'd started it when I was in high school and added to it over the years; bits and pieces of my life, scraps of charms and other found objects, all arranged to look like a crowd of people of various shapes and hues.

The witnesses of my life.

For years, I'd kept it under my bed; but when I moved into my current house, it was the first thing I unpacked and hung.

"That corner is empty." He pointed to the plain white paper that peeked glaringly from the bottom right side.

"Yeah, that corner has always been empty. I'm waiting for the right thing to put there to finish it off. I'll know it when I see it." I did not feel like explaining that the missing element in the picture was me, that I had not yet found the right piece of paper or object that would best represent me at the edge of the crowd.

Laz studied my collage a few moments more, one finger resting on his bottom lip, before turning to face me fully.

"So, clearly, Ms. St. James, I did not come wake you just to discuss your hidden art talents." His tone was light, but his demeanor was somber.

"It *is* early." I nodded.

"Yes, but it's important." He paused, and I wondered what this man, who barely spoke to anyone at our church, had come to say to me. Did he somehow know that I had studied his news report about the kidnapped girl? That his filed story had been running and rerunning through my head? I realized that despite seeing him on television daily, I never knew he was so tall in person. His eyes were a subtle shade of gray, his skin as smooth, rich, and brown as apple butter. A fresh fade with precision-cut sideburns and a meticulous goatee rounded out his face, giving him a sharp definition that seemed to match his pointed on-air persona.

Should I say something to him about Silver?

I was still trying to make sense of this early morning interruption. Laz did not have me waiting for an explanation for long.

"Sister St. James, about an hour ago, I got a call from an old colleague of mine who now works for a television station in Las Vegas. He was about to break a story and contacted me for some background information, which I did not want to give before speaking to you first."

"Um, Brother Tyson—"

"Please call me Laz."

"Okay, Laz, I have absolutely no idea what you are talking about."

Laz looked away and sucked in a deep breath before meeting my gaze again. "Sister St. James—"

"You can call me Sienna."

"Sienna, are there some young people from our church missing along with a rental car?"

"Wh . . . what? What are you talking about?" I felt my heart skip two beats as a strangling feeling began crawling up my spine and stopped at the base of my neck. "Do you know where my son Roman is? Las Vegas? And who is this reporter? What breaking news? Is it on now?" The questions came out my mouth as quickly as they formed both in my mind and in the pit of my stomach. "Is my son okay?"

"Whoa, whoa. Slow down." Laz offered a calming smile—a smile that almost calmed me until I reminded myself that this man was a skilled investigative reporter who knew how to get the answers he wanted.

He had not shown up at my front door at almost half-past six in the morning if he did not want something.

"Ms. St. James—I mean, Sienna—I am not trying to alarm you, or get you prematurely worked up. Yes, I am a reporter, but I am a fellow church member as well."

Was the man reading my mind? Probably my body language, I decided, forcing my shoulders to relax so as not to look defensive. He may have come here looking for answers, but I needed to get answers of my own.

Where is my son?

"Perhaps we can sit down and talk. I'll tell you what I know, and you can tell me what you know."

I glanced at the mahogany grandfather clock—a housewarming gift from Ava—that graced the other side of my basement level entry foyer. *6:31.* My first client was not due for another two hours, and I had already been planning to cancel while I tried to figure out where my son was.

And Laz apparently had answers. *And questions.*

"Come on up to my kitchen. We can talk while I fix a quick breakfast." I finally closed the door behind him. I was nowhere near hungry, but my gut told me I needed strength for the journey.

Chapter 12

"The artwork continues." Laz nodded as we left the entry level of my townhome and headed to the kitchen/living/dining area of the second floor.

At my old home, I'd kept on display the many artifacts of RiChard: trinkets; indigenous handmade crafts; colorful, mysterious pieces from every corner of the world that dotted my residence like scattered puzzle pieces that were supposed to make the whole of my life.

My new home had none of that.

I'd been brave, willing, disgusted enough to instead hang out the four major paintings I'd completed over the years, oil portraits I'd created based on random snapshots I'd taken; one of Roman as a sneaky toddler thinking he was not being watched as he stuck his entire little hand into a freshly baked cherry pie; the Wildwood, New Jersey seashore; an elegant elderly black woman dressed in all white, sitting at a bus stop in downtown Baltimore; and a purple, orange, and black-spotted butterfly I'd spotted years ago on a nature walk with my son.

"You're gifted, Sienna. These pieces are exquisite." He was standing in front of the lady on the bus stop picture, his head cocked to one side, his finger resting back on his bottom lip.

In the nearly two years since I'd been in my new home, nobody had commented—or even seemed to notice—my work, not even Roman. Not even Leon. A part of me wanted to feel honored, flattered at Laz's observations, but there was too much business at hand that needed addressing for me to give in to vain glory.

"Coffee or tea?" I mumbled as I slammed a metal skillet on the stove to fix a quick batch of scrambled eggs.

"Hot chocolate."

"My kind of man," I replied without thinking, feeling immediately embarrassed for such a flirty response that I had not meant. I closed my eyes, as hot tears seared the back of my eyelids for some inexplicable reason. "I mean"—I opened my eyes again to face him—"I have no ill will toward anyone who respects chocolate."

"Now that's *my* kind of woman." Laz was all smiles as he nestled onto one of my breakfast bar stools at my extended granite kitchen island. His eyes seemed to pierce through mine, as if he was looking for something in them that would tell him all he needed to know.

I turned away and let out an overdone chuckle, hoping that was the end of the awkwardness I'd created; but as I reached for my secret stash of Godiva hot cocoa, *The Soul Mate Show* flashed through my mind. *Chocolate. Kwan/Brayden's licking lips. Silver.*

Bang.

I jumped at the memory of Brayden's last words on the show, so much so that I dropped onto the floor the collection of mixing bowls for which I was reaching. The loud clatter of metal sent both of us springing into action, our heads and hands bumping as we gathered the bowls from the floor.

Oh no, he thinks my nerves are rattled because of him. I could tell by the subtle smile of victory that lingered on his lips as he settled back into his seat. I rolled my eyes to myself, opting to fix toast and whatever was ready-made in my refrigerator instead.

I needed to get some answers and then get this man out of my house.

"Yogurt? Fruit salad?" I grabbed some containers out of the refrigerator. "You can make your own parfait."

"You are a beautiful woman."

His directness caught me off-guard, but I was not going to be thrown anymore.

"What do you know about the whereabouts of my son?" I sat in the chair next to him, ignoring his comment and refusing to try to figure out why his finger was resting on his bottom lip again as he studied me. Whatever he was studying, he came to a quick conclusion because he straightened up in his seat, cleared his throat, and began talking like the reporter I saw on the news every night.

"An old colleague of mine works as an investigative reporter for an affiliate out in Las Vegas. He's been working on a story about underage gambling at some casinos. I got a call from him a couple of hours ago telling me that he was following a story about three boys from Baltimore found at a blackjack table at one of the high-end hotels."

"And you know that—"

"It was your son, his cousin, and the pastor's nephew." He leaned back in the chair.

"Okay, so we get them on the first plane back home and punish them for the next decade. I don't get what the big deal is. Why the 'breaking story' as you called it?" I was minimizing how I felt about this revelation, but I had to for the sake of this man. I did not know where this was going.

"It's not that clean or simple, Sienna."

"Clean?" The word jumped out at me.

"The rental car they were driving would be considered stolen if reported."

"I'm sure my son was not driving it." Like that meant anything. I knew it wasn't a good situation.

"And there was . . . a large amount of money and some illegal substances hidden in the trunk."

I grabbed the edge of the counter, willing myself not to faint. "The police . . ." I couldn't get out the rest of my question.

"There are no police involved. Yet." Laz spooned a large glob of vanilla yogurt into the tall glass I'd put in front of him and then dropped several grapes and melon slices on top. The fruit salad had been left over from Ava's impromptu lunch, I recalled, the same lunch when she'd told me I needed a man.

Why do these thoughts come up at such inopportune times?

I knew why. I wanted Leon there with me. He would know what to do. And he would find a way, a reason, to hold me close to him, I imagined. But he wasn't there. I had to handle this moment on my own. First, I exhaled. Then I tried to make sense of what Laz was saying.

"The police aren't involved *yet?* What does that mean?" I held my breath.

"Like I said, my friend is an investigative reporter, like me. He was the one who found the boys and brought it to the attention of the casino security, who made the other discoveries, the cash, the drugs. Now, it is *not* in the hotel's best interest for the police and media to get involved because they freely let the boys come and play without checking IDs, which is supposed to be their policy. And, to be honest with you, Mitch is only interested in breaking the story if the boys had major dirt on them, so it doesn't just look like he's reporting about some teen boys trying to have a night on the town in Las Vegas. That's not the type of breaking news that will boost his career. At least the kind of career Mitch is aiming for."

And the kind you're aiming for too, I wanted to say. "Okay, I'm still trying to follow you," was what I said instead.

"He called me to see if I could unearth any dirt on them that would give him a real story."

"If you came here to find out if Roman is a mass murderer or a drug kingpin, you can go ahead and finish your breakfast and leave. There is no story here for you." I tried to find the name for the emotion I was feeling, but I could not even begin to get my thoughts organized enough to get beyond one word.

Roman!

"Sister St. James, I know Roman is a good kid and that the last thing he needs is to have his name smeared all over the news. That's why I came to you. And only you. The other two? Not so clean."

"Clean. There you go with that word again." I shook my head, wondering why I even let that man into my house at six-something in the morning. Talk about a day crasher. Then, I realized what he was really saying. "Wait a minute, is this some kind of threat . . . no, I mean, warning? Did you come here to try to warn me that my son is about to make the news somewhere across the country because of who he is with and what they have in their pasts, and you're trying to help me brace for the onslaught of gawkers and media that's coming—that you have a role, a helping hand, in?"

"It's not my job to judge the news, or mediate the news. It's just my job to report it."

"So you are giving your journalist friend the dirt, and then going to produce your own story here since there's a Baltimore connection." I wanted to believe that I knew all there was to know about my nephew given his positive changes as of late, but who knew? And Tridell Jenkins? I'd had a bad feeling ever since Roman told me he was going. "Get out my house, Laz. No, Brother Tyson. No *Mr.* Tyson. You are not acting very brotherly toward a church family member right now."

He must have already known that he was about to be kicked out because he was already standing. Before he left the counter, he dropped his business card next to his untouched yogurt parfait. I marched behind him, escorting him to my front door. He opened it but then turned back around to face me.

"I know it may not seem like it, but I really am here not to wrong you or your son, but to provide support. Why do you think I came here first before calling Mitch back?"

"You haven't called him back yet?"

"No, I haven't, and for the record I was not planning on telling him anything about your nephew, Skee-Gee's, record, or Tridell Jenkins, um, other life; but it's only a matter of time before Mitch gets his own information, and once he does, the news market here in Baltimore will catch on and I'll be obligated to report, whether I want to or not."

His eyes pierced mine as he continued. "I came here first thing today to warn you about what is coming down the pipes because I respect you. I've done enough investigating to know that you've been through a lot yourself and I know you are simply now trying to live a peaceful, quiet life. It's about to get a little loud right now, and I want you to know that I am here for support."

Without a warning or a blink, he grabbed me in for a quick hug; not a full-frontal hug, but still a little more than the harmless shoulder-to-shoulder embraces typical of Sunday morning greetings at church. It was over before I could protest or realize that he'd already let go and was heading down my front steps.

"And I meant what I said, Sienna. You are a beautiful and gifted woman." He looked back.

I was frozen, but I realized what was bothering me about what he'd said, aside from the beautiful/gifted remark. I unfroze long enough to call after him.

"Wait a minute, what do you mean you know that I have been through a lot?"

He didn't bother to answer me, just bounded down the steps.

I think five minutes passed before I realized that I was still standing in my doorway; that Laz had finished running down my steps, had gotten in his car, and pulled away.

I think another five minutes passed before I realized that another car had pulled away right after Laz left. A familiar face that had been watching out of earshot the whole scene—the hug—at my front door from a few parking spaces down.

Leon.

Leon!

He'd come to talk to me, but had not even bothered to get out of his car after seeing Laz leaving, hugging me at sunrise.

Too much confusion for a Friday morning.

I slammed my door shut.

What was I supposed to do with the information Laz had given me? Call Yvette? Call my mother?

Call Leon?

I crawled back into my bed.

Chapter 13

Hiding under my covers only lasted about two minutes. I knew it would only be a matter of time before my phone started ringing, and I wanted to be proactive, ready for what I knew would be a long day.

In retrospect, I would have never imagined how bad the day would get.

Bad.

I tried calling Roman first, and, as I expected, his phone was turned off.

"I know what's going on. Call me immediately," I yelled into his voice mail.

I decided against calling Yvette. She would want more answers than I could give, and I figured she would learn of her son's fate soon enough.

Leon.

I had to go see him. He'd been trying to talk to me since yesterday. Thankfully, I'd kept my Friday appointments light, so I could cancel all of them quickly. I grabbed my work notepad to get phone numbers, and a large wad of bills fluttered down to the floor.

Jenellis and Brayden.

"Twenty-four hours," Brayden had said. "By this time tomorrow, both of you will understand why we are so pressed for time."

I had no idea what that meant, or what I was supposed to do. All I knew was that at the moment, that was secondary on the list of concerns of my life. A fleeting thought of Silver crossed my mind, but I had already submitted my tip on the Crime Stopper's Web site.

My hands were clean of all I could think to do.

I picked up the money and decided to put it back into my notepad for now. I'd deal with it later. I needed to get to Leon.

At seven in the morning, I knew that I would find him at a small diner where he went daily for coffee, pancakes, and bacon. An accomplished cook himself, breakfast was the one meal of the day he let someone else cook for him, opting only to fix it for himself on the weekends, usually including me in the fare.

I threw on some clothes and left, determined to make the day one of answers and moving forward, fully knowing, sensing that my plan was a lost cause.

I pulled up to the Twenty-fifth Street diner a little after seven-thirty. As I expected, Leon's gold Altima was parked at a meter near the front door. The smell of grease and waffles drifted in the slight breeze as I parked around the corner in the first open space I could find. As I cut off my ignition, I realized that I was not so sure what I was supposed to say to Leon, or was even prepared for whatever he had to say to me.

But I was there now, and it was time to talk.

For whatever was going on with Roman, I wanted to have Leon's support for the day, with the awkwardness between us gone completely.

As I was getting out of my car, I spotted him through the window, sitting at a cushy booth. He could not see me, and I smiled at how relaxed he looked. He was laughing at something, and in my mind, I could hear his hearty chuckle, something, I realized in that moment, I had not heard in a while.

I wondered what he was laughing at, and figured that the flat-screen television that hung on the wall was the source of his delight. A national morning news show was airing and the anchors appeared to be laughing as well. A funny joke, a light story. *I could use one right now myself.* I shook my head.

But then my head stopped shaking.

As I neared the restaurant, I saw what had Leon's attention. Or rather *who.* A young woman was on the other side of the booth, laughing along with him.

She had sandy brown hair that flowed down past her shoulders and finely chiseled features that made her look like an airbrushed supermodel on the cover of a fashion magazine. A natural, knockout beauty. And several, no, many years younger than both me and Leon. Maybe twenty, twenty-one years old.

Barely legal.

My heart sunk.

My mind became like a DVD on rewind as I mentally reviewed the last few months, searching for a moment when Leon looked as alive with me as he did sitting, laughing in that diner with that young girl.

Why should I care?

I tried to convince myself I should not. After all, wasn't I the one who insisted we just be friends? Leon had never been subtle about his desire for us to be more than that over the past two years, frequently telling me to take my time getting to where I wanted to be emotionally before delving into a serious relationship, or whatever, with him.

Maybe he had grown tired of waiting.

Duh! I wanted to kick myself at the obvious sign of his finished patience on the other side of the glass window.

Or maybe it was not an obvious sign.

Hadn't he left my house not even an hour ago seeing another man hugging me, and I knew there was more to the story that Leon would not have known?

There might be a completely legitimate reason I was not privy to that explained why Leon was enjoying breakfast with a knockout beauty on a Friday morning. Believing that was a stretch, but enough of a hope to keep me afloat for the moment.

I got back in my car, both thankful and grieving that he had been too engrossed in his conversation to even notice me outside the diner.

As I pulled away, my phone began ringing. It was a local number, but not a familiar one. I did not answer, but then it began ringing again. I remembered how that happened last night during my dinner with Leon, and it turned out to be people from church trying to let me know about Roman. I grabbed the phone and pressed talk, putting it on speaker.

"Hello?" I said, breathless, into the receiver.

Silence.

"Hello?" I asked again.

There was more silence, and then the phone clicked off.

I dialed the number back only to hear the line keep ringing. Not even voice mail picked up.

"Strange." I shook my head to myself, throwing my phone back onto the front seat.

I was on my way to my parents' house, feeling like most of my issues for the day somehow revolved around me being there. The radio was on. A local AM gospel station that offered both inspiration and morning news updates filled my car with light banter and spiritual songs. I was only half listening until a news story caught my ear.

"Police are continuing their investigation into a kidnapping in the Fells Point neighborhood last night. An anonymous tip has led investigators to believe that the victim is nineteen-year-old Anastasia Denise Simmons, an exotic dancer on The Block, better known by her stage name, Silver. Police are asking for your continued help in locating her as her whereabouts and status are still unknown."

I slammed on the brakes as the news continued with weather and traffic updates. My gut told me 100 percent that Brayden was somehow involved. Was this what he was talking about? That we would know everything we needed to know in twenty-four hours? Was this it?

There were still too many questions, though. Like, why was I involved in their drama? Why me?

"You passed," he'd said. *Passed what?*

As I began driving again, it occurred to me that Brayden would not have known that I'd seen Silver and him on the dating show, and I didn't know if Jenellis even knew about it. As far as they were both concerned, I would not know that Silver's kidnapping had any significance or connection to them.

That's when I knew there was more to come.

First things first. I had to keep my hands clean and share my suspicions and concerns with the authorities. I made a U-turn and drove down Howard Street on my way to the 400 block of East Baltimore Street, where, ironically, both Baltimore's infamous red-light district, better known as The Block, and police headquarters sat side by side.

I was almost there when the call came.

My sister, Yvette.

My gut told me she knew about the boys.

I didn't bother to answer, knowing that her rants and accusations would make it impossible for me to drive straight. I did another U-turn to go back to my original plan of going to my parents' home. I decided I would submit another anonymous tip from their computer as soon as I had an opportunity to do so.

Forgive me, but my son came first.

Chapter 14

At the end of Roman's freshman year, his basketball coach held an awards banquet to recognize all the efforts of each player on the junior varsity team, which placed third in the county. Roman invited Leon and he proudly came with us, braving a torrential downpour that nearly threatened the evening event. The ceremony was held at a restaurant in Charles Village. When it was over and Leon drove us back home, he quieted as we sat at a red light near Greenmount and Thirty-third Street.

"What's wrong?" I remember asking, seeing the anguish on his face in the traffic lights that shone through the rain-streaked car windows.

"My brother died right there." He'd pointed to a nondescript, overgrown lot in front of a colorful mural painted on the side of an abandoned house. "He was beaten up by five young men and then shot four times, twice in the head."

Roman and I were quiet as the wipers swished furiously on the windshield.

"I was working on homicide back then, and had been following a lead on a case the night that it happened. I wasn't even scheduled to work, but thought I was on to something based on a conversation I overheard on the street." Leon sighed as the light turned green and he started driving again.

"The crazy thing is that my brother actually called me a couple of hours before it happened, asking if I wanted to catch a movie with him. I rarely talked to him at the time because I was angry with his choices. He'd broken my grandmother's heart, and I was tired of his lies, his stories, his broken promises. I told him no." Leon paused. *"I never talked to him again. And the lead I was following? Led to nothing. I wish . . . If I had put my brother first . . ."*

He never finished his sentence. Roman and I stayed as quiet as he did the rest of the way home.

"Where have you been?" Yvette glared at me from my parents' front porch as if I were the one who had taken a forbidden trip to Sin City. I walked right past her and directed my attention to my parents, who were both sitting on their sofa. A couple of church members, some parents of other youth who had gone on the mission trip, were sitting with them. I guess they were somehow afraid that our three musketeers had contaminated the whole lot and coming over here was the best thing they could do to make sure their charges were in line.

"Minister Howard called." My mother spoke before I could think of what to say. "He said the boys drove the rental car to Las Vegas and they got caught by some security personnel at a casino. Minister Howard is with them at the airport right now and putting all three of their tails on the first plane back to Baltimore."

"Children can really take you through some things, can't they?" a woman named Sister Beverly Niece piped in. Her daughter, Alison, was a straight A student and track star at an elite private school in the city. The only thing I'd ever known Alison to "take her mother" through was changing her mind about which college she wanted to visit out of the many courting her.

"That's why we got to get them in line early," another parent, Brother Elroy Brown, chimed in, one eye narrowed at me. "The devil is busy and if we don't set them straight young, we're in for trouble. If our children are not our priority, then this is what happens."

I understood now why Yvette was standing out on the porch. I could feel my hand reaching for my hip and my forefinger about to wag the air, but my mother was giving me the same look I'm sure she gave Yvette: "keep your peace and keep it moving."

Now my mother was not one to back down from a good fight, especially when it came to something as personal as family, but a quick look to the dining room let me know why she was content with letting these people rip apart my parenting skills, and encouraging me to find contentment as well.

Mother Sadie Spriggs.

She was sitting at my mother's formal table in the darkened room, her eyes squinted at me, her lips moving furiously in silence. I knew if I said the wrong thing, or even said the right thing in the wrong way, the tambourine in her lap was going to come to life.

I could not handle it.

It was enough to almost make me want to go join Yvette on the porch.

Almost.

With everyone crowded on my parents' main floor, a thought occurred to me. This might be the best chance I had to get that lion's head ring out of my father's safe. Everything in my life felt like it was spiraling away from me. The ring was something I could hold in my hands. Control. I needed it. Right then.

"Mom, I need to use your computer."

It wasn't a lie. I fully intended to get back on the Metro Crime Stoppers Web site as soon as I had that heavy ring back in my hands.

"Mmm." My mother grunted from the living room, letting me know that she was going to be too preoccupied with whatever was going on in there to care what I was up to in her basement.

I felt like I was a teenager sneaking around my parents' home as I crept down the steps. The smell of my father's worn burgundy leather sofa and loveseat filled my nostrils, bringing a small comfort, a distant memory of my childhood as I descended into the wood-paneled den where my father housed all of his sports treasures.

All the things and issues and concerns going on in my life, and all I could focus on was getting the lion's head ring back in my hands. Don't know why that one piece of jewelry, which caused so much upheaval for me and my son two years ago, was such a source of calm right now.

Control.

It took me all of sixty seconds to spin the combination lock on Pop's safe to the numbers my father did not know I knew, to push my hand through the crush velvet interior, to grab the heavy ring in my hands, to press it deep into my palm and hold it tight.

A rush of tears filled my eyes as I collapsed into the swivel chair in front of my parents' old, large black box-shaped computer. As the ancient machine hummed to life, the screen slowly considering whether it should turn from black to solid blue, I studied the jeweled-encrusted mane, wiped the tears that had dropped off my face onto it, making the emeralds and rubies glisten in the gold.

The computer was taking forever to boot up, giving me too much time to think, to feel, to wonder. I had turned on the machine with the goal of submitting my hunches about Brayden to the Metro Crime Stoppers Web site; but another Web site was jarring my memory.

Two years ago, when the ring showed up inside the package from Portugal, my emotions had gone in a tailspin. I had received a call out of nowhere from a woman who did not speak English, telling me that my husband's ashes were coming to me. No further information, details, names, addresses, circumstances given.

When the urn was delivered, there were no ashes inside. Only the ring. The ring given to RiChard by a village chief as a gift for vindicating his son Kisu's murder. The ring RiChard first promised to give to Roman for his eighteenth birthday, but then said he lost while assisting with rescue efforts during the tsunami disaster in Indonesia.

And yet it was here in my hand.

I tried to get answers when it came. I called the number of the sender repeatedly, but did not get a response. I even went to a Portuguese language class at a community college to attempt to get a native speaker to make the call for me.

Answers.

That was all I wanted.

Back then.

Without looking at it any further, I pushed the ring into the side of my purse.

Out of sight once more, but within reach of my hand. Within reach of my control.

I had to focus.

The computer start page finally came up and I logged on to my dad's outdated dial-up Internet service. I waited three agonizing minutes for the Metro Crime Stopper Web site to finally upload. I logged in with my anonymous username. *Now what to say?* My fingers danced half an inch above the keyboard as I struggled to remember what it was I wanted to type.

A man named Brayden Moore, who went by the name of Kwan on The Soul Mate Show, may be involved in the situation with Silver. I am a therapist and he and his fiancée . . .

I backspaced and deleted the words "and his fiancée." No need to implicate Jenellis in a possible criminal situation; she had not done or said anything that made her look suspect, at least to me.

I am a therapist, I continued typing, and he came to my office this week and did and said things that lead me to believe he might be involved in the kidnapping.

Satisfied with the words on the screen, I clicked submit.

RiChard.

His name dropped so suddenly and violently into my consciousness, I had to look around the basement to make sure he wasn't there.

The ring.

I had tucked it into the corner of my purse, but its presence had awakened something in me that I had been trying so desperately to keep asleep.

The desire to find out what happened.

When the ring had shown up two years ago, a letter written in Portuguese followed about a week later. I had scanned and e-mailed it to the community college teacher to translate.

I'd saved the e-mail, though I had not looked at it since.

The blinking cursor on the screen beckoned me, dared me, begged me to give it purpose. I surrendered and pulled up my e-mail account, logging in before I could talk myself out of it.

The e-mail from the Portuguese teacher, Tomeeka Antoinette Ryans, was in its own folder. I opened the folder, ready to click open the e-mail when a sound to my right startled me.

"Our God is an awesome God," Mother Sadie Spriggs sang to herself as she plodded down the steps. The turban on her head was black, and not white like the one she'd worn the evening before. She'd gone home and come back sometime over night, I realized.

I minimized the screen as Mother Spriggs finished her descent into the basement. I didn't need anyone asking me any questions. Mother Spriggs, for her part, seemed to be willing to go along with my attempts of avoiding conversation. Her singing turned into hums as she meandered around the room, studying the posters and jerseys, autographed balls and gloves that made up my father's treasures. I sat frozen at the computer, wondering how long she planned to pretend to be interested in sports.

The humming got louder.

I grew impatient.

I'd wanted this moment to be private. After two years, I'd finally braced myself to look at the last big clue I'd had of RiChard's whereabouts. And I wanted to experience it alone.

Two years.

The only thing that had changed from two years ago to this moment was seeing Leon with someone else.

He had been waiting for me. Waiting for me to have my sense of complete closure. And I had been avoiding the inevitable.

And now it may be too late.

The humming had stopped. Mother Spriggs had stopped in front of a signed Baltimore Ravens jersey. I could see her lips were moving. Honestly, the woman creeped me out, but she was reminding me that I had a resource greater than an old e-mail.

Prayer.

My finger still hovered over the mouse, poised and ready to open the e-mail that I thought held some key to what I was searching for; but a realization, a basic revelation, that there might be another way to closure struck me.

Prayer.

I shook my head at the thought. Yes, of course I believed in praying, but my situation felt too silly for such a serious solution. I mean, really, God had the whole universe to hold together; sick people to minister to; hungry children to feed. In the scope of tragedies and disasters, the space in my heart that had once belonged to RiChard, and that I had been trying in vain to keep empty, seemed like a non-issue for the attention of the Most High.

I'd spent two years trying to tell myself that I was satisfied with staying in a state of love-life limbo, two years keeping Leon at bay with the excuse that I was enjoying my life alone, that I had moved beyond RiChard so successfully, I didn't need *any* man. At least not until I said I was ready.

As I thought about the lion's head ring that I had kept out of my reach for so long, I thought about Ava's words from the other day. She thought I needed a man. What was stopping me?

Fear.

The word dropped into my consciousness like a winter snow, silent but impactful, enough to change the landscape of my soul.

It made sense. I'd tried love before, and where had it left me? Though Leon seemed genuine, who was to say that he would not abandon me like RiChard had?

Mother Spriggs was staring directly at me, her lips now still, her gaze steady. Such a posture from her would have normally left me feeling intimidated, but for a reason that I could not explain, I was not afraid. I did not take it for granted that my train of thought had suddenly changed with her presence.

She'd been praying. I knew it, felt it; and as silly as the concerns of my life felt, something in me had changed.

"Mother Spriggs," I asked, "what do you think is the opposite of fear?"

"Doesn't matter what I think. Only matters what He says, and 2 Timothy 1:7 tells us plain as day: the opposite of fear is power, love, and a sound mind."

Love.

The word jumped out at me.

"You call that reporter from our church?" Her eyes squinted at me. "You call Brother Tyson?"

"I spoke to him this morning."

She nodded and then she turned toward the stairs.

Why is she asking me that? Her question bothered me, but I did not have time to consider it.

"Sienna!" My mother called me from upstairs. Though I heard the panic in her voice, I was still unprepared for what she shouted next. "Roman is not on the plane! Minister Howard just called to say that Roman walked off the plane right before take-off. "

I shut down the computer. The e-mail had to wait.

My son was losing his mind.

Chapter 15

I was seven years old when I tried to run away from home. Yvette was five and had laid claim to one of my favorite dolls. My mother, who believed in solving all household crises in a diplomatic way, dropped the ball on this one and sided with the party who had the loudest tears.

She told me I had to share, but I knew from past experience and the quick stick-out of Yvette's tongue behind my mother's back, that my beloved doll was effectively no longer mine. Tired of the injustices that had taken over my life the moment Yvette and I were forced to share a bedroom (my mother turned my old room into her craft room), I stuffed my book bag with my favorite pair of stone-washed jeans and pink jelly shoes, grabbed a handful of chips, and set out to my best friend Cherie's house. I made it as far as three houses down before my mother's call turned me right back around on my heels.

I feared my mother too much to go one step farther.

I think that was what bothered me the most about Roman's disappearance. Did the boy not respect me? Did he not care what I thought, how I felt? What had I done to make him think it was okay to act like he did not have a house to come home to?

"Ma'am, will that be credit or debit?"

"Huh?" I looked at the bag of sponges, spray bottles, and disinfectants that filled my shopping cart.

"Credit or debit?" The cashier popped her chewing gum and patted the side of her hair where the remnants of a blond weave clung on for dear life.

"Credit," I whispered, swiping my card, realizing that my thoughts were holding up the express lane at the supermarket.

That's why I had to get home and start cleaning.

Thinking slowed me down.

Cleaning picked me up.

"Ma'am," the cashier spoke slowly as if I could not keep up, "you need to press the red button twice and then the green button once so that we can finish this transaction and I can move on to the next customer."

Maybe I *couldn't* keep up. I blinked back tears, trying to remember the number of times I was supposed to press whatever color button. The cashier popped another bubble and the woman behind me who smelled like moth balls and cinnamon sticks groaned loudly.

"I'm sorry, the red button once and the green button twice?" I didn't trust my voice so I continued to whisper.

"Whatever." The girl rolled her eyes and whipped the credit card machine around to face her. "Just give me the card. Old people and technology never mix," she muttered.

"Um, Star'Asia," I read her name badge, glaring at her. I was ready to tell this girl-child a few things about young people and respect, but then a thought occurred to me. "I got this." I swung the machine back, swiped my card again and finished the transaction before she could think of another cutting insult. "Thank you." I smiled genuinely at the cashier named Star'Asia and headed for the parking lot.

Roman was not answering his cell phone, but phones weren't the only way teenagers stayed connected to the world. I'd made Roman take down his Facebook page after finding out that several girls in his class were posting pictures of themselves fully clothed but in inappropriate positions. He'd fussed and carried on about how he was unfairly being penalized because of others' actions, but he'd followed my directions and deleted his page.

Now, I hoped that he'd actually gone behind my back and started another one.

When my mother broke the news that Roman had run off from the return flight home, I knew that I was not going to be able to stay in that house with all those people looking at me like I was an unfit mother. After filing a new missing child report with Las Vegas authorities, I considered calling Leon, slapping Yvette, or running around the block, screaming.

I chose to clean my house instead.

I was still committed to that task as nothing cleared my head better than the smell of pine and lemons, the scents of my favorite cleaners.

I just had to pray that he had some kind of online trail, then think like my son and figure out his screen name.

As I pulled out of my parking space, I noticed a red Lexus driving parallel to me in the next parking lane. I slowed down, and the other car did so too. "That's weird."

I did not want to add feelings of paranoia to the stew of emotions that were simmering to a boil inside of me; but the thought of Jenellis and her red Lexus and the whole Brayden/Kwan/Silver fiasco were nudging me in that uncomfortable direction.

"I did my civic duty and reported my suspicions to the police." I attempted to calm my nerves as I pressed down on my accelerator. The red Lexus lagged behind.

Seriously, I need to get it together. I shook my head at myself as I turned out of the parking lot and the Lexus stayed put.

I was almost home when my cell phone buzzed with a text message from a blocked number.

One hour, it read.

"One hour?" I scratched my head, pulling into my assigned parking space. It was 9:54 a.m. "One hour for what?" I yelled at an unseen texter. "One hour? Is that a threat? Roman? Brayden? What is going on?" A million and one thoughts flashed through my head, none of them comforting.

"I don't have time for this." I threw my phone onto the passenger seat, fully intending to leave it in my car, but then I remembered that Roman might call. I grabbed it up and marched into my house, and threw it on the kitchen counter. Armed with antibacterial spray, rubber gloves, and heavy-duty sponges, I began fighting the war against the dirt and germs in my house. From the kitchen sink to the counters to the stainless-steel pans that hung from the hook over my island, the sponge in my fist turned into a disintegrating mound of pink fuzz, my world turning into a dizzying spiral around me.

"Gonna run from here? You're going to take off and leave here without a trace? Not caring enough to tell me where you are? Got me worried about you on purpose? What are you doing? Where are you, Roman?" I pushed harder onto my granite countertop, not caring if the cleaner I was using was even the right one. I threw the pink shreds of my sponge into the trash can and threw my hands up to my forehead. "Think, Sienna. Think, Sienna. What is he doing? Where is he going? Oh, God. Oh, God. What am I supposed to do? What do I do?"

"Breathe, Sienna."

The deep voice from the edge of my kitchen caught me off-guard, knocked me off balance, and made me stumble.

"Wha . . ."

"Breathe, Sienna. Start with that." Leon was in uniform, his police radio a mass of static, his eyes solely on me.

"Where . . . where did you come from?" My words came out in short bursts as I tried to catch my breath.

"Your front door was unlocked, and when I heard all those pans banging and clanging, I came up to make sure you were okay." He paused. "I heard about Roman."

I felt weak, close to fainting. Leon was suddenly next to me, his arms about to wrap around me, to help me stand.

No. I am a strong woman. Fearless. I straightened myself up before his fingertips made it to my shoulders.

Fearless.

Was that really what I was demonstrating by not letting Leon hug me and hold me up? I blinked the thought away as I stood up even taller, calmed my breathing, and stared directly at him. "Who told you about Roman?"

"Your mom called me. Said you left her house the moment you found out that Roman ditched his flight back home."

Strong, fearless, I told myself as I continued my tight stance. I noticed Leon had taken a slight step back from me. I ignored the pang of sorrow that threatened to sear through me at that observation, reminding me that even the Bible said power and a sound mind were the opposite of fear, and I was showing my power.

But the verse also says "love."

I could feel the bottom corner of my lip start to tremble, but I cut that out immediately. Everything about and in me felt like it was falling apart, but I could not, even now, let Leon see me break.

I did not want him to rescue me. I did not want anyone rescuing me. Rescue of some nature was what I had searched for in RiChard. Rescue from the routine of my life. Rescue from a feeling of purposelessness. He was like a savior to me, and then he abandoned me in the name of his noble mission of saving the world.

And I was not going down that path again.

I already knew there was another woman in Leon's life who made him smile—saw her with my own eyes. There was no way I was going to let myself become emotionally dependent on a man who wasn't promised to be with me tomorrow.

"Thank you, Leon, for stopping by to check on me." My words felt like dry cotton in my mouth as I forced a smile. "I'm okay, and I'm sure that Roman is okay. I only need to wait to hear from him. I am sure he will get in touch with me soon with a reasonable explanation as to why did not want to come home just yet."

"Sienna, I am with you. I want to help." Leon seemed to see right through my act, but he did not step any closer.

"I know. Thank you. I will be okay." I let my smile grow wider. "I merely needed a moment to get myself together so I could plan out what to do. And I have it now, a plan." I did have a plan. I just could not remember it at the moment. I turned toward the staircase that led down to the lower level where my front door was. Leon took the hint and followed, but before going outside, he turned to face me again.

"Sienna, you know if you need me to do anything—"

"I know." I cut him off, about to shut my eyes to block the tears that were threatening to form in them, but my unfinished collage in the entry hallway caught my eyes. I stared at it as Leon continued to stare at me.

"You know I started this when I was in the tenth grade." I traced a copper spoon I added sometime in my twenties, around the time my grandmother passed. The spoon had been part of her special occasion dinnerware and it fit perfectly in my three-dimensional collage as a part of a brown angel hovering over the empty corner that would eventually be me. I gave my full attention to the collage as Leon simply stared at me. *Brother Tyson is the only person who ever commented—or even seemed to notice—this entry statement of my life.* A fleeting thought.

Leon stared at me blankly. I watched as he pressed his lips together. He partially shrugged and then fully stepped out of the doorway. "I care about Roman's well-being too. Let me know how I can help and keep me posted."

He was gone.

I had gone back up the steps and plucked out a new sponge, this one yellow, from my shopping bag, when a heavy knock sounded on my front door.

"Roman?" I called out, knowing even as I heard myself that my hope that it was him at the door was both ridiculous and impossible. Even still, I smiled as I swung it open.

Leon again. I did not hide my heavy sigh.

"I'll call you to keep you posted." Why was I talking so short to him when what I really wanted to do was collapse into his arms?

Fear.

"No, Sienna." Leon shook his head. "I'm responding to a call." He patted his radio. "A 911 caller just identified your address as the place where a woman named Anastasia 'Silver' Simmons is being held against her will. I know that's completely unfounded, so I wanted to get here first before any other officer did."

I looked at my watch. 10:54 a.m.

One hour, the text from earlier today had read.

Chapter 16

Of all days, of all moments, this was not the time, and yet there was a swarm of police cars, emergency response vehicles, even a SWAT truck circling around my front door.

So much for trying to look like the ideal neighbor.

As countless men and women in various uniforms tore through my house, a man in a black suit kept asking me to repeat the story I first shared with Leon and then shared with him three times already.

"So, Ms. St. James, you're saying that a man named Brandon—"

"Brayden," I corrected.

"Right, Brayden Moore came to your office this week and said and did things that made you suspicious, and then you saw him on a television show with the victim. What else can you tell us?" The shape of his head reminded me of a toad, warts, wrinkles and all. His leathery white skin spoke to sun exposure. Perhaps he was a fisher, or a hunter. Definitely an outdoorsman.

The details I noticed when I was distressed.

We were sitting at my kitchen island, my cleaners and sponges tossed on the floor. Leon stood behind my chair, outside of my view.

I wished I could see his face.

"That's really all I know. Without consulting an attorney, I don't have anything else to add." Someone's life was in danger, so I knew that client confidentiality could be violated to protect Silver from harm; however, I wasn't sure where the line was drawn. I did not want to do or say anything that would get me into some kind of trouble when all was said and done.

That's why I had said nothing about Jenellis. She had not said or done anything suspicious. She'd looked as confused as I did when Brayden talked about us both understanding "why we were so pressed for time" within twenty-four hours. He knew something was going to happen. Jenellis did not. These were cops. They could take a name and do their own investigating, I reasoned. It was true; I really did not know anything else.

My main concern was my son.

Forgive me, Lord, if I I'm being selfish, but I want these people out of my house so I can figure out how to find Roman.

"There's nothing here." A woman entered the room with a small army of officers behind her. The black-suit man nodded and then turned back to me.

"Okay, Ms. St. James. You're clear for now, but if you think of anything or hear from this man, Brayden Moore, again, call me directly." He handed me a business card. DETECTIVE SAM FIELDS, it read.

As he stood, another man approached where we were sitting with my work notepad in hand.

"We found it," he said, opening to the back where I had tucked the large wad of bills Brayden Moore had given to me the other day. "Fifteen hundred two dollars exactly."

"Oh, I'd forgotten about that." Though it was true—in the emotional upheaval of the past two days, I *had* completely forgotten about the stash of cash—even I heard how weak my voice sounded. "Brayden gave me that money and refused to take it back when I tried to return it, saying it was payment for therapy sessions. I never even counted it because I wanted nothing to do with it."

Detective Fields took my notepad and started flipping through the pages.

"Wait, that's confidential information. I keep notes of *all* of my clients in there." I reached for it. Fields hesitated but then returned it before standing.

"We'll be back with another search warrant, Ms. St. James. I wouldn't go too far today if I were you." Everyone was filing out of the house.

I did not like the way this was going, the way he looked at me.

Neither did Leon.

"Sienna St. James is as clean as they come." The mere sound of his voice was a comfort as he stood next to me in the doorway. "We are not sure why she is being targeted, but I can promise you she has nothing to do with this situation."

We.

He had removed any thought I'd had about feeling alone with any of this.

The detective studied Leon for a few moments, his head cocked to one side. "Officer Sanderson, you used to work on homicide before you took up the kid gig, right?"

"Police Athletic League," Leon corrected. "I work at one of the PAL centers when I'm not working my other shifts." Recent department cutbacks had forced Leon back on part-time patrol duty. "Sorry that I have not had the pleasure of meeting you before, Detective . . ."

Fields did not bother to introduce himself to Leon. He merely grunted. "I would suggest that your girlfriend here examine every corner of her life and past if you really think she is being targeted."

"I am not his girlfriend," I said, maybe a little too forcibly.

"I will let you two work that out, but we'll be back with another search warrant. If you think of anything else you've 'forgotten,' Ms. St. James, you have my card."

The door closed and I had more to clean. Muddy footprints on my carpet, some knick-knacks knocked over and broken. A couple overturned houseplants.

Leon's fingertips were on my shoulder, and this time I gave in.

"I've got you, Sienna," he whispered in my ear as I melted into the folds of his arms. "Everything will turn out okay."

Whether or not it would, I did not know. What I did know was that the warmth and strength I felt leaning my head against his chest was the most genuine, comforting, safest place I'd been in a long time.

And then his cell phone rang.

I felt his body stiffen as he fumbled to check it, then turn it off.

"I've got to go, Sienna. I'm still on duty." The hug was over, and he was looking away from me.

"That was your phone, not your radio."

"Yeah, but . . . but I have to go." He reached for the door handle. "There's an unmarked car out there that's watching you, so don't worry about your safety. I will be back as soon as I can. Everything will work out okay."

I watched him run down the steps, pause at his car, and then take off.

In all the vulnerable moments I'd had over the past two years, Leon had never left me standing alone to face them, even if I had not been welcome to his presence.

One unanswered phone call had done just that.

Taken him away.

Chapter 17

Roman SJ
R StJames
RoRo Man
Manny James

Nothing was working.

Sitting in front of Roman's laptop, I tried every combination of names, nicknames, and otherwise I'd heard Roman call himself over the years. Facebook was turning up nothing. I'd checked his computer history and it had been cleared.

"Roman, what are you hiding?"

Hiding.

I wasn't hiding anything, and yet there were police officers and other authorities combing through my history and affairs at that moment. That thought stirred a recollection. Earlier in the morning, Brother Laz Tyson had said he knew something about my past. Maybe he could help me figure out some things about my present.

My mother had called to tell me there were no new updates about Roman. Really, she was calling to see if I still was in my right mind, I knew. My mother, the respected elementary school principal, was a nurturer by nature; she simply did not show this side of herself through frilly words.

Despite my many calls, there was nothing new the Vegas police could share with me. And Roman's cell phone was of no help. I regretted not putting him on my cell phone plan. When he took initiative last fall to get his own prepaid phone with his part-time job money, I was thrilled at his use of economy and independence. Now, the cheap, cut-rate phone provider he'd chosen was living up to my low expectations. I wanted someone to track down his phone's whereabouts, but the customer service phone number repeatedly only led to a web of computerized messages that redirected me to e-mail addresses that led back to more phone numbers that led to nowhere.

I just wanted to speak to a real human being who could help me.

I just wanted my son home.

It was too much going on at one time. And I was all over the place.

The lion's head ring.

That was the one thing I could hold, the one thing I could control. It was still safe in my purse. The e-mail about it was still safe out in the virtual world.

I pulled up my e-mail account. Within seconds, my breathing was easy, steady. I was in control again, the e-mail with the translation of the letter from two years ago on the screen.

My name is Beatriz. I spoke to you yesterday by phone to tell you that a package with your husband's ashes is coming. My brother does not know that I am writing you, and he will be very upset if he finds out, because we promised not to tell, and we needed the money.

I am a pottery maker in Portugal. This is our family business, and we are not doing well. A few weeks ago a man came to view our wares. After quietly studying our best work, he paid us great money to craft an urn. He came back for it yesterday, and then after inspecting it, he put a small box inside of it and told us that he would pay us twice the amount he'd given us for the urn if we would only call you to tell you that your husband's ashes were coming and then mail the urn to you. My brother agreed, because we greatly needed the money, and to make the story more authentic, my brother used the address of a crematorium in a neighboring town for the delivery. When you asked for the phone number during my call to you, he meant to give you the one for that crematorium, to keep you from finding us, but he instead accidentally gave you our number. I took that mishap as a sign from God that it was meant for you to know the truth, especially with what happened last night.

Late last night the same man who asked us to mail the package was found unconscious in a hotel room near our town. The news media here put out a story to try to get more information about him, since he appeared to be traveling in this country alone and illegally. I do not know his name, but a link to the newspaper article can be found at this Web site. There is a picture on the Web site of the man.

I do not know what was in the small box that the man put inside the urn. If it is truly your husband, I am sorry for your loss. What I do know is that I cannot live a life of dishonesty, no matter how much money is offered, and I have not had peace about staying quiet regarding this.

Please do not try to contact me. I do not want my brother angered, as he does not usually get involved in such affairs. I am telling you all I know.

The words "Web site" were hyperlinked. I remembered from before that the link was to a Web site that had a picture of an unconscious Kisu, RiChard's best friend, who was supposedly murdered years ago. At least that was the story RiChard gave Kisu's family and me. He'd had the blood on his hands—revenge of his best friend's death—to prove it.

But Kisu had been found unconscious in Portugal two years ago, according to that picture I'd clicked on back then. He was the one who'd sent the ring, claiming it to be RiChard's ashes. It was too much to figure out back then, and I'd left it alone. Really, it was too much to figure out right now, but the idea that some detective might soon stumble on my connection to RiChard made me want to get a head start.

I clicked on the link and my heart sunk.

"Where's the picture?" I blinked, trying to make sense of the blank screen. Only a few words filled the screen.

Desculpe a página Web solicitada que você está procurando foi removido.

"Great, here we go with the Portugeuse again," I groaned, but then I realized I had an option I had not considered last time.

Google Translate.

I copicd and pasted the sentence into the translation Web site and saw what the problem was:

Sorry the requested Web page you are looking for has been removed.

"Great." I threw myself back in the seat, ignoring the squeaks and squeals Roman's old desk chair made under the weight of my heavy hips. "I should have followed up with this back when I first got it."

Oh well.

I guessed I had reached the end of the road as far as getting answers about Kisu and his connection to RiChard. I shut down the computer, disgusted that I'd failed on two missions, two attempts to find answers about the two males in my life who had walked out on me.

RiChard and Roman.

I looked around my son's room. His bed was made. His stuffed NUMBER 1 pillow, a prize he won at the state fair last year when we went with Leon, was perched perfectly on top. The theme "number one" continued throughout his room as he had actually picked up, sorted, and arranged various trophies and certificates with the "number one" moniker on his desk, book-shelves, and windowpane. Was my son conceited, or was this his way of hiding some insecurity?

His clothes, which usually covered his floor like a patchwork quilt, were folded and put away out of view, or hung up in his closet. There were no empty cereal boxes or crushed soda cans.

How had I missed all of this?

I hadn't seen my son's floor since the day we'd moved in, I think. Not only was his carpeted floor cleared, but it looked like he had even vacuumed, as no crumbs were sticking to the bottom of my socks.

I should have known that he was up to something the day he left.

I sat down on his bed, and tried to smooth down the single lump that kept his baby blue comforter from sitting flat. Years ago, among RiChard's many deliveries to our delicate family unit, he'd sent a mola quilt, handmade in Panama. I'd used the colorful quilt to wrap Roman up as an infant, and Roman had used it to decorate his room since then. Thrown across his bed, rolled into a ball on his desk, hanging off a hook on his wall . . . He always had the bright and colorful patterned quilt somewhere in view.

It occurred to me that I had not seen the quilt since we'd move to our new house. Indeed, I had not seen the quilt or the other little treasures from RiChard that Roman had held on to from his toddler years anywhere since taking up our new address.

I should have followed through with finding out what happened to RiChard. I had been so busy staying numb to avoid feeling pain that I'd neglected to address Roman's take on his father's absence.

As I thought about Roman's feelings—and my lack of attention to them—a thought occurred to me. The e-mail that hyperlinked to the now defunct Web page had been typed up and sent by that helpful Portuguese teacher I had sought to assist with translating.

But the original letter that came after the urn showed up would have had the Web site written out. The teacher simply had not bothered to write out the full name of the Web site in her translation, choosing instead to hyperlink to it using the words "Web site," to make it easier for me to click it open at the time.

Like a newborn babe inhaling to take its first breath, new wind filled me with enough hope to continue on the journey for answers.

My bedside table drawer.

That's where I had put the letter after I'd scanned it to e-mail to the Portuguese teacher two years ago. When I moved, tired as I was, I'd kept the drawers intact, not seeing the point of boxing up a bunch of

loose ends only to dump them back into the single mahogany pull-out. Without hesitation, I nearly ran to my
room, pulled open the drawer, and poured the entire
contents of the drawer—loose change and all—onto my
bed. However, whatever wind had filled my sails slowly
began leaking away, leaving me to feel like a two-day
old party balloon.

The letter was gone.

Where else could I have put it? There was nowhere
else, I was sure of it, just as I had been confident that
I'd put the lion's head ring in my father's safe, and now
in the corner of my purse.

My head dropped into my hands as tears fought to
come out again.

"I'm sorry I failed you, Roman," I whispered, "I
should have pursued what happened to your father for
your sake, to make sure you could come to terms with
him abandoning us."

Roman wasn't there, but I went back to his room
anyway, my maternal instincts leading me to believe
that sitting in his personal space was the best way to be
close to him at this time.

Maybe that's why he had run away. He was angry at
me for not finishing the course and finding his father.
I sat back down on the bed, and tried again to smooth
down the one lump at the foot of his bed that kept his
bedspread from looking catalogue perfect.

I now knew the boy had it in him to keep his room
clean. I shook my head.

I smoothed down the bedspread again, but the lump
was not going away.

"I'll help you this one time." I smiled sadly, as if
Roman were there to hear my offer of assistance. "Let
me show you how to make up a bed."

I peeled off his pillows, pulled back his sheets, ready to tuck them all back in more tightly.

But the lump . . .

What is this? I snatched the comforter and the top sheet off and then grabbed the top of his neighboring desk chair to keep from falling.

The letter from my drawer.

Roman had it, had hidden it.

But why?

How'd he even find it? How'd he even know *about it?*

I had a million and one questions, but I had to stay focused—focused, I realized, to help both of us finally get 100 percent full closure.

I plucked up the wadded envelope from under his bedspread, pulled out the yellowing letter, picked out the Web address from the sea of foreign words, keyed the first part of it into Roman's waiting computer, and held my breath.

A newspaper.

The root site was a newspaper and although the entire Web site was written in Portuguese, I made out enough of the contact information at the bottom of the screen to pick up my cell phone. I was hopeful that someone at the other end of the international phone number would be able to speak enough English to help me.

Someone picked up on the first ring.

"*Olá?*"

"Um, hello," I responded, realizing I had not planned a script for the call. I had not been expecting an actual answer. *Here goes* . . . "I need to speak to someone about an article you ran on your Web site two years ago."

There was a long pause. I held my breath, wondering if the words to come would be in a language I could understand.

They were.

"Uh, what was the article about?" The responder stumbled with her English, but was understandable nonetheless.

"An unidentified man who was found lying unconscious in a hotel. There was a picture of him on your Web site."

"I don't recall that, but I'll transfer you to our archival department. Perhaps someone there will be able to help you."

The phone was transferred three more times before I got through to someone who was able to help me.

"I remember the story because I covered it," a man with a thick accent responded. "The file with the photo was corrupted not too long after we put it up online. That's why the page is gone. The man in the photo was never officially identified. He was taken to the hospital, but apparently woke up on his own and left without notice."

Kisu is still out there.

"You said *officially* identified. What do you mean?"

"The story was a non-story. Nobody came forward to claim him and the link to the story only got a few hits before it became corrupted, so when he was identified, it was never posted in our paper, or anywhere else as far as I know."

"So he was identified?"

"The hotel eventually found a photo ID that had been left between the pages of a book in the room."

"Do you . . . Can you say what name was on the ID?"

"Sure. His name was RiChard St. James."

Couldn't be. I did not even bat an eye. The man in the picture clearly was RiChard's best friend, Kisu, and not RiChard. *Is Kisu going around using RiChard's identity?* I tried to make sense out of that revelation, but knew the speaker on the other end of the phone had no reason to continue with the conversation. Or lie.

"You have a good memory." I was amazed at how quickly the man recalled everything.

"Oh, that is only because it came up recently."

"What do you mean?" I felt my heart quicken a beat.

"Yeah, it's kind of weird actually. You're the third person in the past several months or so to call and ask specifically about that picture."

Third.

I wasn't sure what to make of that either. I only knew that I needed to keep this man on the phone while I figured out what else to ask.

"When—who?" I could not form a single logical question.

"Huh?" The man turned away from the phone. I could hear another voice talking in Portuguese and the man laughed. "Um momento," he spoke away from the phone before turning his attention back to me. "I have to go. Was there anything else I can help you with?"

Think, Sienna, think.

"Yes, can . . . can you tell me who contacted you?"

"Oh, I don't remember. I just forwarded the information that came from the hotel. This was about five, six months ago, I think. I don't usually give out such information, but I felt bad that the man had not been claimed or identified by anyone else. I thought whatever I could do would help. Did you know this man?"

"Um, possibly. Yes."

"Tell you what, give me your e-mail address, and I'll forward you what I sent out before. It was a public news story, so I guess there is no harm done."

I rattled off my e-mail and before I could make sense of the conversation, it was over.

I was still sitting in Roman's desk chair when my phone chimed. I'd finally upgraded and gotten a true smartphone, but honestly, with all the beeps, buzzes, and chimes that now provided a soundtrack to my day, I wasn't sure if I was getting a Facebook friend request, a text message, an e-mail, or a severe weather alert.

It was an e-mail.

I held my breath as I opened the short e-mail from an Alberto Fernandes, a reporter for a small, daily press in Almada, Portugal. It was a forwarded e-mail with no text, only an attachment. I opened the attachment to discover what looked like a scanned photo of a driver's license with most of the information blacked out.

But what wasn't blacked out jumped out at me. The picture clearly was that of Kisu. The name underneath clearly said RiChard St. James. The street name was blacked out, but the city and town were left intact. Perugia, Italy.

RiChard had been the only child of a chef from the Caribbean island of St. Martin and a college professor from Italy. They'd met in Paris and raised RiChard there before divorcing and seemingly leaving RiChard as alone as they had left each other. *Had RiChard moved back to the town of his mother?* But wait a minute; that was Kisu's picture on the ID card.

Why would Kisu be traveling the world with my long-lost husband's name? I wondered if Kisu had ever been back to his native KwaZulu-Natal.

I pondered all these things, straining to make sense of it when something else caught my attention. I'd already seen that the e-mail was forwarded. What I had not noticed until that moment was the name of the original recipient of the e-mailed photo.

RomanNumeralOne.

Of course.

My son, Roman.

Chapter 18

Years ago, I volunteered to design the flyer for our church's Family & Friends Picnic at Gunpowder State Park. I tried to capture the essence of the event—picnic tables and grills, the playground and beach—as well as the notion of friends and family.

That's where things had gotten sticky.

In my original draft, I'd found a photo of a man, a woman, two kids, a grandmother, and a woman who could have been an aunt or a good friend. A woman named Tina Watson, who served on the budget committee of the picnic, more or less laid me out for having "the nerve" to include such a "traditional" picture of family when many of the families at our church were made up of single mothers and absent fathers, including my own—which I'd pointed out to her. Though she was the only one who'd made a big funk about it, I gave into her demands and revised the flyer with a picture of a mom embracing two kids, a grandfather smiling at their side, and a man and woman in the distance, standing over a grill.

The Sunday that the flyer was distributed in the church bulletin, nobody seemed to notice or care about the picture I had settled on. Even Tina, who was busy with her receipt book at the main doors collecting payment for the event, said nothing about my revisions. I thought nothing else of it myself until after service ended and Roman and I were driving home.

He was about five or six at the time, I remember, and the flyer lay in a crumpled wad at his feet where he sat in the back seat.

"What's wrong, Roman?" I smiled at him through the rearview mirror, always tickled at how his fat cheeks back then looked even fatter when he pouted, like a chipmunk who'd stumbled on a bag of sour gumdrops.

"You changed the picture," he sulked.

"Picture? What are you talking about?"

He picked up the crumpled paper, smoothed it out, and pointed to the smiling mother and her two kids. "Daddy's supposed to be right there and you took him out."

If an arrow had pierced right through my heart, I don't think it would have felt any more painful than the merciless sting that pierced through me at his words.

Roman went on to have a great time at the Family & Friends picnic. We stuffed ourselves with hot dogs and hamburgers, potato salad and sweet baked beans, played softball and dodge ball, and stayed in the shallow, rocky sand waters of the Gunpowder Falls swimming beach until the sun gave up on us. However, the entire time, I could not forget the devastation on his face at the idea that I had taken Daddy out of the picture.

And it hadn't even been my idea.

It was hard to believe that police had been in my house only two hours earlier, looking for a kidnapped dancer named Silver. Sometimes I felt like my life was a reality show, and the cameras were constantly rolling.

At the moment, all I cared about was that my son had run away and was somewhere in Vegas with the false idea that his father looked like Kisu and had an address in Italy.

I was standing in my living room, for some reason studying the picture of the purple, orange, and black-spotted butterfly I had painted years ago, like it held the answers to all my questions. I remember painting it from a picture, thinking that I would never be able to replicate the intricate pattern and brilliant colors. Some say "pictures are worth a thousand words," but is the message only meaningful if the picture is correct?

Roman had never seen a picture of RiChard, me having shredded every photo and written memento from him before Roman was barely out of Pull-Ups. I'd described him in detail to Roman before, talking of his café au lait skin, curly hair, peridot-colored eyes; a far cry from Kisu's dark-as-midnight complexion and piercing dark brown gaze. Kisu hailed from the KwaZulu-Natal region of South Africa, a direct descendant of proud and strong Zulu warriors. RiChard was the salt to Kisu's pepper, but Roman had only the picture ID e-mailed to him from a reporter in Portugal to give him an (inaccurate) visual.

Perhaps Roman thought I lied about how RiChard looked, and thereby had lied to him about everything he knew about the man who fathered him.

Perhaps that's why he'd run away.

He did not trust me anymore. He did not trust me enough to talk about his father, to believe I would ever find out what happened to him.

The e-mail had been sent to Roman last September, a full six months ago, three months before the trip to the Native American reservation in Arizona had even been mentioned. Roman had been eager to go on the trip, I remembered. Overly eager, hindsight told me. How long had Roman wanted to get away? How long had he planned his exit, his escape? *What was his ultimate destination?*

My heart told me it was not Las Vegas. Vegas—that was Skee-Gee, that was Tridell. For Roman, Vegas was a means to an end, the first starting point on his carefully planned trip.

I remembered then that he'd gotten his first job at the end of September. I had assumed it was his attempt to have money to buy the high-priced tennis shoes and jeans I refused to buy him.

But, I realized, he never did get those things.

He'd been saving his money.

He'd packed heavily for the trip, I recalled, reflecting on Leon's jokes about the multitude of Roman's baggage. He never planned to return with the rest of them, I realized.

Is Roman on a mission to find RiChard?

The thought winded me as I collapsed into my love seat, the bay window next to it offering a clear view of the unmarked police car guarding, really, watching, my residence.

He'd been doing his own research—probably way beyond the little bit I'd stumbled into—made careful plans, and had probably dismissed whatever information I'd given to him over the years. Did he see me as a liar? Or a hider, as he had obviously found the letter I'd kept secret in my nightstand drawer? What else had he come across? What other information had he dug up? I thought again of the e-mailed picture ID he'd had since September. I just saw it today, but Roman had had a six-month head start into the journey he was now on.

I needed to do my own research to find my son.

I needed to find RiChard.

Where did I begin again?

Roman had at least a six-month head start. The thought repeated itself and frightened me.

I went to the kitchen to fix a cup of chamomile tea to help calm my nerves. The opposite happened. As I reached for my teapot, a business card that had been left on the breakfast bar caught my eye.

LAZARUS TYSON.

He'd dropped it there before he rolled out at my command early this morning, and miraculously, the card had survived the invasion of Detective Fields and his team.

I picked up the card, fingered it, felt my anxiety rise even as I knew that I had to use it. Laz was an investigative reporter. He knew how to dig deep, had sources probably all over the country, maybe even the world. He'd said he knew that I had been through something; perhaps that meant he knew about my dealings with RiChard somehow.

He was an answer. A risky answer—he thought I had the hots for him—but an answer nonetheless. I wasn't sure if Leon saw the hug Laz had given me that morning, but I was sure that Laz could help me.

I picked up the phone and dialed, holding my breath as his line began ringing.

He picked up on the eighth ring. "Sienna St. James. I knew you would be calling."

I could hear the smile in his voice and was immediately irritated, but what choice did I have?

"You knew it was me?" I shut my eyes as I asked him the obvious.

"Caller ID." His voice was all bass, his tone was all flirt. I ignored it.

"Laz, I need your help."

"Oh, so we're back to first names now. The last time we spoke I was Mr. Tyson."

I opened my eyes just so that I could roll them. "Listen, don't mistake my call for something it is not. I need help investigating something, and I think you can help."

His silence told me his interest was piqued. I knew a man like Lazarus thrived on a word like "investigating." I thought quickly of how else to reel him in without sounding like I had ulterior motives.

"For reasons I can't get into at the moment, there are police watching my house and I'm expecting more to return at any moment. However, I have another issue going on that affects my son, and I think you may be able to point me in the right direction to find the information I need, but I don't think I can get out of here unnoticed, and I don't need a recognized news-man knocking on my front door."

"You say the police are outside your house?" He spoke evenly without missing a beat or being thrown off at the idea of a police stakeout. The investigative reporter was in full swing.

"Yes." I exhaled, waiting.

"Do you have a back door?"

"I have a walkout basement."

"Okay," Laz continued. "Your development backs to trees and on the other side of the trees is Rossville Boulevard. I can pick you up from there in about ten minutes."

"You're that close?"

"I'm at the Panera Bread off of Route 40, near Sam's Club."

"Oh, I didn't know you hung out in these parts. Do you live near here?"

"Heavens, no. I don't do the east side." Laz immediately caught his insult. "I mean, I live in Howard County. Ellicott City to be exact."

"So what are you doing all the way out here?"

Laz chuckled. "I was following the breaking news story about a certain someone who was allegedly holding hostage a kidnapping victim."

"Why didn't you say that at first?" I gasped. "Am I all over the news?" I barely breathed, realizing that I had not turned on my television all day, and had not done my news Web site checks in hours.

"No, Sienna. Calm down. The police have asked the media to avoid any reports due to undisclosed sensitive information about the case that could affect the safety and well-being of one of Baltimore City's finest strippers."

I rolled my eyes for the second time, trying to keep my disdain for his condescending tone from stopping me from seeking the help I believed he could offer. "Okay, ten minutes. And you better be there."

I hung up before he could get another word in, grabbed my purse with the lion's head ring tucked inside, the letter from Portugal, and a heart full of ache and a head full of memories, and headed out of my basement door.

Within moments I was pushing through tree branches, fighting through tall weeds, nearing the sound of traffic zooming up and down Rossville Boulevard.

The escape had been easy. Too easy. I wondered what troubles were coming next. I wasn't sure but the first sign of it was driving a silver BMW and heading straight toward where I stood on the side of the road.

"You made it." He grinned through the open window. "Get in."

Chapter 19

He took me to a dimly lit establishment that sat off of a winding back road in Cedonia, a neighborhood in northeast Baltimore that sat on the city/county line. It was one of those dining places that suffered from a confused identity. Through one entrance off of its gravel lot was a restaurant that had an extensive menu with plenty of house specials, private party rooms, and old-school chandeliers. The other entrance led to a grungy-looking packaged goods and liquor store.

He'd taken me to the restaurant side and without even a wait, we'd been escorted to an overly cushy booth with solid, tall walls. Most of the light that reflected off the real silver and china on the table came from a flickering candle between us and a low-wattage yellow light bulb that barely shone through the frosted sconce on the wall.

I had been in a place similar to this one just the other night with Leon.

The date that didn't happen.

The comparison made me uncomfortable.

"Thanks again for getting me, Laz." I stared at him as he flipped through the menu. "But again, let me be clear. I'm only meeting you here to get your help and direction."

Laz looked up from his laminated menu. "Don't worry, Sienna. I am not trying to wine and dine you. Forgive me for thinking that a dark restaurant off the beaten path was the perfect place for a woman being watched by the law to spill her secrets."

I glared at him, wanting to say something back, but knew that he knew there was nothing for me to say.

He was right.

"Afternoon, folks. You here for one of our lunch specials?" A curly redhead with a name tag that read MELINDA stood by our table, a notepad in hand. Even from my seated position, I could tell she was at least a head shorter than me, but her smile seemed bigger than life itself.

"What are your specials, dear?" Laz asked as if we really had come there for a casual lunch date and not an urgent investigative session. In all fairness, I realized, Laz had no idea why I had called him, though a part of me believed that with all the research he'd supposedly done on me and my son—and Skee-Gee and Tridell—he probably had an inkling.

As the waitress rattled off about the crab and shrimp omelet and hot roast beef sandwich specials, I pondered what I would say to Laz, how I would begin, *where* I could begin. By the time she'd taken our orders and filled our glasses with ice water, I was no clearer on what to say, so I went with what was in my mind.

"So, what was the dirt you found on my nephew?" It was random, but Laz didn't seem bothered.

"If you don't already know about all your nephew's side hustles, I don't know what else to tell you."

"I guess you have a point." I shook my head with a slight smile. Laz had ordered a thick chocolate malt as an appetizer and the way he was sipping off the side of it reminded me of a six-year-old Roman. I'd ordered some mozzarella sticks that sat untouched. "What's the deal with Tridell Jenkins?"

"Now that one should interest you." Laz set his glass down. "I won't get into the details, but let's just say that he has found a way to fuse modeling, street drugs, and online gaming into a creative venture. If you are really curious, I'll give you the link to his Web site; but I should warn you, if you click on it, you might be added to a group being monitored by the FBI."

"Okay. I don't think I even want to know more about it. Sounds like I could get in trouble for simply knowing it exists." We both chuckled and Laz picked up his chocolate malt again.

"How do you do your research?" I began again. "Where do you get your information from?"

"Well, you know a good journalist never reveals his sources."

Forget the small talk. My son was out there. I needed information. Now. "What do you know about my past, Lazarus?"

"Thank you, Sienna. Finally." Laz put his glass back down and waved away Melinda, who had come to take the order for our entrees. "I was wondering how long it would take for you to stop your tap-dancing routine and be the strong, passionate, and direct woman I have studied you to be."

"You have studied me." I repeated his words, feeling my eyelids blinking at rapid speed.

"Look, a woman who would risk all to chase a self-proclaimed revolutionary around the world is no pansy. I don't know what happened to you to take such a back seat to your own life, but I'm glad to see the real you finally start standing up, digging deep, not even letting me go unexcused in my own mission for answers."

I shifted in my seat, aware of the sweat pooling on the backs of my knees. Nobody had ever talked to me that way before.

"You know about RiChard." Again, a statement, not a question, as I stared him down.

"It wasn't hard. A quick look at your records—education, marriage, passport, don't ask how I got that—I saw the brief history you had with him."

Brief. I knew then that he didn't know everything. Nothing about RiChard's mark on my life felt brief. I tried not to let my disappointment show.

"Let me get your orders now." Melinda returned with a polite smile. I welcomed the distraction of pretending that I wanted to eat. It gave me a moment to draw my thoughts together, to regroup, to gather my feelings into a less messy pile. However, after Melinda walked away, I realized I was shaking.

So much at attempting composure.

"What do you know?" I did not try to hide my unease.

"Not much," he admitted, "just that you were married to him, traveled with him, had a child with him, left him, but never divorced him."

"No, he left me." I felt confused and I could not stop my finger from wagging. "And I didn't divorce him because I didn't know where to have the papers sent."

Laz shrugged, suddenly looked bored. "Whatever you tell yourself. Anyway, exactly what is it that you need from me? I'm sure you did not go through all that trouble to leave your house just for me to tell you about your own life."

"I need you to help me find him."

Laz raised an eyebrow. "You're looking for RiChard? Why now?"

"Because my son is looking for him. If I can find RiChard, then maybe I can get my son back home."

"I thought Roman was put on a flight back home with the other two musketeers?"

My silence answered his question. He slurped the remnants of his malt, let out a short belch, then put his glass down for good.

"Look, I don't know where RiChard is, or even Roman, for that matter. I only did a little research, but I did not look any further at him after your documents stopped cross-referencing his."

"That's fine. I just need you to tell me where to begin. My son has had at least a six-month start on his attempts at finding his father. You research people, places, and things for a living. Surely you can tell me how to do this."

"I research for news stories, Sienna. What's the angle for me? What am I going to gain out of this search?" Laz narrowed his eyes, and I knew we were at a critical stage of negotiations. He knew that I needed him, and in a way, he needed me. After his journalistic fall from grace, Laz appeared to be chasing that one breaking news story of significance that would earn him back full respect.

I realized then that was probably the real reason why he didn't offer any information to his colleague in Vegas. It had nothing to do with protecting me or Roman; it wasn't a big enough story. It wasn't *the* story.

I needed his help. I needed him to care.

I reached into the side of my purse and pulled out the lion's head ring. Then I took out the faded letter from Portugal, smoothed it out on the table, and patted it in front of him.

"Murder. Lies. False identity . . . I don't know. I've never known with RiChard. This is international, Laz. My husband, or whatever he is—if he's even still alive—could be anywhere in the world."

I watched as he picked up the lion's head ring, tilting it toward the flame of the candlelight, trapping a myriad of brilliant, colorful flashes in the gems. He set it back down on the table, and raised an eyebrow at the letter written in Portuguese.

"I have a translation for that," I said quickly. "And I—"

He placed a single finger over my lips to silence me. "Sienna, I do not know where all of this will lead." He paused, squinting at me. "But I will help you. If helping you somehow means reclaiming that fierce woman inside of you, I don't mind helping."

If I were white, I knew that my face would be bright red. And it wasn't merely because his words held layered meaning. The idea of me blushing was embarrassing, but it had been well over a decade since any part of a man had touched my lips. Leon, respecting my stated wishes of staying in the hug zone, hadn't even crossed that barrier.

Laz had just gone for it.

It was a finger, a single finger that he'd pressed against my lips. Was I that messed up that just the index finger of a man touching my face was enough to send me into a spin cycle?

Laz was looking at me as if he had a question, but Melinda was back, our orders in hand.

She was placing my plate in front of me when my cell phone rang.

It was Leon.

"I . . . I'm sorry, I have to go," I stammered, though I wasn't sure why, or where exactly I was going to go. I could not answer my phone, and could not stay at the restaurant either. I put away the ring and the letter and pulled out my check card as both Laz and Melinda looked at me curiously. "I'm sorry . . ." My words faded away as I stood. Laz waved away my card.

"No, I definitely am not letting you pay for me." I pressed my check card into Melinda's hand.

"Again, I think you're misinterpreting my actions." Laz pulled out a hundred dollar bill. "Think, Sienna, do you really want a paper trail? Here, Melinda. I'm paying for appetizers, our meal to go, and the rest is your tip for being so wonderful."

Melinda looked from his single bill to my check card and back to his bill.

"Sorry, Benjamin wins." She laughed a loud, hearty laugh that reminded me for some reason of family potluck get-togethers on cold winter nights. Her laughter was still in my ears as I marched out the front door of the restaurant and my ankle boots crunched on the thick gravel of the parking lot. Laz was right behind me.

"Don't mind me." He grinned mischievously. "I wanted to see where you were going to go."

My phone began ringing again and Leon's name flashed like an alarm across the face of my screen. Why did I feel so sick? Guilty . . . I had not done anything wrong, I assured myself, remembering that I had seen him earlier that day having breakfast with another woman.

My lunch with Laz was purely business. If anything, the business it was addressing could help me finally get true closure from RiChard and closer to Leon.

If it wasn't already too late.

"You're not answering your phone, and you're not talking to me." Laz sighed. "Tell you what. Take my car. Go wherever you have to go. I can call a driving service I use from time to time. I want you to be okay, Sienna, and I can tell you want to handle things on your own for the moment. I respect that. An independent woman." He winked, and I felt icky and warm all at the same time. "I'll get our food boxed and get it to you later today. Here, my keys." He tossed them and I had no choice but to catch.

As he stepped back into the restaurant, I stepped into the driver's seat of his top-of-the-line BMW. As I debated why I was even sitting in his car and where to go next, one of his last sentences echoed through my mind. *Think, Sienna, do you really want a paper trail?*

Paper trail.

Laz had not offered any reaction over the Portuguese letter I laid in front of him. Indeed, he barely glanced at it as he'd picked up the ring. Of course, that could be the steel journalist in him, trained not to show any bias or emotion; or, more logically, the multi-carat gems of the ring had commanded all of his attention.

But, it occurred to me that the man I'd spoken to from Almada had said there had been three inquiries into the link that led to who I knew to be Kisu.

Three.

A part of me could not help but wonder if Laz had done more research about RiChard than he had let on; but if he had, why would he not tell me?

It was a passing thought in the midst of stormier ones, but a thought nonetheless.

Chapter 20

Laz's car had hints of citrus, sandalwood, and other aromatic hints of leathery spice I could not identify. As I sat in the driver's seat inhaling, I could not help if I was working under some kind of intoxicating effect of Laz, some craze that was affecting my better judgment.

I did not like the man.

Something about his cockiness, his sharp tongue, his know-it-all demeanor grated my nerves like nails on a chalkboard. And yet I was sitting in the driver's seat of his car, inhaling the scent of him, when my phone rang a third time.

Leon.

This time I picked up. "Hey," I answered, afraid that saying more would incriminate me of some crime I wasn't aware that I was committing.

"Sienna, where are you?" I heard panic in his voice. "I talked to the detail sitting out in front of your house into letting me take over, but I've been knocking on your front door for the past twenty minutes. What's going on?"

"I . . . I had to run an errand. A friend, a friend came to pick me up, but I'll be back home soon."

"An errand? Sienna, what could you possibly have to do that is more important than being home right now? A woman is missing and the police think you have something to do with it!"

I tried to sort out an acceptable answer to respond to his loud sighs and groans but could not come up with a single word.

"Sienna, is there something you're not telling me?" Leon was nearly yelling. "Of course there is; what am I asking?"

The silence that ensued for the next several moments was the most intense conversation we'd ever had. It ended with him speaking again.

"Sienna, you need to get back here as soon as you can." His voice was quieter, calmer—but full of exasperation.

"I will," I whispered as he hung up in my ear.

Another first.

In my lifetime—and especially it seemed over the past couple of years—I'd had a lot of people hang up on me, clicking off on my request for answers, making statements of irritation, attempting to assert some form of power over me.

But none of those people had ever been Leon.

Shock, grief, sorrow, ache filled me as I pondered what to do next. I picked up the phone to call him back, to tell him that I was on my way back home, that we could work together to make a grand meal of my Hawaiian chicken recipe and his crab cakes, pop open a two liter of cranberry ginger ale, and finally have the big talk we had been prevented from having the past few days.

I wanted to believe that despite my conflicting feelings and conversations with Laz, in spite of the pretty young girl who had Leon laughing in a diner booth, that I was ready to wholeheartedly move past my past and embrace my future with him.

The phone was still in my hand and I was poised to dial him when it rang again. The phone number was not familiar, but I had a vague recollection of the weird call I'd gotten earlier that day, when the caller had not spoken but simply hung up.

"Hello," I answered, almost certain that it was the same number.

My suspicions were confirmed as only silence greeted me.

"Hello?" I asked again, but then decided to hang up before I was forced to hear another dial tone in my ear.

Let me get home, I decided, throwing my phone onto the passenger seat. I didn't even feel like calling Leon, deciding just to do the talking in person.

Laz's BMW roared to life and I began the fifteen-minute drive back to my house. As I turned onto Rossville Boulevard, it occurred to me that I had no idea how I was going to get back inside. I couldn't just pull up in front of it, and I wasn't going to abandon Laz's luxury car on the side of the road.

And there was no way I could call Leon back to ask for help. How would I even begin to explain the car I was driving?

Maybe Laz really had not meant for me to take his car. Perhaps he really didn't think I would drive away. I wanted to kick myself. *Or maybe he thought I was going to go somewhere that held clues to finding RiChard.*

The second option seemed more plausible. But where would I go? And what did I do about getting myself back home where Leon was waiting?

I was two blocks away from my home at a stoplight, imagining an entire sequence of me driving down to the main Enoch Pratt Free Library downtown on Cathedral Street to begin an intensive research-and-find mission, when my phone rang once more. This time the number was blocked. I let it ring, with no intention of answering, but then reconsidered at the slight possibility it was my son deciding to reach out to me.

I answered on what was probably the last ring.

"Hello?" I held my breath, hoping, praying to hear my son. Instead it was a young woman's voice who answered me.

"Hi. Hello?" There was a brief pause. "Sienna? Sienna St. James?"

"Yes, this is me. Who is this?" My hope had not diminished. Perhaps this woman knew where Roman was.

"This is Anastasia Simmons."

"I'm sorry, who?" My face wrinkled as I tried to think of why that name sounded so familiar.

"Anastasia Simmons," she stated again, "but everyone calls me Silver."

Chapter 21

"Silver?" My heart instantly burst into a quick pace. "Um, who . . . How . . . What . . . what is going on?"

The light had turned green, but I was too frozen to go. A large semi honked behind me, jumpstarting me back to movement. I made a left turn into a parking lot that faced a small strip mall and pulled into a free parking space.

"Ms. St. James." Silver's words tumbled out quickly but softly, maybe a slight decibel louder than a whisper. "I need help and you are the only one who can help me."

"You . . . you are kidnapped. The police are looking for you." I felt like a bumbling idiot, knowing that, at a minimum, I sounded like one. But how was I to make sense out of this? "Let . . . let me call the police. I mean, where are you?"

"No, no!" The woman who called herself Silver gasped. "You can't call the police. I'm okay, I promise I'm okay, but everything else is not."

"Well, then you definitely need to call the police, if only to let them know you are okay."

"No, no, no. That's not an option." Silver pleaded, "I need to explain everything to you, but I need to do so in person. Please, I will tell you where I am, but only if you promise not to tell anyone—at least not yet."

"I'm not comfortable with this." I shook my head. "The police think you are a victim of a crime and my name keeps popping up all over their investigation. Why are you calling me? How did you even get my number? I want nothing to do with this. I am hanging up and calling the police."

"No, please, listen." The woman who called herself Silver sounded desperate. "I promise if you come to where I am I will explain everything, and then, if you want, then you can call the police. But please, hear me out. I would tell you now, but . . . but I need to talk to you in person for any of this to make sense."

"Jesus." I dropped my head into my hands, saying the only prayer I could get out in such a tight, time-pressed situation. "Silver, I will meet you in a mutual place and then I am calling the police."

"No, it's not safe for me to leave where I am."

"Then how do I know it's safe for me? How do I even know that you are really Silver? I don't know you!"

"I need you to trust me," she whispered.

"You are a complete stranger and I ain't no fool. Somebody is setting me up for reasons I do not know and I am not getting any more involved." I meant it. I was going to dial 911 the moment our call ended. "Why on earth do you think I have any reason to trust you?"

There was a long pause—so long, in fact, I thought the call had dropped. I was about to check the signal on my phone when the woman's voice weakly sounded.

"Please trust that I mean you no harm, even if there are others who do."

"Others who do what? Mean me harm? What are you talking about? I haven't done anything."

"No, you haven't, but you're involved now. I need you and once I can explain everything, you'll see that you need me."

At that, I burst into laughter and hung up the phone. The conversation was so ridiculous, her request so outlandish, her assumptions so over the top, I was surprised I'd even entertained the call as long as I did. Now, I *wanted* to get home.

Leon.

He would know what to do. *That is, if I'm even able to talk to him.*

Or should I just call 911?

As I sat there struggling to decide whether to talk first to Leon, the cop I knew, or dial 911 and deal with cops who thought I was in on it, my phone chimed that I had a new text message. Of course, the number was blocked again, but the sender was obvious as I read the all-capitalized text: PLEASE! 18181 PANORAMA CT.

It was an address in nearby White Marsh. I remembered the street name from my days of touring model homes before the housing market crashed. There was no way I could afford the nearly million-dollar homes that were being built in that particular development as they were priced back then, but the models were so luxuriously designed, I used to tell myself I was getting decorating ideas, and not merely daydreaming—or house-lusting.

But why would Silver—if that was even really her— give me an address when she knew I was going to take it right to the police, especially since she was saying that she was trying to avoid the authorities? *Maybe it's a trap!* Now that made sense. Clearly, someone wanted me in the middle of this madness, and texting me a phone number with the assumption that I would simply pass it along to the police could only mean more trouble for me.

I had no idea what was going on or why, but I was 100 percent certain that giving the address to the police would be a mistake against my own well-being.

"You think I'm going to send the police to you, but I'm a step ahead of you." I pressed down on the accelerator and turned toward the suburb of White Marsh, Maryland. I wanted to scope out the address myself before the police got wind of it and found something that implicated me of wrong-doing, as I was sure that had been the sender's intention.

The neighborhood was as lofty and grand as I remembered. Driving down the narrow back roads of Baltimore County, I passed by homes with three-car garages, brick courtyards, and multiple balconies. I recalled the model I had practically slobbered over. It had an extra finished space over the garage, which I loosely dreamed of making my own art studio.

But Roman and I did not need a five-bedroom, four-bath house. Not that I could have afforded it anyway.

I shook my head at the elaborately manicured lawns and the collection of high-end cars and SUVs parked in front of some of the residences. What kind of jobs did these people have to live like this? I shook my head again and reminded myself to stay focused.

I needed to figure out what was going on.

When my GPS indicated that I was only a few houses away from the address that had been texted to me, I pulled to a stop, ready to sit and watch. However, my gut told me that this was the kind of neighborhood where people would probably be looking out of their windows, wondering about the stranger sitting out in front of their homes.

"I'm here now. I might as well go all the way and see what trap is being set out for me."

Maybe I wasn't in my right mind, but could you really blame me? I had police picking through my house earlier that morning; I was actively losing the one man in over a decade who I knew I had a real chance at love with; my son had set himself free from me and was somewhere on the other side of the country looking for a man who'd set up his life to keep us from finding him. *And now I have to deal with a stripper name Silver telling me that she needs me and I need her.* Like I really had time for any of this.

I slammed on my brakes right in front of 18181, a massively large stone-front colonial with red double front doors and trim. I shut off the engine, got out of the car, and heard my own anger and frustration being punched by my boots into the stone pathway to the small porch. I banged on the door, really feeling like I could kick it in, but controlled myself enough to simply step back and wait. Sharp footsteps approached on the other side of the red doors, and that's when my common sense returned.

What was I doing? I had no idea who lived here or who didn't. What was I supposed to say? Who was I supposed to ask for? I looked around frantically for a clue, an answer. And I got one.

The attached three-car garage to the right of me was partially open. A shiny, bright red Lexus peeked out. That quick revelation gave me enough confidence and composure to greet the person who opened the door without blinking an eye or missing a beat.

"Hello, Jenellis. We need to talk."

Chapter 22

Her hair weave was pulled back in a ponytail. She wore a pink and gray running suit, black sneakers, and her face was fully made up in shades of wine and plum, which complemented her natural bronze tone.

But there was nothing made up about the shock that stared up at me from behind her fake-color contact lenses. Today, her eyes were light brown.

"Ms. . . . Ms. St. James," she stammered. "What are you doing here?"

When I did not immediately answer, she seemed to collect herself and settle down. The reason I did not immediately answer was also probably how she knew she had regained the upper hand—I was too busy gaping at her foyer.

The single showpiece in my foyer was the decades-old collage I'd been working on. Jenellis's foyer showcased a staircase-length silver and gold kimono in the most elaborate jeweled flower pattern I'd ever seen. It hung from a satin hanger at the top of her cascading stairwell with the train pinned to the wall at a flattering angle that allowed the natural sunlight from the skylight above to reflect off of the jewels.

"My wedding gown," she answered my unasked question and grinned mischievously. "I had it commissioned by a spectacular gown designer I met during one of my trips to the Orient years ago, long before I even had a fiancé or a rock." She waved her left ring finger as if I had never seen the multi-carat diamond that graced her manicured hand. "All those trips back and forth to Hong Kong to get measured—talk about a reason to keep off the weight." She twirled around in her running suit. "But now I finally get to wear it in two weeks."

I did not miss the quick drop of her smile.

"Come in, Ms. St. James, please. Good, we finally get to talk."

As I stepped into the foyer, I noticed her scan the neighborhood behind me before shutting the door. She smiled at me as she led me down a narrow hall. Our footsteps echoed on the polished hardwood floor, the only sound that filled my ears. At the end of the hallway was a two-story family room and she directed me to sit down on one of its plush couches.

The room was done in shades of red with a single wall painted black. Two spotlights artfully placed on the lone black wall across from me shone on a framed sword. What looked like Chinese writing filled both the blade and the handle. My head was cocked to the side, looking at the writing as if I would somehow understand it.

"It's an authentic *jian* from the Qing Dynasty." Her smile continued as she sat in a couch cater-cornered to mine. She smoothed her hands back and forth over her legs as I continued to study the framed sword. I noted that the frame was more than a frame. With a cover and a keyhole, it was apparent that it was a specially crafted display case. The fact that it was locked and secure gave me cautious comfort.

I did not really know this woman.

And, more importantly at the moment, I did not know why I had been directed to her home.

"What does it say, the writing on it?" I asked. Small talk to get us ready for the big talk.

"'Red is the color of love and blood,' or something like that." Her tone was unreadable as she spoke.

"Interesting." I turned my attention away from the framed sword and smiled back at her. Silence flooded the room and I felt like she was waiting for me to talk, waiting to see where I would begin.

But I was a therapist. I was used to awkward silence, and trained enough to not feel uncomfortable with long breaks in conversation such as the one happening between us now.

After several rounds of the minute hand swirling around the face of my watch, Jenellis finally gave in.

"Would you like some tea?" Her smile had diminished in size and her eyes blinked almost rhythmically, but she otherwise remained quite poised and proper.

"Sure," I said flatly.

"Tatyana, tea!" she yelled, her eyes still glued on me.

I heard some tinkling noises come from what I assumed was her kitchen and in a matter of mere moments, a short, slouching, mousy-looking woman entered the room, carrying a wooden tray of porcelain teacups and a teapot. She had Slavic features, wisps of gray hair, and she was actually wearing a blue pincord housekeeping dress.

Really, Jenellis? I wanted to roll my eyes at her overdone display of wealth. Had that poor old woman in here working like a darn slave, I could imagine. She disappeared back to wherever she'd come from before I even had a chance to make sense of her.

"So, you seem really into Asian culture." I decided to bring a real end to the silence as I poured a steaming hot cup of black tea laced with ginger into the quaint white and blue teacup.

Jenellis shrugged me off. "One of many cultures I study."

"What kind of work do you do?" The question occurred to me. Jenellis only stirred her tea and took a sip before looking back up at me with a tight smile.

"Ms. St. James, I'll be honest with you. I'm still trying to figure out why you are here. I did not realize that I had even given you my address when we met."

"You didn't. I got your address from a text message I just received."

"A text?" One of her arched eyebrows rose slightly.

"There's a girl who's been flashing all over the local news, allegedly kidnapped while coming out of an alley in Fells Point. Her name is Silver." I paused, wanting to read any slight reaction.

There was none.

Her non-reaction told me she knew exactly what I was talking about.

"And?"

"And she called me a few minutes ago asking me to come see her, but I told her that I was going to go to the police and then she sent me the text with your address."

"So an alleged kidnapped victim calls you with an address of her supposed whereabouts. Well, I can assure you she is not here, and, I see, neither are the police. You didn't call them?" Jenellis took another sip of her tea. Tatyana returned with a plate of sliced oranges and then scurried back into the kitchen after a quick wave of Janellis's hand.

"Thank you," I offered to the older woman. She did not seem to notice.

"She doesn't speak English," Jenellis explained.

She was way too calm and collected for the entire situation as far as I was concerned.

"I didn't call them. The police. I did not call them. Not yet." I was kind of wishing I had. Everything felt wrong.

"Hmmm." Jenellis put her cup down.

"Ms. Walker, what is going on with Silver? It is obvious to me that you know something. You know who she is."

Jenellis stood and walked over to the mantle of her fireplace. Her back was to me as she fished through a short stack of mail that sat on top of it. "'Silver' Simmons." She shook her head. "You're talking about that nasty skank of a woman who was mouthing all over my fiancé in front of a studio audience."

"So you did see that episode of *The Soul Mate Show?*" I watched her carefully, wishing I could see what she was searching for out of my view. "I thought you said you didn't care about Brayden's infidelities."

She spun back around. "I don't, at least when it comes to physical affairs. Brayden's a man, and, let's face it, a man's going to be a man."

"I don't share your views."

"That's fine. You don't need to. What you do need to know is that I couldn't care less what Brayden does in his free time, but Silver apparently cares what he is doing with me." She turned back to the pile of papers on the mantle, picking them up one by one and examining each as she continued. "Ms. St. James, mark my words, a woman who is desperate enough for money that she will take off her clothes in front of a crowd for it is a woman who is desperate enough to pull drastic tricks to get more of it."

"Let me get this straight." I eyed her closely though her attention was elsewhere. "Are you saying that Silver staged her own kidnapping to somehow get more money out of the whole situation?"

"That's exactly what I'm saying." Jenellis huffed. "It's no secret that both Brayden and I are persons of great wealth. I'm thinking that if she can't have my man, she's thinking she can at least have my money."

"So she is setting you up to look like you had something to do with her supposed kidnapping? That's why she wanted me to send the police to your house?"

"Look at this." She finally turned around for good, an envelope between her long, fuchsia fingernails. I took it from her as she continued. "It was delivered to me this morning. Open it."

A single sheet of paper was inside. $1,502 was typed on it.

"A ransom?" I looked up at her.

"A *fake* ransom." She slid back into her seat near me. "Remember, she's not really kidnapped.

"Blackmail?"

"That would probably be the more accurate term."

"So she has dirt on you."

"No, on Brayden."

I tried to put it all together in my mind, but the pieces were just that. Pieces. "I'm sorry, Jenellis. I'm not following you."

Jenellis sighed loudly and sat back farther in her seat. "Remember yesterday, Brayden said we would both understand within twenty-four hours. I think he knew about this, he knew that she would be demanding money from me. And since he did not try to stop it, to stop her, and would not come clean with us at the counseling session yesterday, he obviously has something worth hiding."

"But $1,502? That's hardly enough to qualify for blackmailing two millionaires."

"I agree."

I pondered it more, wondering if she knew that was the exact amount Brayden had given me, the exact amount that the detective confiscated from my notebook that morning.

What did I have to do with any of this?

"It's not about the cash," I murmured. "1502, the number itself, is significant, I bet."

Jenellis was silent again.

"What is it? What do you know? What does 1502 mean? What does it symbolize or stand for?"

For the first time, I saw Jenellis's lip quiver. "It's complicated."

"So you do know what it stands for? You do know, and you understand what Brayden has to lose if you don't follow through with whatever demand Silver is making?" When Jenellis still did not answer, I could feel my body temperature rising. "What does any of this have to do with me?"

"Ms. St. James, I'm sorry you are in the middle of this. It was not my intent—or Brayden's for that matter. It is what it is."

"Okay, well, what it is now is time for me to call the police. You are not going to have me entangled anymore in your foolishness. I don't know what y'all have going on, but I'm out." I stood, ready to walk out, drive home—yes, march right through my front door—and get the detective's business card, which I'd left on my counter.

"I understand why you feel that it is necessary to call the police." Jenellis did not move from her seat. "But I should at least warn you. I've looked into Silver's past, done some research. She's dangerous, Ms. St. James. Before you catch the authorities up on everything, let me finish protecting Brayden. The situation he finds himself in, it's not his fault. He is a good guy, honorable. Let me finish my business with Silver, and then feel free to call. Two hours. That's all I am asking for."

I shook my head as I headed to her door. These people thought I was crazy if they thought I was just going to go along with their ploys.

"Funny thing is that two days ago you were begging me to find out if Brayden had any history of violence toward women in his past. Now, you're practically canonizing him as a saint." *Or she could be lying about everything,* I considered. Maybe the dirt, if there was even any, was really about her. Either way, I was not staying to find out. "Bye, Ms. Walker."

My hand was turning the knob on her front door when she suddenly rushed toward me. "Wait, Ms. St. James." Her hand rested on my shoulder. "Please don't call yet. I need you to trust me."

"Funny." I brushed her off. "Silver said the exact same thing." I felt her eyes on me as I walked back to Laz's car. A million and one thoughts about my day, my life ran through my head as I started the motor. As crazy and bizarre as it all had been, not one thought had prepared me for what happened next.

I had just sat down in the seat, closed the door, started the car, and reached for my cell phone when a hand came from behind the driver's seat. I heard the click of a gun, and felt cold metal on the base of my neck. My rearview mirror showed me only the top of a black knit cap.

"Drive." The single word came from a muffled voice.

Wasn't nothing else for me to do but drop the phone and put my foot on the accelerator and obey.

Chapter 23

"Make a U-turn. Now turn left at the light."

His face was hidden from me, but his voice served as a menacing GPS, weaving me in and out of the suburbs and finally into the narrow side streets of East Baltimore. I felt like we were going in circles, like my captor needed the services of a real GPS himself as he directed me down familiar blocks and boulevards again and again. Any lessons I'd had about self-defense, whether to scream, whether to fight back or keep still, had gone out of the window the minute I'd felt that cold metal on my neck.

"Make this turn here. Okay, right." His voice sounded youthful, but the gun told me he was not playing games. I eyed my cell phone, which I had dropped on the passenger's seat the moment I'd first felt the chill of the revolver on my skin. My phone had even buzzed a few times during our quiet tour of Baltimore—Leon's number then Laz's filled the screen—but there was nothing for me to do but keep driving.

Finally, after almost an hour had gone by, I found courage to speak.

"I'm going to run out of gas."

"Shut up and turn left at the stop sign."

We drove for ten minutes more as I wondered if these were my last moments. I looked at the people, buildings, homes, and cars around me anew, trying to savor small details that I probably would not have even noticed any other time. I counted trees that grew out of small patches of dirt in the concrete; noticed the handwritten store signs on some corner stores; listened to the loud laugh of a woman with a short, scruffy ponytail sitting on a stoop with a group of giggling toddlers; imagined Roman never knowing what ever happened to either his mother or his father; Leon never knowing that my heart wanted to love him; Laz wondering what ever happened to his beautiful silver BMW.

"Right here. Stop. The third house down," the man's voice interrupted. "Get out. Go straight to the door."

We'd stopped in front of a narrow row house near East Biddle Street, I think. My mind had gone numb and my memory evaded me. All I could see were crumbling brick steps, a dingy front door, and a single potted plant on the cement porch. He used a key to open the door and used the gun to beckon me inside. My eyes adjusted to the dark interior of a living room in shambles.

"David? Is that you?" A large woman in a wheelchair sat in the darkness, an oxygen tube running from her nose, her hair done in two sloppy, graying cornrows, her eyes staring off into space. She appeared to be blind. "You picked up my medicine?"

"Yes, Grandma. I'll get your water in just a minute." He walked behind me, pushing me forward, the tip of the gun now at the center of my spine. His breaths were as labored as mine.

Both of us were scared.

He seemed to be pushing me toward the kitchen, toward a closed door that sat right beyond a large pantry.

"David," the woman's shrill voice called out again, "someone with you?"

"It's okay, Grandma. I'm getting your water."

He reached from behind me and opened the door, and I saw that his hands looked massive, powerful. "Go down there," he whispered, nudging me down unfinished wooden steps. I took the first one and the door clicked closed behind me. I heard him lock it.

The basement was well lit. I took three more steps down and saw that there was a twin bed, a mini fridge, and an old television with a movie playing, *Jesus of Nazareth* it looked like. I remembered that Easter was coming soon. Roman was supposed to be volunteering on a Native American reservation for spring break. He was looking for his father instead. Maybe he planned to come home at the end of his break, the thought occurred to me. *Why all these thoughts right now?*

Blue, shaggy carpet covered the floor and the slight scent of laundry detergent filled the air. Shaking and not able to put any logical plan of escape together, I sat down on the corner of the bed.

"I'm sorry I had to do it like this." A voice from the crawl space behind the stairs whipped my head around. There in the shadows of the stairwell sat a pretty young woman wearing a black halter top and tight blue jeans.

Silver.

"David would never hurt you, but my mother would. I told you I needed to talk to you in person and this was the only way to get you here."

"Your mother would hurt me?" I recoiled at the thought of the sickly, disabled woman upstairs having some kind of death wish against me.

"No, not David's grandmother." Silver seemed to be reading my thoughts. "I'm talking about my mother, whose house you just left. Why didn't you call the police?"

Chapter 24

"Your mother?" I blinked in disbelief. "Jenellis Walker is your mother?"

"Unfortunately." Silver was staring at me with the same intensity with which I was staring at her.

How had I missed the resemblance? I wondered. Both women had the same flawless deep cocoa skin, the same high quality use of weave, the same almond-shaped eyes. However, I noted, Silver appeared to have had some work done on her nose and there was a hard edge to her expression and posture that spoke to a rough life. Jenellis may have had that same edge to her but she had learned to disguise it as arrogance.

"Jenellis didn't say anything about you being her daughter."

"Of course she wouldn't. She probably told you that I had faked the kidnapping."

"In so many words. And she also told me that I needed to trust her, just like you have told me to trust you."

"Trust can be a two-edged sword. It can cut you coming or going. Without it, you can get hurt, but if you trust the wrong person, you still can get hurt."

I looked around the basement. Aside from the television and bed, there were also several posters on the wall: rappers, athletes, and barely dressed women.

The den of a too-mature adolescent or an immature young man.

"So is this where you live or are you being held here against your will?"

"This is not where I live. As far as my will, well, let's just say I am in hiding."

"Hiding from what?"

"I'll get to that in a moment."

"And David . . ."

"Is a loyal fan. He's smitten with me. I knew he would help me."

"Fan?"

"Don't pretend that you don't know my business. It's been all over the news." She yawned and stretched, then moved closer to where I was sitting, pulling a pillow to her chest and leaning on it like we were two schoolgirls at a sleepover.

"What is going on, Silver, and why am I in the middle of it?" I decided to trust her at the moment, seeing as she was the one with an armed man on the floor above me and I needed her to be relaxed enough to tell me what I needed to know.

"My mother and her men issues." Silver had a look of resentment on her face. "She wanted me to go on that dating show to get more info about Brayden. She knew he was going to be on the show, something he'd agreed to doing awhile ago, and my mother got me on there to pick him as my date. Only he figured out who I was and, of course, was not pleased at my mother's lack of trust in him. From what I understand, they agreed they needed counseling—and quickly, since they'd already booked their wedding and didn't want to reschedule. My mother told me that they found you after a Google search for therapists in their area."

"So my involvement is pure chance."

"Yes, Ms. St. James. You were chosen as the lucky contestant. Or unlucky, I guess, from your perspective."

It was a very neat story she told.

Too neat.

"What are you not telling me?" I asked her directly. "I get the whole trust issues thing spiraling out of control and your mom and soon-to-be stepfather agreeing to premarital counseling. What I don't get is the kidnapping caught on camera, your mother's statement that you are somehow blackmailing her, and your telling me that you are hiding. What is really going on?"

"What is going on is that my mother is not the only one with trust issues." Silver's eyes filled with tears. "You are right. There is more. But if I can't trust my own mother, how do I know that I can trust you? I brought you here by force, so when I let you go, how do I know you aren't going to go run to the police?"

"But don't you want the police to know you are okay? What or who exactly are you hiding from?"

Silver shut her eyes and tears flooded her fake lashes. "It's a life-and-death situation. We are not safe. We will never be safe."

"Who is not safe? What are you talking about? And why are you so adamant that I not go to the police?"

"Listen, I called you because you are the only person I could turn to for help. The police cannot know where I am because then my mother will know. And if she knows, then Brayden will know, and then it won't be good for any of us. If you talk to the police, keep them focused on my mother, regardless of what she tells you or anyone else." Her tears were gone and a resolve that I recognized as reckless courage had taken its place.

I'd seen the same look in Roman's face once before, when he was willing to face a group of armed wannabe gangsters to get back the lion's head ring, which was briefly stolen at that time.

She was telling me her truth, I was sure of it.

"1502. What is the significance of that number?" I put it out there.

Silver gasped, throwing her hand over her mouth. "You have to go. You have to go now. It's not safe for you to be with me. Please, I beg you, please, please do not tell anyone where I am. I need you to trust me on this." She grabbed my arm as she pleaded, directing me back toward the steps. "I need to trust you." She used her fingertips to lightly scratch the door. "David will let you out." She turned back to face me. "Thank you. Thank you for coming."

"I did not exactly have a choice."

"I'm sorry, but *I* did not have a choice. With any of this. There's more, I wanted to tell you more, but it's not safe. I'm scared."

Everything was moving fast. Too fast. I wasn't sure what was even going on. The basement door cracked open and a pimple- and scar-covered face peeked through. The knit black cap was still there, but the gun apparently was not.

"Let her out, David."

The door opened wider and I took a step toward freedom. Just as David started to close the door behind me, Silver grabbed my hand.

"Here, take this." She pushed something cold and metal in my palm and closed my fingers tight around it. "I need you to keep this in case something happens to me. I was holding on to it for a reason, to give it to someone, but I am not sure I will get a chance. When it all makes sense, you'll know what to do with it."

"Come on," David grunted. I was beginning to wonder if he was capable of saying more than two-to-four-word phrases.

Loud snores sounded from the darkened living room where his grandmother still sat in her wheelchair. A paper plate that held a baked chicken leg and a heaping mound of cabbage struggled to balance on her knees as she slept. I noted a tall pitcher of water and a glass full of ice on the floor next to her feet.

"Get out," David murmured as he quietly opened the front door and pushed me through.

The sun had begun its evening descent. I was alone on their porch. The door shut tight behind me as I tried to gather some sense of time, some sense of sense, period. It had been a bizarre, emotional, crazy day, one that could have easily left me off my rocker for the dangers, questions, and confusion I'd had to endure.

Maybe that was why I waited until I was back in the car to finally open my hand and see what Silver had pressed into it.

A necklace.

A simple silver chain with a charm dangling from it.

I waited until I was at a red light to examine it.

The charm on it appeared to be half of a butterfly, a broken butterfly but one nonetheless. It had been split down the middle so that only one wing was left. On the back of the wing were the words WITH FAITH ALL. *The other half of the butterfly must have the rest of the sentence,* I concluded.

Something about a butterfly . . . I shook my head, too worn to even begin trying to figure out what it was about a butterfly that was bothering me.

Silver had seemed desperate when she'd pushed the necklace into my hand, but I understood the power a piece of jewelry can have when it has meaning. I didn't know what meaning it held for her, though she seemed certain that one day I would get it.

I had no responsibility to this woman, didn't know whether I should trust her or believe a single word that had come out of her mouth. Shoot, her mother had sung a whole different tune when I met with her. Obviously, one of them—maybe even both of them—was lying. Whose melody was pitch perfect?

I slipped the broken butterfly necklace into the side of my purse and heard it land with a loud plink near the lion's head ring.

A ring and a necklace, both with their own stories to tell, tucked away in a dark, quiet corner of my world . . .

Chapter 25

I pulled up to the front of my house right as the sun had nearly made its way down to the treetops that surrounded my development. The horizon had rays of deep purple and pink, just enough light to remind me that my cell phone still sat on the passenger's seat.

I'd missed eight calls. Five from Leon. Three from Laz . . .

None from Roman.

I walked up to my front door, almost expecting a group of uniformed men and women to jump out of my bushes and tackle me to the ground.

It had been that kind of day.

I put my key in the lock, but the doorknob turned before I could open it.

"Sienna! Where have you been?" Leon's nostrils flared as I stepped into the foyer. I'd given him a key as an emergency backup when I first bought the house. This was the first time I'd known him to use it. "I've been waiting here for you all afternoon. It appears that detective and his crew moved on to another lead and don't seem particularly interested with you anymore. I've called you I don't know how many times. I even had one of my friends in the department track down your phone. I was about to have some patrol cars sent down to where it looked like you were in East Baltimore. I didn't want to leave here in case you came back."

"Wait a minute." I only heard one thing in his rant. "You have a friend who can locate phone numbers?"

"I mean, it's off the record, and he's a stickler for the rules, but since you were being monitored by the police and had some kind of connection to this kidnapping case—which I'm still waiting for you to explain to me—I was able to talk him into quietly tracking you down."

"Can he find Roman?"

Leon paused, exhaled, leaned back against the wall. He closed his eyes, shook his head, reopened them, and then shook his head again. "Let's go sit down in your living room, Sienna. We need to talk."

"Do you know something, Leon? Do you know where Roman is? Tell me."

"No, Sienna, I don't, but we need to talk. About everything." He turned toward the steps that led from my entry foyer to the living area upstairs. I had no idea what to think, what to feel. In the few years that I'd known Leon, he had been a rock. Steady, composed. Constant. I was always the one having meltdowns, breakdowns, but something in Leon's voice, something in his eyes—which were avoiding mine—looked menacingly close to the edge. I was not used to this Leon. I didn't know him; didn't know what he would say or do; didn't know where this was going.

I was terrified of what we needed to talk about, what he needed to say. I wasn't ready for this talk that I knew was coming, but the moment was now. Ready or not, I followed him up the stairs, sat next to him on the sofa he helped me pick out; the sofa he, along with my dad, had helped carry into my house.

Leon took immediate charge of our talk. "Sienna, you know that I care very deeply about your son, as if he were my own. If there was anything I could do or could have done to help locate his whereabouts, I would have done so already. As I said, my connection in the department is a straight shooter. He is only going to help if there is a clear legal pathway to doing so. Roman is considered a runaway, and at his age, and because of his own choices, I did not even consider asking my friend because I know that he will not help."

"Leon, I—"

"Let me finish please, Sienna." Leon blew out a loud sigh. "Look, for the past two years, anything you've asked me to do, you know that I have done it. I want to, and I will continue to do whatever I can to help you with anything. Anything. What I need you to understand, however, is that as much as I try to answer your questions, I need you to answer mine.

"You don't answer me, Sienna. My questions, my needs, my wants, you don't answer. And it hurts, Sienna. It hurts because I love you, Sienna. *I love you* and I care about you and I *want* to know your answers. The questions I ask you, especially about your basic safety, your whereabouts, your feelings, I need them answered. I want to share life with you, but right now, no, this whole time, these entire past two years, everything has been one-sided. I understand, and I have waited, and I am willing to keep waiting, but not if there is nothing to wait for. I have been feeling like you do not have the same commitment to sharing our lives together that I have, and, Sienna, I don't want to waste your time anymore."

He was breathing hard and I could barely breathe. When I did manage to inhale, all I could focus on was the faint smell of pine and lemons, a reminder of the vigorous cleaning I had done earlier that day to deal with the crazy turn my life had taken. I had been falsely accused, abandoned, lied to, and physically threatened all within the past twelve hours. I wanted to tell Leon about the cold metal that had been pressed on my neck, but all I could smell was lemons. Lemons and pine.

"Am I wasting your time, Sienna?"

No! my mind screamed. My mind was in full motion, the daydreaming part that imagined me jumping from my seat, collapsing on top of him, holding him, him holding me, feeling alive, safe, comforted.

Feeling love.

Laz had touched my lips with his finger and awakened something in me, something that wanted to live out loud with Leon.

My mind was in full motion, but my body, my voice were not. I was frozen, as if the gun were still on me. I could not talk. I could not see.

My eyes are closed, I realized. And I was rocking, my arms wrapped around myself. Leon wanted answers, and I just wanted something in my life to make sense. I wanted to tell him this, to tell him everything, but all I could do was shut my eyes and rock, shake, and quiver.

"Am I wasting *my* time?" His words were a whisper, but they may as well have been a knife. Piercing. Cutting. Stabbing. Not because of how much it hurt me to hear, but because I knew this was the question he needed answered the most; this was the unspoken answer that pierced, cut, and stabbed him the most. My distance toward him had been what kept us close over the past two years.

But I'd pushed him too far away.

"Am I?" He actually wanted an answer.

I wanted to tell him of course he was not wasting his time; that I had taken steps that very day to move forward, to move closer to him; but all I felt at the moment was pain, and I needed it to stop.

I was a therapist, and a decent one at that, but I had not yet learned the lessons I shared with my clients. I was facing the most emotionally difficult moment of my day, the culmination of the disasters in my life and the prospect of bearing them alone, and all I could do was run away to avoid the pain, the fear.

"So you don't think your friend will help me find Roman?" I whispered, opening my eyes, but looking only at his feet. I could not give him the answer he wanted, the answer I knew he needed. Leon stared at me in silence. Several moments went by before he opened up his mouth again.

"He's looking for his father." He'd accepted that I had no answer for him. I saw it in his eyes, read it in his posture, heard it in his voice.

It was over. Whatever we had, whatever we didn't have, it was over.

"You knew?" I gasped, playing along. "You knew Roman was looking for him?"

"I figured it out. He told me that he was going to find him one day. I did not know he meant he was actually going to leave to do it, or that he was going to do it now."

"Roman talked to you about RiChard?"

"All the time."

At this, I quieted for a moment. Roman had not so much as mentioned his father to me in, what, two years?

"And you knew he was going to run away?" I finally asked.

"No. I knew he was going to look for him. I never knew he was planning to run away to do it. I always assumed it was a long-term goal for him, something he would do as an adult. I never pictured this."

"Where is he?"

"I don't know where Roman is."

"No, I mean, where is RiChard?"

"I don't know, Sienna. You said you were going to find out."

"I never said that."

"Then why am I here, Sienna? Why have I been here?"

We glared at each other. This scene, these feelings, the silence was foreign to me. Nothing about it seemed right. This was me and Leon, not me and a stranger. *Oh, God, help me!*

"Sienna," Leon broke into my thoughts, "I need an answer. Why am I here? Can you please answer me?"

My stomach hurt. I wanted to throw up. I wanted to scream. I wanted to do anything but answer his questions.

Only because I did not know how.

Strong, passionate, direct woman. That was what Laz had called me that afternoon. I had the sudden urge to laugh, but I contained it. *Is this what a nervous breakdown feels like?* I wondered.

"Why can't you answer me?" There was no humor in Leon's eyes. Only hurt.

"Roman," I stated flatly. "I am his mother." My voice was hoarse, unrecognizable even to me. "You should have told me he was planning to look for his father. You should have told me the first time he even said anything about RiChard."

His head dropped into his broad hands. I watched as he wiped his eyes with both palms. *Were those tears I saw?*

"I can't do this anymore." He stood, paused, and then walked toward the stairs to my front door. I followed.

We were quiet as we went down the steps, defeated as we both stood in my doorway. Neither one of us looked at each other. I think only thirty seconds passed, but it felt like thirty minutes. He turned to leave, to disappear into the night.

I remembered how he came to my rescue one dark night a couple years ago, when an angry drug addict tried to attack me with broken glass and dirty needles in an abandoned house. I had gone there looking for a little girl named Hope. I thought I'd found my own hope, but now part of it was about to walk away. And I felt too weak and tired and stressed and powerless to stop him from leaving.

"Leon," I tried. "I'm sorry."

He stood sideways next to me, his face only inches from mine. I moved in closer. So did he. I held my breath. Waiting. Hoping.

And then he stepped away.

"Bye, Sienna." His words were softly spoken, soft enough to seemingly disappear into the frost-tinged night air. "I hope everything works out for you. Everything."

As he jogged down the steps, each footstep away from me felt like a dagger piercing my heart. The slam of his car door was the final, fatal wound.

It was my fault.

I had him. He was there for me.

But I could not get it together. And now he was gone.

"Bye, Leon," I whispered as his taillights joined a sea of others on the main road off of my cul-de-sac. "Thank you for being the man I needed even when I could not be the woman you wanted."

I closed my door, closed out the night; but the inside of my house held no light for me either.

My son was still gone.

Chapter 26

The flames crackled and danced around in the outdoor hearth like the ceremony we had witnessed only hours earlier. Some of the villagers had broken into spontaneous dance to celebrate Kisu's visit—Kisu, RiChard, and me. We were there to tender the fires of revolution. Apartheid had recently ended and RiChard had convinced us we could help ensure Kisu's home village in KwaZulu-Natal, South Africa shared in the most basic of human rights being promised to all. Kisu had not been back home since leaving for his university training in London.

I'd met Kisu's fiancé, Mbali, only once, that night of our arrival. As the oldest woman in her bustling household, she rarely seemed to stand still, was constantly at work out of view. I barely remembered her. What I did remember was that first night she came out to greet me by the fire. Sensing my discomfort at sharing plates with total strangers as part of their communal meal, she flashed me a wide smile and gave me my own plate, piled high with cabbage, yams, and corn meal porridge, or *phutu,* instead of the kidneys, lungs, and brains, or offal, of some livestock that had been slaughtered for the celebration.

She'd spent a short time at the London university with Kisu, so was not offended by my Western bias. In the crackle of flames, she giggled with me as I discreetly passed along the gourd filled with *utshwala,* or Zulu beer, without drinking from it. A lot of mouths had been on that single gourd.

Mbali, whose name meant "flower," had a smile and a spirit that rivaled the majestic mountains that surrounded their village. I remembered feeling slightly jealous of her beauty, her will, and strength. *"The fire is alive, so it makes our traditions alive. We are nourished and fed by the foods that we prepare and share together. Come, taste, Sister Sienna. Life taste good, does it not?"* *She laughed and we all joined in, the men and I, as I bravely sampled amazi, or curdled milk, and took a bite of cow's head off of RiChard's plate.*

I did not see her again, not even the night Kisu did not return, the night RiChard returned with blood on his hands, fighting, defending what he called justice. Avenging the tragedy of Kisu's murder; a murder, RiChard claimed, that was done by some who did not appreciate their message of revolution. Kisu's mother trembled at the news that her only son was not returning. His father had been eerily solemn and still as he gave RiChard Kisu's ring as a gift for his action of reciprocal vengeance. Someone said Mbali had locked herself in her home, refusing to let anyone witness her grief.

But RiChard had apparently lied.

Kisu was still alive.

I wondered what other lies he'd told me, told the world.

I woke up startled, a downpour of sweat making my clothes stick to my skin, hot like I was still standing in front of Mbali's living fire. I did not remember getting into my bed and hiding under the covers. The moments after Leon's departure were a blur to me. My light was still on and I sat up, catching a glimpse of myself in my dresser mirror.

I looked like I'd had the worst day of my life.

My hair was all over my head. My eyes were red and puffy. My face looked swollen, as if all the ingredients that had made my day horrid had combined to create an allergic reaction inside of me. I felt sick, itchy, hot, heartbroken. I collapsed back down into my layers of blankets, wishing, hoping that my recent memories had all been a dream, but I was still wearing the same clothes I'd been wearing when living out my nightmare.

It had all been real.

The clock next to my bed read 2:17 a.m. Leon had left sometime between six and seven p.m. last night. Had I really been asleep for over seven hours? Had the day really ended and a new one begun? I groaned at the realization, wondering what horrors awaited me. My hope for a better day was dimmed.

Laz's car!

The spicy-smelling BMW crossed my mind and I sat back up. Surely that man was probably in a panic, wondering why I had not contacted him about returning his car. I looked at the clock, then decided that a text message would not be too intrusive this time of night. I imagined that he would at least wake up knowing that I'd had enough decency to thank him again for the use of his wheels when he checked his phone.

> Thank you again for letting me use the car. Sorry I did not get back to you last night, but feel free to let me know how to get it back to you.

I crashed back down into my bed after pressing send, too awake and shaken to fall back asleep, but too uncertain to know what else to do. My phone buzzed with an incoming message almost immediately.

No worries, it read. I already have it. I came by around eight and when you didn't answer your door, I figured you were getting some rest. I have an extra key to my car.

As I sat there wondering if my text had woken Laz up, or if he was a night owl, another text came through.

You up? You rested? If so, let's get started. The best work happens under the cover of darkness.

Was the man suggesting a late-night booty call? I frowned, thoroughly offended and completely turned off—and not sure how to respond. I typed slowly.

Not sure I get what you're saying.

His reply was again immediate.

Calm down, Sienna. I'm only talking about helping you find RiChard. I have some sources that may be helpful.

I tried to recall our conversation over the lunch that didn't happen, but only one question came to mind.

Do you know a way to track someone's cell phone?

This time, several minutes went by before my phone buzzed with his reply.

Let me come over. We'll talk. We'll plan. We'll figure out where your son is. It's easier to get a lot of work done when no one else is moving.

The idea of having a man over to my house this time of night was out of the question for me—but he sounded willing to help me find my son. I was desperate and he was available to help at the moment. The man had a busy life, I told myself, and if this is the time he could help, then so be it. Plus, I was too awake after my seven hours of straight sleep.

Okay, I pecked into the small screen of my phone. I deleted it and retyped it twice before finally sending it through.

Great. Be there in forty minutes.

I remembered that he'd said that he lived in Ellicott City, no short ride from my residence, if that was where he was coming from. Surely a drive from that far away this time of night was not just for charity. I may have been out of the dating cat-mouse game for years, but I had enough insight to remember the unspoken rules.

I didn't care if I was falling into some kind of trap. I was grown enough to stop an unwanted advance and panicked enough to accept any kind of help.

I was desperate and he was available to help at the moment.

Chapter 27

By three a.m., I had showered, combed my hair, and changed my clothes. I had turned on my coffee maker—something I rarely did—and flipped on the television. I nestled onto my sofa, waiting for the knock that I knew was coming any moment, wondering what the heck I had just agreed to do with Laz. I had on my "ugly" outfit: an old blue and white plaid flannel shirt and worn black leggings. It was what I wore when doing yard work, the times that Leon's schedule didn't allow him to help me with mowing my lawn, trimming my bushes.

Leon.

The wound was still too fresh as I blinked back tears.

I turned up the volume on my television to mute my thoughts, to drown out my vision of him stretched out emotionally bleeding somewhere.

I'd hurt that man and all he ever did was genuinely love me.

I love you, Sienna. I could still hear him. *I love you and I care about you and I want to know your answers.*

Answers. That's all I wanted now. That's all he wanted then.

I turned the volume on my television up even louder.

"Good evening, all you lovers and ladies in TV land." A man's voiceover sounded. "It's time for the one, the only, *The Soul Mate Show.*"

I leaned forward on my sofa as the theme music of another episode began. A man was the main contestant this time, and the trio of women he could choose from were variations of low-cut, too-tight, overly made-up teases. Sex à la carte. I rolled my eyes at the parade of desperation that flashed on the screen. *Where are the regular-acting and regular-looking women who are quietly seeking lasting love?* I was about to snap the foolishness off when a quick still caught my eye. As part of the opening credits, the grand prize was previewed.

"A fantasy date at La Chambre Rouge . . ."

La Chambre Rouge.

I remembered that Jenellis and Brayden were hosting their wedding at that very same location, the same spot where Brayden was supposed to take Silver for their prize date.

What's the connection? I wondered, but I didn't have more time to ponder it. A light knock sounded on my door. It was a gentle knock, but I knew that the man behind it was anything but that; and, as he'd told me, he didn't think I quite fit that bill either.

"Stay focused, Sienna," I reminded myself as I stood to answer it. I peeked through the peephole, and he seemed to be staring directly back at it.

"Hi, Laz." I gave a half smile as I opened the door for him.

"I'm surprised you let me come." He grinned as he stepped in. He was wearing his signature brown trench coat, and his fedora was in his hand.

"You said you could help me find my son."

"I thought we were looking for RiChard?"

"Same difference," I muttered as I shut the door behind him. We headed up to my living room and I was suddenly embarrassed that I had chosen to wear my "ugly" clothes. I realized that it was obvious that I had tried to make myself look as unattractive as possible. If Laz had an opinion about my blue flannel and black leggings, he hid it well. I curled up in an armchair and he sat down on my sofa.

"So, what information do you have so far?" He pulled out a notepad, a laptop, and an hourglass, and set them on the coffee table between us.

"What's the hourglass for?"

"Ah, I'm going to turn it over and you are going to tell me everything you can think of regarding your last contact with RiChard."

I raised an eyebrow and he chuckled.

"I've found that the element of pressure sometimes makes the human brain work more efficiently. Let's go."

I shook my head, but played along. "His father is from the Caribbean, his mother is from Italy, and I last saw him in California when Roman was less than two months old. He said at that time that he was headed for somewhere in South America. He's called a few times over the years, sent packages"—but no money, I left that part out—"and the last time I heard directly from him was when he called on Roman's thirteenth birthday."

I closed my eyes at the memory of Roman's elation that his father had called to pronounce him a fully grown "warrior." When he finished talking to him, I'd gotten on the phone and finally had the courage to challenge him somewhat about not being a part of our lives on a regular basis. He'd excused his absence as usual by stating that he was doing "what was right" for the sake of the universe by fighting for social justice for all. *I have to make the world a better place for you and our son, Sienna. This is my duty.*

"Bitter are we?" Laz interrupted my memories and I realized I was probably frowning.

"Huh? Oh, where was I?"

"You were filling me in on how RiChard was a deadbeat dad."

"That's not what I said."

Laz studied me for a moment, his finger resting on his bottom lip. Finally he said, "What . . . what else do you have for me?" He looked down at his notepad. I could see the boredom stretching across his face and I imagined that he was thinking that I was simply a scorned, angry woman looking for her child's father to demand support.

No breaking news story here.

"The package." I hesitated, but then walked over to my china cabinet where the box hid out of view behind the bottom right door. I brought it over and added it to his supplies on the table. "I received a call almost two years ago from a stranger in Portugal who said my husband's ashes were being mailed to me."

Laz's eyebrow rose quickly. "So I am trying to find the whereabouts of a dead man, okay, continue."

"No, I mean, when I got the package, it was an urn, but there were no ashes inside."

"So the urn was empty?"

"No. The ring I showed you earlier today was inside of it, wrapped up in a thick wad of bubble wrap."

"That ring was crazy ridiculous. I've never seen anything like it. It has to be worth a pretty penny. Was it RiChard's?"

I nodded my head. "You know, I don't think I have ever seriously considered how much the lion's head ring is worth. I've never looked at it in terms of its monetary value. When I look at it, all I see is loss."

"How so?" He put down his pen.

Did I really want to tell Laz that the ring had originally belonged to RiChard's best friend? That he'd only gotten it when he told Kisu's father that he had killed the men who supposedly killed Kisu? That seeing the blood on RiChard's hands on that fateful day forever changed the way I looked at him, the way I looked at his self-defined life mission?

I did not want to talk about it. The stew of emotions that simmered in me from merely *thinking* about it was enough to make me feel like I would break into a full-blown boil.

But I was determined to find Roman.

"He'd told my son about the ring once during one of his phone calls to us. Told him he'd give it to him when he was eighteen, but then later said it got lost when he was assisting with clean-up efforts in Indonesia after the terrible tsunami in '04. Seeing the ring in that urn after all these years, after being told it was forever lost, was a great surprise."

"Do you know where RiChard got the ring? That might be a good clue to start from. A piece of jewelry that big has got to have a story, a paper trail, something behind it."

"It was his friend's, Kisu's." I struggled with what to share. I shut my eyes, seeing anew the blood on RiChard's hands, feeling anew the queasiness in the pit of my stomach that came every time I remembered that RiChard had admitted murder, "for the sake of what was right," for supposedly avenging the death of his good friend. I opened my eyes, swallowed the bile taste in my mouth, and did my best to continue.

"His friend Kisu was . . . was killed, and Kisu's father gave RiChard the ring before Roman was born; but that package that came from Portugal two years ago was initiated by Kisu. He was never dead. The letter I showed you earlier that was written in Portuguese? Well, here is the translation." I'd printed both the translation and the picture that had been e-mailed to me by the helpful newspaper editor. Laz looked at both.

"So Kisu is going around claiming to be RiChard," he commented. "Do you mind if I make copies of these?" he asked even as he took out his smartphone and scanned both the letter and the picture of Kisu's fake ID.

"What is Kisu's last name?" He was writing something down.

"I don't remember. Started with an O, or maybe an A, or R, or, I really don't remember. It was something really long. I could never pronounce it. He and RiChard used to laugh at how I stumbled over it."

"Where was he from?"

"His village was somewhere in KwaZulu-Natal, in one of the most scenic, mountainous areas of South Africa, but he studied and lived part-time in London. That's where RiChard met him, during a study-abroad experience he had when he was an undergraduate."

"So you don't know any of his people, his family?"

I shut my eyes again, remembering the strong, austere look of his father, the pride and humility that somehow balanced on the face of his mother. But I could not recall their names. I shook my head, opened my eyes again.

"All I remember is that he had a fiancée named Mbali. I dreamt about her last night, and I hadn't even thought about her once in years." I smiled. "She had been a student at Kisu's university but then dropped out to help her family at home when her mother died. She was the oldest girl, and was ordered to come help care for her younger siblings, despite having two older brothers who lived right there, or so I remember. I remember thinking she had every reason to be angry, to be bitter; but she truly lived up to the meaning of her name: flower. She was very nice toward me when I was there, and the way she and Kisu looked at each other . . ." I stopped as a stinging sensation that filled my chest threatened to bring me to tears. "We did look at each other like that once, RiChard and I," I whispered.

Laz was too busy scribbling down notes to notice my sudden spell of heart sorrow. "Perugia, Italy," he mumbled before looking back at me. "You said his mother was Italian. Is that the city she was from?"

"Yes. I never met her though. His father, either. RiChard showed me a picture once of them that he kept with him. It was a picture of all three of them together, all smiling. They looked like an ad for the United Colors of Benetton," I said, chuckling. "All of them were beautiful, his dad with his dreads, his mother with her long, dark hair, pale green eyes, and freckles."

I paused, thinking of when RiChard showed me the photo. It was the same night that I'd introduced him to my parents at Thanksgiving dinner my freshman year of college, when I told them I was dropping out of school to marry him and travel with him around the world.

After the firestorm of my mother's wrath and my father's silence, we'd sat in his old, rusted car and he showed me the one picture he had of his parents. RiChard was about sixteen years old in that photo, from what I remembered him saying, the same age Roman was now. He told me that the events that led to his parents' divorce happened shortly after the picture was taken and all three of them more or less went their separate ways, leaving RiChard on his own. I never knew what had happened to his parents' marriage. I never asked and he never volunteered that info.

"Okay." Laz was back to writing. "Can I see a picture of RiChard?"

"I don't have one."

He looked back up at me with a question on his face; but I guess he saw the look on mine and left it alone.

"I know you said you never met his mother, but do you know anything or anyone in Perugia? I guess I'm trying to figure out the significance of Kisu using this address."

"I don't know a living soul in Perugia or any other parts of Italy." I shook my head. "No, wait. Well, that's not really anything."

"What?"

"The person who translated the letter from Portugal for me two years ago was a teacher at a community college. I briefly signed up for her course solely to seek assistance with getting answers about the package from someone who could speak the language; and the night I went, the only other student there said he was originally from Perugia. He seemed willing to help, but I had too much going on at the time." I could still see in my mind the young man with the tight jeans and white tee, looking a like a cologne or underwear model, his accent thick, his manner casual. "His name was Luca. Luca Alexander. He signed up for the class because he was planning a trip to Rio and wanted to learn basic Portuguese before then."

Laz dismissed my comments with a quick wave of his hand. "Unless he is someone you really know, or are in touch with, I don't really see how that is helpful. So, anyway," he moved on, "you've given me a lot to start with. I'll check some of the resources and sources I have and will see if I can come up with some clues of RiChard's whereabouts." He looked me squarely in the eye. "That is, if he is even still alive, and is willing to be found."

"Roman obviously found something to make him willing to leave and look."

I could tell Laz was weighing what I said as he began packing up his things.

"You're leaving?"

"Yeah, unless you want me to stay." His face unfolded into a wide smile that made me uneasy.

"No, I mean, it's . . ." I struggled to find words. "I thought you were going to help me. I just told you all I could about what I know, or don't know, as it is. How are we going to do this, find him?"

"I am helping you. You gave me info, and I'm going to follow up on it. That's what I do."

"I thought we were going to work together."

"I get my best work done alone.

"Laz—"

"Let me do my thing, Sienna. I promise I'm good. I mean, really good." His grin at the moment reminded me of the Cheshire cat.

"Okay, yeah, you do need to go."

He winked as he put his fedora back on his head. "I'll be in touch very soon."

Chapter 28

As I closed the door behind him, a new wave of exhaustion threatened to break my momentum. I'd never told anyone even a quarter of what I had shared with him. Talking about it all had worn me out. Though it was only early morning, I felt like I'd already lived through the whole day and was ready to go to bed.

But too much had been triggered in me to stop now.

Pieces.

That's what my heart felt like. What my life looked like. What my understanding of what was going on was. Bits and pieces, no coherent whole.

I changed into a more presentable outfit, grabbed my keys, and stepped outside.

The night's chill was still in the air. My breath crystallized in front of me and I was glad I had on my leather gloves. I got in my car, and sat in it until the sun finally finished its daily climb to the top of the morning sky. As the morning's temperature began rising, I started my car, not sure exactly where I was going, but putting it in reverse just the same to back out of my parking space.

I needed answers, directions.

Peace.

A sound mind.

Sadie Spriggs had shared a verse about power, love, and a sound mind being the opposite of fear.

I was afraid.

For my son.

For myself.

Heck, I was scared for Silver and her mother because something was clearly off and wrong and desperate, but I did not know what to do for them. I didn't even know if I was supposed to go to the police. Leon had said something about the detective moving on to some other lead.

Leon.

Tears burned my eyelids, but I blinked them away.

I was halfway to my destination before I realized where I was going.

There was a public garden in the city off of Northern Parkway that had acres of greenery, open space, and walkways. Every now and then, when I was exceptionally stressed, or sad, or otherwise out of sync, I would go there to meander through the landscaped grounds, to sit on the cement benches. To think. Pray. Cry. Meditate.

I hadn't been there in a few years. Actually, now that I thought about it, I had not been there since the day after Roman's thirteenth birthday.

The day after the last time RiChard called us.

I guess I'd subconsciously known even then that something significant had just happened in our lives.

The gates to the gardens had opened only minutes earlier. It was the near the beginning of spring, a Saturday, and the first day of the season that I could recall that the early temperature was already over fifty degrees. Despite the chill from earlier, I believed the forecasters who'd called for a dry, sunny day with a high in the sixties.

It would only be a matter of time before other people starting walking through the arboretum's manicured gardens.

I parked my car on a lot near a modern-looking glass visitor's center that had not been there the last time I'd visited. Right beyond this building sat the stately Victorian mansion that had graced the grounds since the 1800s. Lion statues that framed the porch seemed to watch me as I walked by. I stopped at the first garden and sat down on a bench nearly hidden by shrubs and bright flowers. Crickets, birds, and other wildlife competing for attention at the start of the day serenaded me. I inhaled and the scent of sweet flowers calmed me.

"Jesus."

It was the best prayer, the only prayer I could get out. With all the questions, confusion, and turmoil I faced, one thing I knew for certain. God would get what I could not say. I was certain of this, realizing that as my sanity threatened to break from under the pressure of the past few days, the only thing keeping it from doing so was a smidgeon of faith that held on to the belief that somehow, someway, everything would turn out okay.

I recalled driving by a church marquee once that had a phrase that stuck with me: THE OPPOSITE OF FAITH IS FEAR. I wondered why I had not remembered this the other night when I asked Sadie Spriggs what the opposite of fear was.

Power.

Love.

A sound mind.

Wasn't faith needed for those three things to take root, to grow, to thrive? It would take faith for my mind not to break; faith to believe that I could experience true love; faith to have the power to address the situation with my son, to figure out what to do about the circumstance surrounding Silver.

Without faith, it is impossible to please God. I remembered a verse my pastor had shared with me once.

Without faith, I would have every reason to be afraid.

"God, I trust you." I whispered as a slight breeze rustled through the leaves. "Even if I can't see you, or understand what is happening, or know for sure what will happen next, I am confident that my life and times are in your hands and this too shall pass."

I thought of Ava's flowers and realized why I had not been in this garden for so long. For the past few years, when I faced disaster, I usually ran to her. A smile filled my face even as tears filled my eyes. Ava would be proud to know I had grown up enough to run to my source. A peace I could not explain took hold of me. Peace and strength.

I was ready to face the day and whatever it held.

I stood and decided to take the long way back to my car. The serenity of the moment was too precious and rare to rush through. As I passed a couple of smaller gardens on the pathway back to the lot, a sudden flurry of color caught my eyes, startled me, and then made me chuckle.

The butterfly garden.

I paused at a small area of butterfly-loving flowers and bushes, finding a youthful pleasure in the fluttering of black, purple, orange, yellow, and white wings. One of my three paintings that hung on the walls of my house was based on a snapshot I'd taken at this very spot during a nature walk with Roman when he was a wee little thing: the purple, orange, and black-spotted butterfly. It warmed my heart both then and now to see the carefree beauty of the insects flittering over the flowers. I stared in admiration at them a few seconds more before turning back to my car.

That is when it hit me.

Butterflies.

I'd been instinctively bothered about something ever since Silver had given me the necklace with the broken butterfly charm.

The woman in the police footage of the kidnapping had a butterfly tattoo on her neck. It had caught my eye when I reviewed and paused the news story on my computer the other night. I had met the woman allegedly kidnapped just yesterday and *she did not have any tattoos.* She had been wearing a barely there black halter top with plenty of open room to see her neck.

Nada. No butterfly.

"So either the woman I met was not Silver . . ." I said out loud as my pace quickened to get to my car. "Or"—I gasped—"the kidnapped woman was someone else." I dug in my purse for the necklace, pulled it out and studied it anew. I looked at the broken inscription on the back: WITH FAITH ALL. I wondered what the rest of it said—where the rest of it was. There had to be another person involved.

"I need you to keep this in case something happens to me. I was holding on to it for a reason, to give it to someone, but I am not sure I will get a chance. When it all makes sense, you'll know what to do with it." These had been the words of Silver, or whoever she was, as she had pressed the necklace into my palm. As I reflected on it all, I was convinced that someone else was involved.

I was winded again as I plopped down in the driver's seat, unsure of what to make of this revelation, uncertain of what to do, where to go with this thought.

The detective.

He had given me his name and number. Perhaps I could call him and talk to him about my concerns. However, I wanted more information before I approached him. I was tired of sounding like a bumbling fool and did not want to open the door to looking like a person of interest again. I was going to get some answers and then present my suspicions to the authorities. A plan of action began fashioning in my mind.

But first things first.

Skee-Gee and Tridell should be back from Las Vegas by now, I realized. Perhaps they would know something more about Roman. I pulled out my cell phone and dialed the first few numbers for Yvette before thinking better of it. I started over and dialed the first few numbers of my mother's home. As her phone began ringing, I remembered the crowd of church members who had been sitting there, and wondered if any of them were still there. I hung up immediately and settled with dialing my mother's cell phone. She answered on the first ring.

"Well, it's about time you decided to check in with your family." Her tone sizzled and popped like hot oil over the phone.

"Mom," was all I could say as I thought quickly of how to respond to all she was saying and insinuating. But there was no sly talking or soothing my momma.

"Do you have any word on the whereabouts of my grandson? I have been worried sick and you have not returned any messages or given me any updates."

"I was hoping that you had some updates, or rather, Skee-Gee did, if he's back. Is he there?"

"Is he where?" Her diction was sharp and direct. Never a good sign.

"At your house?"

There was a long pause and when she did respond, the air had gone out of her voice. "We're all at Yvette's."

I nearly gasped. My mother, as a rule, never went over to Yvette's house. When Yvette began the series of her purposeful choices that left her living in a rundown row home in the middle of an abandoned block in Lower Park Heights, my mother did all she could to avoid the dwelling; just as Yvette did all she could to prove some point she'd been trying to make since she first got pregnant by a low-level drug dealer, Skee-Gee's late father, at the age of sixteen. What either one of their points was was anybody's guess.

What I did know at the moment was that I was stepping on foreign and dangerous territory if I ventured to explore why my mother was over there. The sizzling steam in her tone told me she did not want me to suspect or ask. Only to come join them.

"I'm on my way," I replied and we both hung up.

Our entire conversation had consisted of only a few sentences, but so much more had been said. Seems like that's how all my deep conversations with my mother were spoken: in the emotion-filled pauses in between.

Chapter 29

I pulled up to Yvette's house around 8:30 a.m. and knew immediately that Skee-Gee's homecoming of sorts was in full swing. The porch was filled with his friends, wannabe gangster-looking types with baggy pants, bandanas, profanity, and sneers that were meant to scare away the timid, all sitting and standing around the covered cement stoop. Whatever lessons Leon had drilled in him along with Roman over the past two years seemed to have been thrown out of the window.

The effects of Leon's absence from my life were being felt already.

I stepped through the mass of directionless young men who barely budged as I pushed through to get to the front door. As a rule, one or two of them were destined to make it. The right configuration of outside help and inside will would somehow join forces to set in motion an escape route for a couple of them from the trappings of the hood. The rest of them would probably disappear into the short news articles, the not-so-shocking-anymore headlines, the negative statistics that seemed to loom over the success of too many young black men. As a social worker by training, I knew that context was everything, and the context, the setting where these young boys' lives were playing out, did not give them the best odds from day one.

I prayed to God that Skee-Gee would be one of the ones who made it out.

"There she is!" Yvette's loud voice blared as I crossed the threshold into her living room. "How you doin', sis? Come on in. We're eating breakfast." She flashed a smile before heading back into her kitchen. My mother, Skee-Gee, and Yvette's other four children were sitting around her dining room table, platters of pancakes, bacon, and scrambled eggs before them.

I froze in my steps. Yvette never called me "sis." Shoot, I could not remember the last time I'd seen her even smiling.

"Good morning, everyone. Welcome back, Skee-Gee." I plastered a smile on my face and headed to the kitchen, fully knowing what I would find in there.

And I was right.

A man.

As Yvette giggled and carried on over the simple task of getting a bag of oranges out of her refrigerator, a man stood at her sink, washing out a glass pitcher and tall glasses.

"Nothing like fresh orange juice on a Saturday morning." He smiled at her, a straight-tooth, bright white smile that sparkled like the diamond solitaires I noticed in Yvette's ears.

"Oh, Sienna, this is my friend, Damari." She patted his arm and they both smiled at each other.

"Nice to meet you." I offered a half-smile back, trying my best not to roll my eyes. I was used to the parade of men Yvette seemed to have in and out of her house; but as Damari led us both back to the table and began a genuine prayer of thanksgiving for the food that had been prepared and for Skee-Gee's safe return, my slight disgust turned into slivers of sorrow.

Yvette had a good man there.

And from the way she fussed over his plate and patted his shoulders every time she passed by him, she was making sure that he knew that she knew it.

Everyone at the table was laughing, smiling, sharing jokes and stories of good humor—including my mother, who I realized had probably sought shelter at Yvette's for the same reason I had avoided calling her house phone. Too many people were over there waiting to tell us how screwed up our family was.

I looked at my screwed-up family: my nephews and baby nieces making a mess of their food and bickering back and forth with each other; my mother doing her best to put up a front like she actually was accepting Yvette's life disasters; Yvette laughing as loud as a chainsaw; the new man at the head of the table who clearly didn't realize what he was getting himself into. I looked at the family who surrounded me and I never felt more clearly both the absence of Roman and the void left empty by Leon.

"I have to go," I whispered. Nobody heard me. Nobody even looked my way as I stood and headed to the kitchen to scrape my uneaten plate. I was opening the front door to leave when my mother called after me.

"We're going over Mother Spriggs's home for dinner this evening."

I started to say something back, but she had already returned her attention to the table, laughing at another story, this one being shared by Damari. I stepped out on the porch, pushed through the throng of Skee-Gee's friends, and was almost at my car when a voice stopped me.

"Aunt See! Hold up! Wait!"

It was Skee-Gee. I waited for him to finish high-fiving his boys on the porch before coming to talk with me. I could not get any words together, but I didn't have to. He was the only one with anything to say.

"I didn't tell anyone this, but I thought you should know. I saw a plane ticket to California in Roman's bags. That's all." He turned around before I could explore any more with him. I watched as he fist-pounded a few more friends before disappearing back into the house.

When I got back in my car, I had only one thought, one destination in mind.

But I had to make one stop first.

Chapter 30

East Biddle Street was closed about a half a block down from the side street where Silver was hiding.

Fire trucks.

The smell of smoke permeated the air. Lights from huge red engines and smaller rescue trucks flashed in a dizzying array of red and yellow beams. I drove as close as I could up to the yellow tape that had been draped around what looked like the entire block and parked my car behind a police cruiser.

"What happened?" I walked up to a uniformed woman who was milling about the perimeter.

"Stand back," she shouted as my stomach turned over in knots.

The equipment and emergency vehicles seemed to be concentrated on the narrow side street off of Biddle where I had been forced to drive down not even twenty-four hours earlier.

"I need to know what happened." I tried to remove the panic in my voice as the officer ignored me. I noted small crowds of people standing around, shaking their heads, whispering among themselves. I went up to a group of three women: one older, two younger. A girl of about eight to ten years old twirled on her toes around them.

"What happened?" I asked quietly.

The eldest of the group narrowed her eyes and studied me before responding. "Fire 'round on Teamont

Street." The other two ladies looked nervously back
and forth between the speaker and me.

"Do you know which house?" I asked, though I felt
like I already knew the answer.

"The middle one, where Ms. Mona lived. Firebombed." All three ladies tsked and shook their heads.

"Daggone shame. Ms. Mona ain't never done nothin'
to nobody," the youngest of the group snarled. The
others looked at her with slight alarm before looking
back at me.

"Are she and . . . and David okay?" I took a risk to
verify that my suspicions were right. The immediate
quiet from all three of them told me I had made a
mistake. These ladies did not know who I was, didn't
know why I was there. None of the people on the
sidewalks around me were talking to any of the police
officers or fire fighters around them. What made me
think they would talk to me, a complete stranger in
their neighborhood?

As if to confirm my line of thinking, the little girl who
had been twirling around the women suddenly stopped
and stared at me, her beads clanking together at the
pause of her spinning.

"Lady, we ain't no snitches. We ain't getting our
house firebombed too!"

"Hush, Neeka!" The middle woman grabbed her by
the ear and all four of them skirted away. I felt like
a spotlight had shined down on me as it seemed like
nearly everyone standing around the street had their
eyes on me.

Snitches.

Somebody had told on someone and the result was a
firebomb.

Nobody else was going to be saying anything to anyone. There was no point in me even trying. As I walked

back to my car, I tried one last time to get some info from the police officer who still stood at the perimeter.

"Excuse me, do you know if anyone was hurt, or . . . or killed in the fire?"

The officer, a short black woman with wide hips but an otherwise lean frame, glanced at me. For a second, I thought she would shoo me away again, but instead she answered me. "Nobody died. Only sent to the hospital for minor injuries from what I understand."

"Oh, good." I exhaled. "I'm so glad to hear all three of them got out okay."

"Three?" The officer turned to face me. "Just two. There were two people who were rescued."

"Okay, thank you." I turned away sharply, wanting to get out of there before I had more people staring at me. I could feel the officer watching me the entire time I walked back to my car. As I drove away, she was still facing my direction.

I needed to find my son, still had a plan to do so, but right now, I needed to get to that detective. I did not have his card on me, but I remembered seeing written on it that his office was located on Baltimore Street. The only police station I knew on Baltimore Street was the main headquarters, right next to The Block. With what felt like an entire neighborhood watching my every move, I sped away to the police station that sat right next to Baltimore's infamous red-light district.

"There's no one here by that name," a man in blue told me. I'd waved him down at the entrance of the headquarters, and after he consulted with another uniformed officer, he came back to me to break the news.

"Detective Sam Fields?" I asked again. "He's kind of short, has a lot of bumps on his face."

"Sorry, ma'am, nobody I know of with that name works here, and believe me, I've been working here for over ten years. I know everyone in this building." He gave me a smile.

"Okay, thank you." I gave up, not sure what else to say to anyone. I wanted to speak directly to the detective so that I would not have to give any back story. I decided to wait until I got back home to pull the correct phone number off of the business card he'd given me. I obviously had the wrong address in mind.

As I walked back outside, I looked to the right of me, where The Block began. It was now late Saturday morning. I didn't know the "prime time" hours of strip clubs and adult toy stores, and wasn't sure that I wanted to find out; but I wanted to get more info about Silver. I walked to the edge of the street, stopping on the corner, trying to decide what to do, where to go.

"Looking for a job, doll?" A skinny, middle-aged white man with stringy blond hair and coarse stubble on his face was leaning against the brick exterior of the club closest to me, puffing on a cigarette and looking at everything but my face. He smelled at a minimum of alcohol and marijuana and his eyes were glazed red.

I thought about where I'd just come from, where I'd scared an entire neighborhood into silence by simply asking the wrong questions. I could not afford to lose an audience here.

"You know where I can find one?" I wanted to laugh. The man had to know I wasn't serious. I was certain nothing about my black slacks and Mary Jane shoes screamed exotic dancer, but maybe he was too stoned to notice.

"Heard they need a couple new girls down there." He pointed to one of the places.

I kept thinking on my feet, kept playing along. "Yeah, I guess they do, after what happened to that young girl . . . What was her name? Silver or something."

"That's right, both of them. Silver and Gold." He shook his head and took another drag of his cigarette.

"Yeah, Silver and Gold." I shook my head, my heart beating faster. *Silver and Gold?*

"Tragic what happened to Gold, but now Silver? Too many animals out here." The man shook his head along with me.

"Yeah, tragic," I replied, though I had absolutely no idea what we were talking about. I was beginning to feel more uncomfortable. "Oh my, look at the time. I'm gonna have to come back later." It was such a weak getaway line, but the only one I could think of. The man did not seem to notice my pathetic ploy to leave.

"All right, doll, be careful out there." He threw his cigarette on the ground, crushed it with the tip of his boot, and turned toward an open, darkened doorway.

I hightailed it out of there, wanting no more than to get home, follow up on my plans to find Roman, and jump in the shower.

I wanted to get the slime and sleaze I felt off of me.

Chapter 31

It was a little past noon when I finally walked into my front door. I did not bother to take off my coat, or drop my keys or purse down into a chair. Instead, I marched straight to my room, straight to my nightstand drawer.

I had already rummaged through it when I'd searched for the letter from Portugal, which I later found under Roman's blanket.

Now I was looking for something else.

The plane ticket.

I'd never told Roman about the cross-country trip we made to California when he was a newborn nestled in my lap. I had discovered some activity back then on a joint account I shared with RiChard and tracked him down at a commune near San Diego. Although he had not called or written following the birth of our child, I guess a part of me naively believed that if he simply saw Roman, saw both of us in person, he would see how much beauty we held, how much help we needed, and that he would decide to come home with us.

It took me fourteen years to realize that was what I had been hoping would result from our trip.

RiChard didn't even hold Roman, a fact I never told my son.

I'd held on to the plane ticket as a testament to our fruitless journey and wrapped it up in a copy of the account statement that had triggered the whole search. I'd buried both in my nightstand drawer years ago.

For the second time that week, I dumped the entire contents of the drawer onto my bed. I flipped through papers, dug through boxes, checked and double-checked odds and ends.

There was no sign of either the ticket or the account statement.

"Roman, what are you doing?" I went to his room and plopped down on the side of his bed, accepting that my son had gone on a wild goose chase based on incorrect and incomplete information. He had a fake ID with his father's name, his paternal grandmother's home city, and Kisu's picture on it. He had an old plane ticket and a bank account number that were both over sixteen years old. Who knew what else he had?

The thought scared me.

My son, my sixteen-year-old son, was somewhere across the country seeking answers without me. I didn't know what scared me more: what he was doing to find him, or what he *would* do once, or even if, he found the answers he sought.

My continual check-ins with the Las Vegas police department assured me that the authorities were doing what they could to help locate him. I considered flying out there myself, but my heart told me that Nevada wasn't his planned destination. Vegas had been a means to an end, I was certain.

It was hard to find someone who did not want to be found. The fact that Roman had not called me said that loud and clear. Like father, like son; the thought stung. I was not worried that something would happen to him. I just wanted him home. I wanted him to *want* to be home.

Now.

I looked around his room. All the trophies, the tidied and folded piles of clothes, the "number ones" all over the place.

Number one.

I recalled that the e-mail from the Portuguese journalist had also been e-mailed to a user with the name "RomanNumeralOne."

It was a stretch, a long shot, I knew, but I went ahead and entered the words into a search engine box. My son was out there and I could not control his whereabouts; but if he had some kind of presence in cyberspace, maybe I could find it and somehow pin him down.

"Please, Jesus," I pleaded, and then pressed search.

Pages—hundreds, thousands, over a million Web site results—came back.

"No." I collapsed my head into my hands, rubbed my temples, and started scrolling through the list of sites. I clicked on some that looked promising, and avoided others that looked like they were waiting to spring out a computer virus on an unsuspecting user. I kept clicking on results, hoping, praying that something, anything about my son would surface from those search words, *Roman Numeral One.*

An hour and a half later I'd made it through the sixty-third page of results with no luck. My anxiety level was beyond a ten, and I knew that I needed to find another way to search for him.

I did not feel like I was moving anywhere sitting in front of a computer screen. I shut it down and called Laz. He answered on the first ring, but not with a hello.

"Hey, babe, I haven't forgotten you, but I'm covering a firebombing in the city. I'll call you back when I can."

And that was it.

I stared at the phone in my hands, trying to figure out why I had not been given the decency of a hello or good-bye or even a chance to say a word. And what was up with the "babe"? I was about to get myself worked up over the entire non-conversation, but the word "firebombing" jumped out at me.

I'd meant to find that detective's card to call him and fill him in about my encounter with Silver and her mother, Jenellis Walker.

If I could not save my son at the moment, maybe I could save someone else.

Chapter 32

The card was where I remembered it to be, on the granite countertop that made up my kitchen island/breakfast bar.

"See, I knew I wasn't crazy." I shook my head, studying the address. It was the same one I'd gone to, the address for the police headquarters on Baltimore Street. "I guess you don't know everyone," I murmured out loud as if the officer who'd directed me away from there could hear me.

As I dialed the number, I thought about what I wanted to say to Detective Sam Fields, where to begin, how to explain why I had not called him earlier. Someone's life was possibly in danger, and even I knew I had been dragging my feet.

My reasons for not making this call sooner were simple. My son had run away. I was confused by Jenellis. And Silver had begged me not to.

In the chaos that had become my life, the only thing that felt clear to me was trusting Silver. Something about her vulnerability made me want to believe her.

And she had begged me not to talk to the police.

I planned to do so anyway, but wanted more information first. Now, with the firebombing happening at the very house where I had talked to her, I knew I could not delay reaching out to the detective. I felt like an irresponsible citizen, an uncaring person.

I did care.

I'd just had a lot going on.

As the phone began ringing, it occurred to me that I had not followed up on a lot concerning this Silver business. I had a vague recollection of Leon saying that the detective and his crew had turned their attention off of me to chase another lead. What was it? And the number 1502? Both Jenellis and Silver looked terrified when I brought it up. What was its significance?

And Silver and Gold?

Maybe the biggest reason I had been avoiding the situation was because I did not like the helplessness I felt trying to understand details that made no sense.

The phone was still ringing. Maybe the detective didn't have voice mail, I considered, as I was about to hang up. My finger inched toward the "end call" button when someone finally picked up.

"Vito's Pizza. Delivery or pick-up?"

"Huh?"

"Vito's Pizza. Delivery or pick-up?" the pleasant-sounding young male voice asked again.

"I'm sorry, I dialed the wrong number." I hung up, checked the number and dialed again, and the same person answered again.

"Vito's Pizza. Delivery or pick-up?"

"Okay, I was trying to reach someone but this clearly isn't the right number. I'm sorry. Thank you." I hung up again.

I was still holding the phone in my hand when it rang. The number I'd just dialed was on my screen. Confused, I wrinkled up my face, but I answered.

"Hello?" I asked into the receiver and then held my breath.

"Ma'am, your pizza is ready for pick-up," the same voice informed me.

"Excuse me?"

"Your pizza is ready for immediate pick-up. You can come get it at 600 Elrush Way, suite 29." The phone went dead and I was left dumbfounded.

"Pizza? Elrush Way? What?" I dialed the number again, ready to demand an explanation for the bizarre call, but this time there was no answer.

"Elrush Way?" I repeated. Aside from not knowing what that phone call was about, I had no idea where Elrush Way was.

Who was this Detective Sam Fields? I looked down at his card again. He wasn't known at his stated address and his phone number led to a pizza shop? No, that's not right. My gut told me that as crazy as it seemed, these were the correct ways to get in touch with him. What kind of detective was he? I started to call Leon to see if he knew anything about him, but then thought better of it.

It wasn't right for me to think I could keep coming at Leon with a million and one questions without being able to answer any of his. He'd made it pretty clear and I could not pretend that our conversation yesterday did not happen.

I put my coat back on. I didn't know where Elrush Way was; didn't know what kind of "pizza" I was about to pick up; didn't even know if any of this was safe; but what else was there for me to do at the moment? If I did not like what I saw when I got there or found that the detective was not really who he said he was, I could always dial '911.'

I'd somehow survived the week so far. No reason to believe I could not get out of today intact.

I noted that my phone was on its last bar of power. I did not want to be in a tense situation without the ability to call for help—or miss a call from or about Roman! I fished through a small basket I kept near my coat closet for a new car charger I'd recently bought since my old one had stopped working. I dropped the charger in my purse and headed outside, my confidence growing that I was taking the right steps to ensure everyone's safety.

The temperature had dropped. I guess the forecasters had been wrong after all. Though the first hints of spring were in the air, March wanted to remind us that it was still a winter month. I wrapped my coat tighter around me and went back into my foyer. Dropping my purse on the floor, I searched for and then found my gloves. As I stood in my doorway adjusting my coat and gloves, I noticed that despite the falling temps, a couple of my neighbors were engaged in Saturday afternoon chores they'd probably been waiting all winter to get to—washing cars, trimming lawns, and the like. And all of them, all of my neighbors who were outside, were staring at me like I had four heads.

"Hi, Kenny." I waved at the man who lived two doors down as he finished adding another coat of wax to his Range Rover.

"Hey, Sienna." He nodded. "That was a pretty Beemer you were driving yesterday. Where'd it go?"

Laz's BMW.

The question caught me off-guard. "Oh, that? It was a friend's. I'm still driving my Chevy." I jingled my keys and shut the front door behind me. I scurried to my car, wanting to avoid any more conversation.

"You must have some generous friends to let you step into their rides like that."

"Yeah, I guess so. All right, I'll see you later." I had to get out of there before more questions I did not want to answer came. I guess my neighbors noticed more about my life than I realized. Didn't know if that comforted or concerned me. I was certain they'd seen all the activity at my house over the past few days. Who knew what they were thinking.

I waited until I pulled out of my development to set my GPS.

"600 Elrush Way." I entered the address. After a few moments of calculations, I saw that I was heading to Glen Burnie, an area in Anne Arundel County, south of Baltimore. It would take about half an hour to get there from where I was.

"I should have enough to make it." I eyed my gas tank, which had been running low ever since my ride around town with David yesterday. "Let's get this show on the road." I turned on some music and headed south toward 895.

My mind was blank as I followed the turn-by-turn directions that took me through the Harbor Tunnel and on to I-97. Airplanes arriving and departing from the nearby BWI Thurgood Marshall Airport glided right over the highway as I neared the exit the GPS was directing me to. Seeing the planes made me only think of Roman. I'd misled him. No, I point-blank lied, telling everyone that his trip to the reservation was the first time he'd flown. I thought about the old plane ticket to San Diego I knew he had, and wondered if he'd figured out that he went on that pointless trip with me as an infant.

Did my son view me as a perpetual liar? Had he given up on getting any truth about his father from me?

The questions burned as much as the potential answers to them did.

Good thing I have this GPS working for me, 'cause I have no idea where I am. I interrupted my own thoughts with this realization.

"Turn right and arrive at destination," the unit said.

"Ain't nothing back here," I answered, frowning. "Oh, I see it." I spoke to the GPS like it was a real person directing me from the passenger seat.

I was on Crain Highway, a long, busy thoroughfare that was dotted by office parks, fast-food restaurants, strip malls, and big-box stores. 600 Elrush Way was an office building that sat way back from the street at the end of a long, curvy parking lot, nearly out of view from the main street. It was an impressive four-story square building covered with opaque glass windows—the kind of glass that looked like mirrors from the outside, but offered perfect views of the outside to those who were within its domain.

I was certain that someone was watching me pull up and park.

The office building was probably busy during the week as I noted a couple of signs for doctors, dentists, and counseling centers. However, at the moment, I did not see another car or person on the lot or nearby. I could hear the roar of traffic on Crain Highway, but not see any passing cars where I was. Even the airplanes that zoomed overhead were out of sight due to the heavy greenery that surrounded the building.

The entire area was desolate.

While I knew I wasn't on my way to a pizza parlor, I wasn't expecting to come to such an isolated area. I sat in my car for a few moments, debating whether I should start my engine back up, turn around, and head back home.

But I'd come this far.

No fear. Only power, love, and a sound mind. The elements of faith. *But will going in this building looking for suite 29 be an act of faith or foolishness?* A sound mind was not a foolish one. *God, I wish I had a sign . . . .* But having a sign wouldn't be faith, right?

I sat there confused, contemplating what to do, not feeling comfortable with any of my options. *What if this Detective Sam Fields is a total fraud?* I considered. No, he would not have had so many cops at his command searching through my house and threatening to come back with another search warrant.

But he never came back. And now that I thought about it, I never saw the first warrant.

However, Leon didn't seem to have any alarm at who they were or what they were doing. His frustration seemed limited to me not telling him what was going on, the parts I did know anyway.

These were the questions and issues that battled within me as I sat there, cutting the motor on and off, on and off, until it was just . . . off.

"I'm out of gas." I kicked myself. I'd pushed my car too far, just like I'd successfully pushed everything and everyone else in my life. Now I was out of gas and . . . and I did not have my purse with my cash or credit cards. The realization hit me like a bag of bricks dipped in concrete. I remembered dropping my purse onto the floor of my foyer when I'd gone back in my house to get a pair of gloves. I'd never picked it back up as I rushed away from my neighbor's questions.

All I had was my cell phone.

With its one bar of power.

I needed someone's help, but who was I to call? Laz was busy with his breaking news story, and there was no way I was contacting my mom or sister or dad right now.

Too much going on in me to add family drama.

Leon.

I felt like he was the only person who would willingly come to help me, no questions asked.

Not wanting to hear the hurt and pain that I was sure would be in his voice, I sent him a text message.

I'm sorry to bother you, but I am out of gas and have no money on me. I am at 600 Elrush Way. Can you help me, pretty please? ☺ I will pay you back.

I looked at the words and the smiley face I typed on the screen, feeling cheap and cheesy, but not sure what else to do. I pressed send. His reply was instant.

On my way. Will be there in about forty minutes.

I exhaled, finding comfort once again in the one constant of my life. Well, near constant. I knew that the meaning and terms of our relationship, or whatever it was we had, had changed. Permanently.

I had forty minutes to kill. The office building still loomed before me. Knowing that Leon was on his way gave me courage. Without a clear thought or plan, I exited my car and headed for the front door of the building. I pulled the handle. It was locked.

"Oh, well, I tried." I turned away, feeling a sense of relief that I had worried over nothing. Even as I turned, though, I heard it: a low buzz, a slight click.

I turned back around to see that the door's lock had given way.

Someone, somewhere in the building, was letting me in.

"Here we go." I grabbed the handle again and stepped into the dimly lit lobby.

Chapter 33

It took a moment for my eyes to adjust to the dimness. Though the outside of the building had a modern edge to it due to the opaque glass windows and walls, the inside of it, at least the foyer anyway, had an old-fashioned feel. With the cushy upholstered couches, Tiffany chandeliers, and floral area rugs, I imagined that the lone elevator probably had velvet curtains on its wall, brass fixtures, and mirrored panels. The real plants that sat around the mahogany tables told me that someone took pride and care in the building, a far cry from the disaster that was the building where I rented office space. *One day, I will have an office in a building as nice as this one.* I smiled.

Suite 29. I willed myself to stay focused, alert. The directory that hung on the wall next to the elevator did not showcase a suite with that number, but I noted that double digit offices were located in the basement.

Wasn't anything else to do but go down.

"This is foolishness," I told myself as I skipped the elevator and headed for the stairwell, a pale green maze of pipes and cement. My heart was thumping so loudly, I felt like it would thump right out of my chest. Thankfully, the basement level, once I entered it, had the same comforting old style to it as the lobby did. I tried to relax, knowing full well that I would not be able to do so until I figured out what was going on, why I was there.

I stopped at an unmarked door between suites numbers 28 and 30 and gently rapped on it. When no one answered, I pushed it in. It gave easily and revealed a well-stocked supply closet.

"You came." A woman's voice sounded from the shadows. A light bulb flickered on and I blinked to adjust my eyes to the sudden brilliance.

Silver again. Or at least this woman who claimed to be her.

She emerged from behind a tall stack of paper towel rolls.

"Umm, why are we inside of a—"

"Shhh." She put a finger up to her plumped lips. "We need to talk in here."

I had not noticed another door. She held it open and I could see a tiny office with a metal desk, a single chair, and a cheap floor lamp. A corkboard hung on the wall with several lists tacked to it, including what looked like a cleaning supply inventory and a "to-do" checklist.

"It's the safest place to talk," she responded in reply to my obvious hesitation. I realized she was whispering. I shrugged my shoulders and followed her into the maintenance worker's office. She clicked off the light in the closet, turned on the floor lamp in the cramped workspace, and shut the door behind us.

The space was even tinier than it had looked from the other side of the door—and cold.

"Want an apple?" She held out a Red Delicious as she crunched into one herself. I noticed a paper bag on the floor filled with more fruit, water bottles, rice cakes, and a large French baguette.

"You're hiding again?" I tried to make sense of the scene before me as Silver plopped down onto the floor, sitting cross-legged on the linoleum.

She nodded.

"Whose office is this?"

She shrugged her shoulders and took another bite out of her apple.

"Why am I here?"

"Because I told him that I would only keep cooperating if he bought you here to talk with me."

"Who is he?"

"Detective Fields."

"He knows where you are?"

"Of course." She took another bite. "He's protecting me."

I cocked my head to the side, as if doing so would somehow make the jumble of details that had been collecting in my brain suddenly come together and make sense. "Protecting you from what?"

"I can't get into that right now. I just want to talk."

"Talk about what? And why can't you get into it?" I rubbed my temples. "This is crazy. What is going on?"

She continued to blink innocently, her fake lashes really starting to get on my nerves.

"You have to tell me something," I demanded.

She threw the apple core into a metal wastebasket, then, thinking better of it, took it out, wrapped it in a paper towel and put it back into her bag of food supplies.

There would be no trace of her once she was gone from this holding spot.

"Well?" I folded my arms.

Silver shut her eyes, laid her head back on the wall, and smiled. "When I was ten years old, I told my mother I was going to be an electrical engineer. I was in the math club at my elementary school and some lady who was an engineer came to our after school meeting to tell us we could be one too. I was sold. " She opened her eyes and looked at me. "Does that surprise you?"

I did not know where this was going, but I played along. "No. Most children have dreams about their future. In fact, I'd be concerned if you didn't." When silence took over the room again, she looked a little irritated.

"Well?" she asked.

"Well, what?"

"Aren't you going to ask what happened? How I went from dreaming about being an electrical engineer to becoming an adult entertainer?"

"Does it have anything to do with why we are sitting in a supply closet in an empty building on a Saturday afternoon?" I wasn't trying to be mean, but Leon was on his way, and I wanted to be out of there so I would not have to answer questions from him I could not answer.

But isn't that what he wanted? Answers? I blinked out the memory of his pain and waited for Silver's response.

"It has everything to do with why we are here."

"How so?" I demanded.

I could tell she was Jenellis's child. The moment she felt back in charge of the conversation, she relaxed again.

"My mother and her men." Silver shook her head, grabbed a water bottle, and twisted the cap. "When I was eleven years old, my mother got married for the first time, unfortunately to a monster. Its name was Sheldon."

"What did he do?"

"What didn't he do?" Silver shook her head again. "I watched that creature punch, slap, kick my mother, spit in her face. She did not know how to get away. She couldn't find a job that paid enough to support us on her own. Listen." She stared at me. "I was a sweet, innocent little girl. I loved my stuffed animals and my bike. I went skating down Shake and Bake on Pennsylvania Avenue, and had dreams of being an electrical engineer. That monster Sheldon came in our lives and destroyed everything." She was breathing hard, trying to catch her breath. "I saw my mother lying on the floor unconscious and him stepping over her like she was . . . was a bag of trash. Nothing. But . . . but she was my mother." She looked up at me, a look of pleading in her eyes.

Pleading to be heard, to be understood.

"He was a monster. And he hurt your mother. And he hurt you." I said what she could not.

Tears suddenly sprung onto her face. "My mother could not stop him from hurting her, or hurting me. That's what it seemed like, anyway. Nobody could stop him. I tried to tell my teachers, but all they could talk about was how my grades were slipping, how I had suddenly become too mouthy, too moody. I went from being the popular girl at school to being teased because I always seemed to smell. I couldn't stop wetting myself. By the time I was in eighth grade, I was taking baths three times a day to try to feel clean. All I wanted was to feel clean, but I never did, no matter how hard I tried."

She was shaking. I sat down in the desk chair as she stayed huddled in the corner, her legs now drawn up to her chest, her head resting on her knees.

"By the time I was fifteen, I had become so numb to my life, I didn't even remember what a dream was. I had dropped out of school, had my first baby." She smiled. "I named him Tracy. He looked exactly like Sheldon, a little monster." Her smile dropped. "My mother made me give him up for adoption, although I was going to try to love him." She touched the end of her hair, twirled a single curl of it as she momentarily disappeared into an unspoken memory. Then she came back.

"By the time I was eighteen, I had tried everything to just . . . just feel again. I was tired of being numb, of feeling dirty. I thought that if I took that job down on The Block, I'd be able to reclaim my body, because then I would be in charge of whatever happened to it, in charge of whatever a man did to it. I put my heart and soul into my work because I did not know what else a heart and soul could do if allowed to dream."

She shook her head as new tears formed. "It didn't work. The girls where I worked were so competitive, so desperate for money, for whatever it was they were looking for, for whatever it was they were trying to prove, that I had to go further, do things that . . . you don't even want to imagine. I thought I could reclaim control, feel clean again, and all I felt was . . ." Her sentence faded away for a second time.

"I'm sorry." She gave a nervous laugh. "You didn't ask to be part of any of this." She looked at me, searching, I could tell, for a sign that it was okay for her to have shared all she had.

"Have you ever talked to anyone else about . . . all these things you've been through?"

"No." She recoiled. "I guess that is why I insisted that you be allowed to come here. When you called Detective Fields, I told him that I would not cooperate any further unless and until you came."

"Why me?"

"You're a therapist." She chuckled before sobering suddenly. "And you trusted me. Yesterday. After all I had David put you through, you believed me."

I didn't want to tell her that me not calling the police on her was more a function of my confusion and distraction than it was my belief in her, but I guess there was a purpose greater than my own shortcomings that was holding things together.

"I'm glad you have begun to share your story. There's nothing wrong with talking to a therapist or someone who can offer you a professional listening ear. Telling your story is important for your healing, and seeing a professional doesn't mean you're crazy." I paused, stepping carefully before proceeding. "It simply means you are committed to being the best person God created you to be."

"God!" She laughed. "People like you who have never had a bad day in your life are so quick to talk about God. If there really is a God, why did He let that monster destroy our lives?" She was laughing, but her anger was evident, raw, and real.

A million and one thoughts flashed through my mind as I considered how to answer her question. I decided on a raw, real response of my own.

"Silver, I have not had to go through anything like you have. I've had some hard days, some pain, some sorrow—nothing like what you are describing, but enough to make me ask questions similar to what you are asking now. I do not fully know or understand why terrible things happen. What I do know and firmly believe is that without faith, without believing that God is still in control somehow and cares, we would have no chance at healing, at wholeness. I don't have the answers, but He does. I think it's okay to ask Him your questions directly, and believe that He will answer you, if you truly seek Him to do so. If He's the all-powerful, almighty God that we want to believe Him to be, then He can handle our questions."

Should I tell her that I have been having my own crises of faith as of late? Repeatedly? As she stayed quiet, seemingly reflecting on what I had just said, verses from the Bible I remembered reading once came to mind. Well, paraphrases of verses as I could not remember the exact wording, or even scripture references. "Perfect love casts out fear" and "God is love." Something like that.

"God is not afraid of us or what we can think to ask Him." I told her in response to my own inner dilemmas.

Silver looked tired. Drained.

"How long do you have to stay here?" I asked, giving up on asking *why* she had to stay there. Seemed like all of my interactions with her were on a need-to-know basis, and I, apparently, did not need to know some things about her yet.

"Just until Detective Fields determines another safe house. The last one was compromised."

"Oh, yes, that's right. Are David and his grandmother okay?" I could not give up on my search for answers.

"They're fine. Detective Fields was able to get me out of there the moment it appeared I was no longer safe. Fifteen minutes later their house was firebombed in a drive-by. Someone threw a Molotov cocktail through their front window. David carried Ms. Mona out their back door, or so I heard."

"What put you in danger there?"

"Contacting you."

"All right, I really need to understand better what is going on."

"Trust me, you don't want to be involved any more than you already are. Hasn't this been enough trouble for you?

"I'm still trying to figure out what exactly I'm involved in. Police say you're kidnapped. You say you're not, that you're being protected. And your mother, as you call her, seems to think you are blackmailing her, and I still don't know what is so important about the number 1502. And what about Brayden? What's the deal with him?"

"Brayden is my mother's new man. What else can I say?" She looked away, smiled sadly, then blurted, "Thanks for coming."

"Am I getting dismissed?"

"You have company."

"Huh?" I stood up, and moved to the corner where she sat on the floor. I saw for the first time that a small collection of monitors were propped up against the desk where I had been sitting. Silent, grainy black-and-white images of the parking lot, front entrance, lobby, and elevator flickered directly in her line of sight.

Now it made sense why she had settled so comfortably on her spot on the floor.

And also explained how I'd gotten into the building so easily.

I wondered what else about her mannerisms had an explanation beyond what I could see from my vantage point. Regardless, I would have to figure that out later as I saw on the screens her reason for my sudden dismissal.

"He's a cop, isn't he?" She was pointing to Leon. He was standing next to my car, a gasoline container in hand. I understood the gasoline container; what I did not get was why a black Pathfinder was parked next to my car and not his Altima.

"I'm going."

"No, wait." Silver jumped to her feet and grabbed one of my wrists. "I need to know—is he a cop or not? Were you expecting him?"

I saw genuine fear in her eyes and I reminded myself that she was hiding from something or someone. "Yes and yes," I said to reassure her, though I did not stay around to see if she was indeed assured.

I had to get out there and figure out what to say to Leon about my whereabouts. How could I even begin to explain to him the happenings of the past three days? I tried to think of an acceptable excuse, a believable reason to have been in the obviously empty office building. I used the time I had jogging up the steps, cutting through the lobby, and exiting the front door to prepare myself for his questions. As I walked up to the car, my mind was still blank for the coming inquiry.

"Hi, Leon."

"I hope regular was okay." Leon recapped the container.

"That's fine. Thank you so much for coming, Leon." I reached out to pat his shoulder through his soft leather jacket, an innocent gesture of appreciation.

"No problem." He turned away from my gesture and placed the container in the trunk of the SUV.

"Where's your Altima?"

"Traded it in." He glanced back at me as he turned toward the driver's side. "Decided to go all out and get the truck I've always dreamed of having."

"Never knew this was in your dreams." I ran my hand over the gleaming black hood, wondering when his questions would begin.

Instead, he opened the door of his truck and got in.

"Leon," I asked as I raised an eyebrow, "that's it?"

He raised an eyebrow back. "You asked for gas and I bought you some." He put the keys into the ignition.

"I mean, it's just that . . ."

He froze for a moment and stared at me as I struggled to find words to a question I could not pose.

"I mean, uh, I guess I thought you'd be curious to know where I was."

His movements came back to life as he reached for his seat belt. "No more questions for you, Sienna. I'm letting you live your life. If you need anything else, call."

I need you, I wanted to say. "Okay, thanks," was what came out.

"No problem." He shut the door, started the engine, and began backing up. As I watched him drive off in his dream truck, I became aware that Silver was probably watching the entire scene from her hideout in the basement in suite 29. I turned toward the building, smiled, then immediately regretted doing so. Who knew who could be watching? Paranoia was eating away at me.

Leon's new truck disappeared out of the lot as he turned toward Crain Highway.

I felt terrible for keeping secrets, and even worse was my silence when the hard questions came. Even my son had not been exempt from my inability to talk when I needed to.

Roman!

I pulled out my phone from my coat pocket, about to pull up my Internet connection and continue my search.

But my phone was dead.

And I'd left my car charger inside my purse. And my purse was sitting on the floor of my foyer.

That revelation was not enough to stop me.

There was nothing more for me to do with Silver and company, I figured. No point in even trying to contact that detective, or whatever he was, again.

I had no idea what was going on with any of them. What I did know was that my son was somewhere out there looking for his father and I did not know where either one was.

But I was determined to find out.

I got back in my car, knowing exactly where I was headed next.

Chapter 34

The main branch of the Enoch Pratt Free Library system was located on Cathedral Street in downtown Baltimore. It was a massive building with architecture that reflected its 1930s construction—tall pillars, ornate cornices, gargoyles, and elaborate trims over every entryway, window, and door. I parked my car about a block south of the main entrance and walked as fast as I could to it.

I could have gone home to do this, but a sense of urgency had quickened my pace as I headed to a public computer in a small alcove and logged on. Besides, something about the vast spaciousness of the high ceilings, the anonymity, and the hushed voices made me feel safe and comforted as I continued the most important mission of my life.

Finding my son.

RomanNumeralOne.

I'd done an Internet search with the terms earlier, but it had crossed my mind to add the name "St. James" to my attempt. Now Web sites referencing historical people, Bible verses, even football, popped up on the results screen. There were still pages and pages of results, but I felt like I was on to something, so I willed myself to start scrolling through them all. At least until my sign-up time was depleted or my paid parking time expired.

"Please, Jesus," I pleaded, as I scrolled through the fifth page of results. I kept going, the speed at which I scrolled through seeming to increase with each new page.

"Wait." I froze. "I missed it." Something told me I had gone too fast, that my eyes had caught notice of something important, relevant. I clicked back to what I thought I'd seen and whatever air I had left in my lungs squeezed out of me.

A blog site.

I clicked on the link and felt my heart jump from my chest to my throat.

> RomanNumeralOne. The life and times of a legend.

There were no pictures on the page, no real name of the blog's author given; but the paragraph describing the author of the blog told me all that I needed to know.

> On my thirteenth birthday, my father told me I was a warrior and called me a full-grown man. And then he never called me again. At first it didn't bother me cuz I knew he was a warrior fighting for right causes all over the world. I accepted my fate as child of a deployed soldier. But when I started realizing that people around me were hiding information about my father from me, I began to suspect there was more I didn't know about.

I reread that sentence several times before continuing, feeling a sharp pang of guilt, knowing that "people" referred solely to me.

> At first I was angry, but then I decided to turn my anger into something more useful. If I am a warrior,

then I must act like one, and join my father on the battlefield. Secrets that have been held from me only prove that my destiny is greater than I imagined. Perhaps, more than a warrior, I am also royalty, who knows? I am going to find out who I am and nobody will stop me. I am going to find my father to prove to him that I am worthy of the mission he started. I will complete my destiny and keep you posted about my discoveries on the pages of this blog.

I sat there stunned, hurt. Seething. My fool child. This whole time, I assumed he was looking for his father out of resentment toward him, to find him to tell him off—or at least question him. In reality, he was resenting *me*. All I had done to raise this boy on my own, to care for and provide for him, without one ounce of help from his father, and yet his father was still who he idolized, who he wanted to emulate, who he was chasing after.

He saw me as the enemy, as the one who'd kept secrets from him, like he had some other identity that I had not wanted him to know about.

I read through his self-description again and again and then began clicking on various posts he'd written. His posts started nearly two years ago, right around the time we'd moved to our new house.

The people have broken all ties to my father and moved to a new location. Now he will never know how to find me again. That is why this mission is so important. I need him to know that I care, but I must do so with discretion so my mission will not be discovered.

I kept clicking through his blog. The posts spread

out with weeks, months between them, rants and
rages about "the people" who were keeping him from
knowing his heritage, who refused to even "mention
his father by name" or "allow him to see one picture of
him."

I could not believe what I was reading. With each
new post, each rant, I felt my anger level rising. I had
started from the beginning and was now at his posts
from about six months ago.

> I found a letter about my father, an old plane ticket,
> and a bank account that shows activity in California.
> It was hidden, not meant for me to find. Now I know
> that the people are trying to keep me from the
> truth. All this time I had been told that my father is
> overseas, and he was at one point right here in the
> country. I'm getting closer to finding him, to joining
> him. I will not be stopped.

After that post, things really picked up, I noted. He'd
started putting posts up at least twice a week from
that point forward, sometimes every other day. I came
across the first picture.

It was the fake ID of Kisu, the one I knew had been
forwarded to him from the Portuguese reporter.

> Finally. I have a picture of my dad. He looks like he
> really could be a prince. Perhaps I am African royalty.
> He lives in Italy now. Maybe he's an ambassador.
> And to think the people who are working against me
> could keep this information from me!

I started to shut down the computer. Or at least leave
a detailed message in the comment section that was
underneath every post. There had not been any com-

ments at all under any of his posts. I doubted that he had any followers. And if there were any followers, they were probably as delusional or wistful about fantasy and legends as my child. He wrote about "levels of understanding," and "hidden knowledge," as if he were trapped in a video game or a fairy tale, or some kind of hybrid of the two. How had I missed any of this?

Here I was a social worker, a therapist, and I had somehow missed the major storm brewing in my own household, with my own child. I clicked on the comment box, but then clicked off. I needed to read the rest of his posts before I posted anything. Who knew if he even had access to a computer, or if he even was still keeping up with his blog? I noticed that the index on the right of the page gave the date to his last post as a week before he left for the mission trip.

Nothing since.

He must have thought he'd found something, or changed his approach. What had he found?

I decided to keep reading the posts in order before jumping to the last one. I needed to fully understand what he was thinking, how his mind was working.

I kept reading, but outside the posts where he had posted the ID picture of Kisu, nothing else stood out. His rants about injustices, and secrets, and "the people's betrayal" of him continued. Once he knew he was going to Arizona with the church youth group, he moaned and whined about it being his best opportunity to make "a clean break" but not knowing where to "break off to."

I finally was at his last post. All I had to do was click on it. *But if there is nothing there that helps me know where he is, what do I do?* In the blizzard of emotions I felt, helplessness was not one that I wanted to add. This last post was it. If there was nothing in it that offered any clues to my son's current whereabouts, I was back at square one.

Lost.

It was too much. I was not ready to be disappointed. To be helpless. I clicked off the Web site, wanting to prepare myself for what may or might not be there. I thought about calling Leon to tell him what I'd found, but was that really the right move? He had not even asked about Roman just now when I'd seen him.

That hurt.

But maybe he was hurting too much to even talk to me about my son, who I knew he loved as his own. Leon was going through his own blizzard of emotions, I knew. I also knew that I'd seen him with another woman—a beautiful, young, smiling woman—yesterday morning. I had to switch thoughts before I sunk even lower in them, if that was even possible.

My phone was dead anyway. I could not call anyone if I wanted to, including Laz. I hated that Laz even came to mind as an option. Oh, well. I pulled the Internet back up, and went to the Web site of the news station where Laz worked. The story about the firebombed house on Teamont Street was the lead article. Laz Tyson was credited as the reporter. I scanned through the article.

There was no mention of Silver or any ties to a kidnapping.

Maybe Sam Fields really was a detective, maybe a private detective, and Silver really was in hiding.

I was too worn out to make sense of their drama, but I was tied to it some kind of way, even if it was merely through the randomness of a Google search for a therapist.

Jenellis and Brayden had shown up at *my* office; Brayden had given me cash in an amount, $1,502, that held some kind of significance. Silver had somehow traced and tracked me down, wanted me to believe her, hear her story.

Abuse, violence, crime, questions . . .

I pulled up a search engine box again. Typed in the number 1502, and added the names Jenellis Walker, Brayden Moore, Silver Simmons.

Of course, nothing that made sense came back.

I didn't know what I was looking for. What I did know was that the number 1502 meant something to all three of them. What was it? An amount? A symbol? An address? A date?

I stared at the number, considering these various options, considering which would be the easiest, most logical to look up. If 1502 was an address, how could I even begin to imagine what street? A symbol? Could be anything. I was back to the idea of a date. 1502. The fifteenth of February? *1/5/02?* It was worth a try.

I entered January 5, 2002 with their names.

Jackpot.

The first result that came up had both the date and the name Jenellis highlighted in the blurb underneath. It was a news article . . . *No, an obituary,* I realized as I clicked on it, a short death notice that had been posted and archived in the *Baltimore Sun:*

LONG, Sheldon R. On January 5, 2002 Sheldon R. Long of Baltimore. Beloved husband of Jenellis Long (nee Simmons); loving stepfather of Anastasia and Contessa Simmons, son of Ramona K.M. Gilbert and the late Brandon Long. Funeral will be Friday, January 11 at Bartholomew Baptist Church on East Chase Street. Interment to follow at King Memorial Park.

"Huh?" I blinked trying to make sense of this new bit of information. I quickly went back to the Web site of Laz's news station, knowing that if there was a news story tied to Sheldon's death on this date, there would be some record.

There was.

He had been murdered.

Stabbed multiple times, the victim of an apparent robbery as he was found missing his wallet and a watch. A young gangbanger had been arrested and charged with the crime, though he vehemently denied responsibility. Sheldon had been found lying next to several trash cans in an alley in East Baltimore.

I felt dizzy, trying to put the pieces together in a way that made sense, uncertain if or what to do with these dots I was connecting.

There was a short video of the news story accompanying the article. I clicked play and a teary-eyed, younger Jenellis filled the screen. As it was a public library, the volume had been set to mute. Didn't matter, no sound was really needed to watch the coverage of Jenellis shaking her head, tears flowing down her face. She pointed to two girls standing behind her, her head still shaking as I imagined her saying, "He's gone. What are we going to do?"

Two girls.

I froze the frame, wishing I could zoom in. Anastasia "Silver" Simmons stood there weeping, a little girl at the time. She was holding the hand of her sister, Contessa, I assumed from the death notice.

Silver and Gold.

The other girl was standing slightly behind her mother, her face partially blocked by her mother's movements, but she appeared to be about the same height and size.

Twins?

It was possible. Very likely, I concluded. *Silver and Gold*. The man working on The Block had alluded to some tragedy happening to Gold. Assuming that she was really Silver's sister, I did another search for Contessa Simmons on the news Web site.

Another story surfaced. The burned body of a young woman with that name had been found in a burnt-out car two months ago. No arrests had been made, no leads, no nothing. There were no pictures of her in the article, and no other information about her life, employment, or family.

My gut told me this was no coincidence, that this was the same Contessa Simmons who had the stage name "Gold."

Silver's sister; most likely even her twin.

Lord, what am I in the middle of—and why? I rubbed my temples, feeling a headache blossoming somewhere in the center of my brain and radiating outward. I realized then that I could not remember the last time I had eaten.

I had been surviving on pure adrenaline and nerves.

"Excuse me, ma'am."

I jumped to a start as a finger tapped my shoulder.

"Huh? Oh, yes?" I turned to face a wiry-looking older white woman who had curly blond hair and a look of severity on her well-defined features.

"Your one hour of computer use is nearly completed. This is your five-minute warning." She walked away, disappearing into the stacks with a loud echo of her heels.

I needed to get back to my son. Thankfully, I'd memorized my library card number back in grad school days and I was certain I had enough prepayment on it for printing. I sent all the news articles I'd found to the printer before shutting down each window.

Then I went back to Roman's blog.
The final post. It was the shortest entry.

I've got $1,000 saved up! I leave for Arizona next week. Haven't figured out where to go from there, but once I do, it's a wrap, folks!

My heart sank as I blinked back tears. There was nothing there that told me where he could have gone. He had not even known where he was going. No clues. No direction.

I heard loud footsteps echoing toward me. I knew the librarian was on her way back to tell me my five minutes were up. I shook my head, and reached for the mouse to shut down this last open window.

But something caught my eyes.

A comment.

The top of the page noted that there was a single comment from a viewer beneath this last post. I started to scroll down to the end to read it, but the footsteps were getting closer. A second set was with them, probably the person who had signed up to use the computer after me, and the librarian was coming as the enforcer.

"Let me print this out," I decided, clicking on the printer icon before logging off.

"Finished," I said aloud, smiling at the approaching librarian and a man in a dirty jacket trudging beside her. I had my things gathered and was out of the way before she even had to say a word. I was not in the mood or mindset to explain anything or interact with anyone.

I just wanted to get to my son.

I nearly ran to the public printer, getting some raised eyebrows and angry snarls along the way as I stepped on a couple of toes, brushed past a few shoulders.

I did not care.

I was close to finding out something about my son's whereabouts. I needed to see that comment I'd sent to the printer. I grabbed the papers that were actively coming out of the printer and started sorting through them.

"I'm sorry." A young woman with long, cinnamon-colored dreadlocks interrupted my task. "I just sent my paper to this printer and I think you might have it in your hand."

"Okay, hold on." I didn't even look up at her as I easily plucked out the news articles on Sheldon and Contessa. *Economic Policies of Eighteenth-Century Maryland. Huh?* I wrinkled my face at the next sheet. "I guess this is yours?" I held it up for the young woman.

"Yes, that's the title page. The rest should be coming."

I watched as the printer spit out more and more sheets, knowing that my son's final blog post with the unread comment underneath would not be coming out until her paper finished printing.

"How many pages is your paper?" I asked as the printer kept rolling out sheets.

"Oh, it's my dissertation." She smiled. "Two hundred and thirteen pages." She beamed. "My printer at home broke, and it's cheaper to print it here than buy a new one. Broke college student, you feel me?"

Don't get me wrong; I was proud that sister girl was about to get her doctorate degree, but as I sat there waiting for all 213 pages to finish printing, a part of me felt like I was going to start rolling on the floor, screaming, shaking.

I needed to see this comment on my son's last blog post.

"Oh, no," the doctoral candidate murmured.

"What is it?" I followed her eyes and felt my heart drop. The printer had stopped.

"Is it out of paper?" I groaned.

"No. Looks worse than that." The young woman groaned even louder than me. "Paper jam."

"Oh, that's easy to fix." I grabbed the last sheet, which was hanging out of the printer halfway and gave it a hard yank. It gave easily, but then the next paper came out in shreds, followed by more shreds and more shreds. I grabbed what I could, started pressing buttons, and banged on the side of the mammoth machine.

"What are you doing?" the woman shrieked.

Red, green, and yellow buttons started flashing all over until a loud beep sounded. Then the machine shook, rumbled, and shuddered before falling eerily silent and still.

"You broke the machine and you messed up my dissertation!" The girl looked ready to do some damage to me as strips and shreds of paper hung from both of her hands. I heard loud footsteps echoing toward us.

"Is there a problem?" The librarian from earlier was marching toward us, her frown directed solely at me.

"I'm sorry. The paper was jammed. I tried to fix it, but, but I need to go."

A small crowd was starting to gather as the young woman began hurling insults at me. I had to get out of there. I needed to get to another computer.

"I'm sorry," I said again as I began pushing past all of them. The doctoral candidate threw up her hands and screamed. The librarian called for help. I pushed my way out of there as what looked like an army of security guards seemed to be marching toward us. *Guess I won't be able to come back here for a while.* I shook my head as I jogged out of the building and ran to my car.

I needed to get back online.

I needed to know what that single comment under my son's blog post said.

As I got into my car, I recalled that we were supposed to be having dinner at Mother Spriggs's house. Skee-Gee would be there, I consoled myself. *Maybe he might remember something Roman said or did that would offer some more clues to his whereabouts.* Plus, maybe the elder lady had a computer somewhere in her house. Perhaps a grandchild or another younger relative lived there with her. Young people always seemed to have a way to connect to cyberspace.

"Sorry," I yelled out at the tiny Mini Cooper I nearly hit as I pulled out of my parking space. As I checked my rearview mirror to ensure that I had not cut anyone else off, I noticed a red Lexus three cars behind me.

I knew it was a long shot, that the events of the last three days had done a number on my nerves; but I firmly believed that I was being followed. I sped up and made a quick left turn onto West Mulberry Street. The Lexus continued straight down Cathedral Street.

"Lord, I think I am officially going crazy." I wanted to laugh at myself for being so paranoid, but I did not have time to do so. I pushed my foot on the gas pedal and headed back to East Baltimore, where Sadie Spriggs called home.

Chapter 35

I pulled up to the tiny stone-front row home on East Preston Street just as the sun was calling it quits for the day. The block blossomed with activity, people walking here and there, neighbors sitting out on their front stoops. The area around Mother Spriggs's front door was swept and tidy, with two labeled trashcans turned upside down next to her steps. A No Trespassing sign was tucked in one of the two front windows, and a small birdhouse painted in multiple pastel colors sat on the side of her top step. Also on her top step lay a bag of candy, an unopened package of hot pink beads and a skinny plastic comb, as if someone had been sitting there about to braid a little girl's hair.

I hope there is a computer somewhere in this house, I prayed again.

The door opened before I even knocked. "My grandma said come in," a little girl of about eight or nine answered. I recognized her from the children's choir at church and remembered that there had been a funeral for the girl's mother last year. I had not known that Sadie had taken the little girl—I thought her name was Jessica—in.

"We're back here," my mother called. I followed her voice to the dining room, where a full-sized dining table was surrounded by my family and several church members. The house was narrow in width, but long in depth.

"Hi, Sister Smith, Deacon Evans, Mother Greene." I nodded at familiar faces from our church. My mother and Yvette were helping Mother Spriggs put out platters of foods.

I had never seen my mother and sister work together so effortlessly without so much as a grumble between them. *I guess Mother Spriggs's prayers and songs really work.* I shook my head, remembering leaving all three of them in the basement of my mother's house the other night for the Spirit-filled intervention. I tried not to feel left out.

"Hi, Mom." I kissed her cheek. "Hi, Yvette, where's Skee-Gee?"

"He found some video games upstairs with one of Mother Spriggs's grandsons."

"Do you know if she has a computer here?"

"I don't know, why?" Yvette looked at me like I was crazy.

"I might have come across a clue to Roman's whereabouts, but I need to get back online."

"Oh, you have to check with Mother Spriggs, I guess." Just as quick as she had looked my way, her words and attention were directed back to my mother. "Mom, can you pass me that bread basket?" she beckoned.

"Here you go," my mother replied. "Sienna, give us a hand with the utensils, please."

My feet were glued to the floor as irritation swelled within me. "Are you kidding me?" My voice was slightly louder than I meant it to be. "Yvette, when you did not know where your son was, you were in a panic, calling every phone number you could think of. Mom, this morning you were fussing at me for not calling you with updates about Roman that I don't even have. My son is still out there, and the two of you seem like you couldn't care less."

"Sienna, calm down." My mother frowned as she opened a gallon of fruit punch to pour into a punch bowl. "The whole reason we're here for dinner is to have prayer for Roman's speedy return. We did not tell you because you try so hard to be independent with these things. We were afraid that you wouldn't show if you knew that's why we were all gathering."

I looked around the dining room, realizing that everyone at the table was staring at me. Sister Angie Smith, one of the ushers who always chided Roman about wearing his hat in church, was nodding and smiling. Deacon Evans, a handsome eighty-year-old man, eyed me solemnly. He wore a hunter green church suit complete with a paisley handkerchief peeking out in a crisp triangle from his lapel pocket.

"Yes, chile, that's why we all are here." Mother Greene nodded, her cane balanced in her hand as she sat at a chair in the corner of the room.

"And, Sienna"—I heard a little bit of the bite back in Yvette's voice—"the reason why I am not worried about Roman is for the simple fact that Skee-Gee isn't. As much as our sons bump heads, you know that Skee-Gee loves Roman like a little brother. If Skee-Gee thought Roman was in danger, you know that he would fight to the death to make sure he was okay."

"That's right," my mother echoed. "When I saw Skee-Gee coming out of the airport and he did not look the least bit worried about Roman, I knew that I need not get worked up either. It's hard, Sienna, but I have faith. Roman is his mother's child. He may be strong enough to go out on an adventure, but he is smart enough to know where his home is, where the people who love him are, and he'll be back home soon enough."

My mother and I stared at each other a few moments.

"Thanks, Mom."

"Mmm, hmmm." She turned back to add a two liter of ginger ale to the punch bowl.

I savored the moment, knowing that was my mother's best attempt at complimenting and comforting me. Even Yvette respected the moment, as she quietly handed me the bread platter to put onto the table, instead of throwing it at me in her usual way.

"Praise the Lord, you made it here." Mother Spriggs came out of the kitchen, a plate of crackers, cheese, and grapes in hand. She was wearing all white again, from the turban on her head to the white orthopedic shoes on her feet. The woman still gave me the heebie-jeebies, but I knew that was simply her style. "Some more people from church are coming. We're going to give them a few more minutes to get here and then we're all going to pray, pray, pray. And because we believe that God hears and answers our prayers, we are then going to have a celebration feast and sing songs of praise. Amen?" She turned back into the kitchen, humming.

I sighed, not quite sure what to do, but wanting to get out of the spotlight of attention. Plus, I still needed a computer. "Excuse me," I murmured as I headed toward the stairs. I climbed up to the second floor and found Skee-Gee in a front bedroom, a video game controller in hand. Mother Spriggs's grandson, a pudgy fourteen-year-old who wore thick eyeglasses and stuttered except when he was singing solos for the church youth choir, sat on the side of a bed. He kept quietly reaching for the controller in Skee-Gee's hands. Skee-Gee, for his part, simply batted the younger teen's hands away.

"Hold up, Vern! I got them bonus points and two extra lives. That's how you do it, son." He swung the controller again out of reach as Vern tried in vain to reclaim his property.

"Aunt See, how are you?" Skee-Gee grinned at me before shooting down something else on the TV screen. The television wobbled on a rickety old metal stand at the foot of the bed. "Bam, got that mutha!"

"Sylvester Grantley III," I demanded in my sternest tone, "do you know where Roman is?"

"Naw, man!" He narrowed his eyes at the screen, shooting down what looked like choppers and tanks. "Got it! Yes!" he shrieked.

I walked over and pulled the plug to the TV.

"Aunt See, what you doin'?" He glared at me, jumping to a stand. Vern blinked quietly, his eyeballs as big as quarters behind the thick frames.

I narrowed my eyes at my nephew, who stood three inches taller than me. "I'm going to ask you one last time. Where is my son?"

Skee-Gee collapsed back down on the bed. "I don't know Aunt Sienna. I swear."

I sat down on the bed next to him. "Just tell me what you *do* know."

Skee-Gee curled up his top lip, and threw the controller at Vern, who flipped it over in his hands. Vern looked at the unplugged TV, looked at me, and did not move another muscle. Both of our eyes were on Skee-Gee.

"Look, Tridell and I told him we were only going to go on the mission trip so that we could get to Vegas. That was our plan all along. First, Roman was talking like he wasn't going to go with us; but then all of a sudden, last week, he told me that he was in, that he was going."

Last week. That was when Roman stopped posting on his blog. My heart skipped a beat. I had to get to a computer! I needed to see that comment underneath his last post!

"First," Skee-Gee continued, "I couldn't figure out why he even bothered to come. It was like he was hanging back, waiting for something. He kept checking the time, checking his phone. Seemed like he was kind of nervous. When we got busted, he almost seemed relieved. In fact, he didn't even seem stressed out again 'til we was sitting on that plane waiting for take-off to come back home. I thought it was only 'cause he was nervous about flying—you should have seen him on that first flight to Arizona." Skee-Gee chuckled. "Well, Minister Howard had a mix-up with his seat five rows behind us. While he was talking with the flight attendant and some dude who was refusing to move, Roman kept checking his phone, and then he got up and scooted right past me and Tridell, who was too busy crying about getting caught. So I says, 'Cuz, where you going?' and he looked at me and said, 'It's all cool. I'm going to find my pops.'

"What was I going to say, Aunt See? Cousin ain't seen his dad, like, ever, right? So I thought about it, and it all made sense, how I had seen that ticket to San Diego in his bags, how he all of a sudden wanted to go with us to Vegas and looked like he was waiting for something the whole time. The way I figured it, if Roman knew something about where his dad was and was determined to find him, how was I gonna stand in his way? I respected him for what he was doing. If my dad was still alive, I'd probably be doing the same thing. Anyways, he got off the plane and Minister Howard didn't even notice 'til we was up in the air. I was like, 'Run, Roman, run!'" He laughed, clapping his hands. "That's it, Aunt See. That's all I can tell you."

"Why didn't you tell anyone this before?" I had to whisper to get out my words to keep from screaming. Everything in me wanted to punch him in the face and I had never had that feeling so strongly before.

And Skee-Gee had done a lot over the years to press my buttons, many times over.

He must have felt my wrath, because he sobered right up. Even Vern had scooted away from the two of us, the video controller left alone on the bedspread.

"What's the deal, Aunt Sienna? I ain't worried about Roman. He knows what he's doing and he knows how to take care of himself. I've taught him well." Skee-Gee tried to chuckle again, but his laugh fell flat.

"You said you saw a ticket to San Diego?"

"Yup."

"It was an actual rectangular ticket, not like a full sheet of paper printed out from a computer?"

"Yeah, it was a real ticket going to San Diego International Airport in California."

"Skee-Gee, that was an *old* plane ticket. A sixteen-year-old ticket that Roman found in my nightstand drawer six months ago. Nobody really uses real tickets to board planes anymore. You print them out from your computer when you buy them."

I could see this bit of information registering in whatever brain he had and his smile slowly faded away.

"So, he didn't fly to California?" He scratched his head.

"I don't know where Roman went."

"So, then where is he?"

"That is what I am asking you."

"Oh." Whatever trace of a smile had been on his face before had completely disappeared. He turned away and looked at the dark TV screen, his mouth slightly agape, before turning back to face me.

"I'm sorry, Aunt Sienna," he whispered.

I looked in my nephew's eyes and saw something I had never before seen in them.

Fear.

Chapter 36

"Father, we know that there is nothing too hard for you."

"Yes, Lord."

"You know the numbers of hairs on our heads, You call each of the stars by name."

"Well, well."

We were all standing in a circle, hands held, heads bowed, the food an aromatic feast on the table that we surrounded. I stood between my mother and my sister. Skee-Gee was leaning against the wall, alternating between closing his eyes and looking around. I could hear his younger siblings, Mother Sprigg's grandchildren, and some other youngsters from church playing in the basement of the home, their shrills of laughter and giggles a stark contrast from the sober pleas that were going up to God for the safe return of my son.

I could not keep my eyes closed.

I still needed to get to a computer.

The one Mother Spriggs had in her house was not connected to the Internet, and my sister had left her smartphone at home. My mother did not believe in such things, determined to hold onto her ancient flip-top until Jesus came back; and the other church members seemed to be confused about what I was talking about.

The prayers were getting louder, more intense, longer. I appreciated them, was confident that God was hearing us and would answer. I just needed to get online!

"Believe, my sister," Mother Spriggs shouted out over the others, both of us looking at each other as everyone else's eyes were closed. "Believe that everything will turn out okay. If faith the size of a mustard seed, the smallest of all seeds, can move mountains, imagine what faith the size of a peanut can do. Just takes a little bit of believing to see things move your way, my sister. Hold on to His hands!" And then she began singing the old hymn about holding on to God's unchanging hands.

It was about that time that the front door of the home opened, revealing a polished, apple butter-colored man in a brown trench coat and fedora.

Laz Tyson.

"Am I late for the prayer meeting?"

Silence filled the room as everyone opened their eyes and looked at the controversial news reporter. I took that moment to break away from the circle and rush toward him. My mother and sister joined hands in my absence and the prayers continued. Mother Spriggs's eyes were still on me, her lips moving quietly as Deacon Evans took the helm of the pleas.

"Outside, please," I whispered to Laz, not caring if I looked desperate at this point.

I *was* desperate.

He opened the door and we scurried down Mother Sprigg's front steps, shutting her front door behind us. It was all the way dark now, and the neighbors who had been sitting on nearby stoops and milling about the sidewalks looked like shadows moving through the night.

"I am sure that you have a phone on you with an Internet connection."

"You don't have one, Ms. Superwoman?"

"Mine is dead and I don't have a charger." I thought suddenly of all the potential calls I could have missed with my phone being dead so long. What if Roman had been trying to reach me? An emotion beyond panic was settling into my bones, my stomach, my heart, my lungs. "Listen, I don't have time to explain all of that right now. Give me your phone!"

"A take-charge kind of woman. That's what I like to see." He took out his phone and slipped it into my hands. I didn't miss that his hands rubbed over mine as he did so.

"How do you pull up your Internet?" I asked impatiently. He reached over and pressed a button and I typed Roman's blog site on to the screen.

Sorry, this Web page not supported on this device.

"Are you freaking kidding me?" I nearly threw his phone to the ground. "Oh, God!" I dropped my head into my hands. "Jesus, please! I just need a darn Internet connection!"

"It's going to be okay, Sienna." Laz spoke softly.

Before I realized it, his arms were around me and he was holding me tightly. For once, this time, not because of who he was, but because I did not want to collapse to the ground, I let my entire body weight fall into his embrace. I was shaking as tears flooded down my face. "I need to know where my son is. I need him home with me."

"Calm down, calm down." Laz stepped back from me, and used his thumbs to simultaneously wipe both of my cheeks. "Look, I found something. It might help, it might not, I don't know."

I held my breath and tried to get myself together as Laz dug into one of his coat pockets and pulled out a sheet of paper. "I looked up something earlier today and came across this. Thought it was worth printing out."

He gave me the single sheet of paper and my mouth dropped.

"This . . . this looks like the lion's head ring." I stuttered at the color picture, not yet making sense of the words around it.

"Looks like it to me."

"What . . . what is this?" I asked, still too frazzled to make sense out of what I was holding.

"I found this on a Web site that auctions high-priced jewelry. As you can see from the description, it was believed to be the only one of its kind, and it was listed and sold over two years ago, just weeks before it showed up in that package you got from Portugal."

"So, Kisu was probably the buyer? And then he shipped it to me under the guise of it being RiChard's ashes." I tried to put it all together. "But where did the auctioneer, the Web site that posted it, get it from?"

"That is exactly what I have been trying to figure out. I contacted the administrators of the Web site. They pulled the file of the ring's history and stated that the ring was given to them for auction as part of an estate sale."

"An estate sale." I sat down on the steps, blowing out a long, hard breath. "An estate sale is usually done after someone dies."

"Yeah, usually. Not always, but usually." He allowed a moment of silence before continuing. "There's more." He pointed to the back of the paper. "I asked them what else had been part of the estate and they were able to tell me a few items. I jotted them down on the back of the page."

Slowly, I flipped it over and skimmed through Laz's list. *Authentic Chinese silk painting. Mayan vase from Belize. Indonesian bamboo stool. A Zulu beaded necklace.* Tears filled my eyes anew as the paper shook in my hands.

"Definitely RiChard. These are definitely RiChard's treasures." I shook my head, biting my lips. "Wow, that man is dead, ain't he? Estate sale . . ."

Laz let out a loud sigh. "Kind of looks like it. Like I said, estate sales can happen for some other reasons, but odds are, this was probably death-related."

I nodded in agreement. "Do you know where the estate originated from? Where he was when he died? Is there an address?"

"Still working on that. The person I spoke to at the auctioneer Web site did not have that information. No worries, there's always more than one way to get the answers you need."

I shook my head in disbelief. "So my son is searching for a dead man. Where is he right now?"

Laz reached out for me again and I accepted his embrace.

"Thank you for your help," I whispered. I was still in his arms when bright headlights pulled to a stop beside us. Too consumed with emotions I could not even identify, I did not even notice the slam of the vehicle door and the heavy, booted footsteps that neared us. It was only when I realized that the car that had stopped next to us was not a car, but a black Pathfinder, that I jumped back out of Laz's arms.

"Leon!" I jumped, startled.

"Hi, Sienna." He stood about three feet away from me and Laz. "Your mom called me to say that you all were meeting here to pray for Roman. I take it there's still no word on him."

"Not yet, but . . . but . . ." I stumbled, trying to figure out what I was supposed to say as the two men looked at each other.

"How are you doing, brother? Laz Tyson." Laz extended a hand to Leon. He shook it.

"Yeah, I recognize you from TV. Channel 55, right?" Leon avoided eye contact with me as he let go of Laz's hand and bounded up the steps. "Your mom and sister are in here?" Leon grabbed the doorknob.

"Yes, but . . ." My mind had stopped working. "Wait, do you have an Internet connection anywhere on you? I need help." My voice was weak, I could barely understand myself.

"I'm sure Brother Tyson can help you out."

"No, he can't."

Laz narrowed his eyes, his head jerking back. "Umm . . ." He shook the paper with the picture of the ring.

"I mean, he is helping me, but I really, really need to get to a Web site. Roman had a blog. I got to the last post he put up last week. There was a single comment underneath that I did not get to read. I need to see it. It might help me find him."

Without missing a beat, Leon turned back around and beeped his truck door unlocked. He opened the passenger side door and pulled out a computer tablet. "What's his site, Sienna?"

His passion matched mine as he typed in what I told him. I stood next to him as he sat in the passenger seat with the door propped open. Laz stood behind me, straining his neck to see what was going to pop up on the screen.

"He's been writing posts for the past two years?" Leon scrolled through the site, moving faster than I had the first time I'd pulled it up.

"Yeah, I went through all of the posts, I can tell you about them in a moment. Right now, I just need to see the last post. The comment underneath."

Leon clicked on it, and the page stalled. "What were the other posts about?"

"Long story short, he thinks he has a picture of RiChard, but it's actually someone else RiChard knew long ago. He also found old paperwork from when RiChard was in California sixteen years ago. I don't know what new information he may have come across to make him think he had enough to leave like he did. That is why I need to see that one comment that was left on his last post last week. Maybe it will give some answers."

"It's coming up now." Leon seemed to be holding his breath like me.

Laz poked his head over my shoulder. "This is it," he stated, as if not knowing what else to say.

"What in the world?" I read and reread the single comment as everything in me wanted to collapse, puke. Scream.

Hi, fellow warrior. I have been following your posts for a while, and you are right. There are many secrets and hidden information in the world out there. Fortunately, I think I can help you. I am going to e-mail you my contact information, and perhaps when you come out to Arizona, we can figure out a way to meet. Talk to you soon, Your Friend, Croix

"I'm on it, Sienna." Leon slammed the cover over his tablet. "I'm on it right now!"

Chapter 37

"Police have initiated a nationwide search for a local sixteen-year-old male who went missing yesterday in the Las Vegas area. Authorities are following up on leads, but need your help. If you have seen this young man, Roman St. James, or have any information about his whereabouts, please call 911. Live from East Baltimore with friends, family, and church members who have gathered to pray, this is Laz Tyson. Back to you in the studio, Brittany."

Laz took off his fedora and handed his microphone to a crew member as a bright camera light clicked off. He wiped his forehead with a handkerchief as Yvette stormed up to him.

"You didn't say anything about this Croix person!"

"The police are asking the media not to mention it until they are able to fully investigate. We don't want to tip off a potential predator that we're on to him or her before we even have a chance to figure out where they are, especially if Roman is with him or her, you know?"

Predator.

The word and my son didn't belong in the same sentence.

I felt nauseous again, and this time I could not hold it back as everything inside of me pelted out into the gutter next to the sidewalk in front of Mother Sprigg's house.

Sweating, hyperventilating, chills, more vomit. *Oh, God.* I felt myself blacking out. . . .

I was lying across Mother Sprigg's couch. Had no idea how I got there, what time it was. Remembered why I was there. Blacked out again. . . .

"We are praying, big sis. Roman is just fine and will be home soon." Yvette was whispering in my ear. I could smell her cheap peach body spray and feel the cool, damp washcloth she was patting on my forehead.

"I failed him. I failed my son." My voice was a hoarse whisper and the taste of bile filled my mouth again. "All this time, I just assumed that he was running away from me and that he would call when he was ready. That maybe he had even found him . . . his father. I guess that is what a part of me was thinking, hoping. He's so independent and strong-willed, it never occurred to me that he could be in real danger. Oh, God . . ." My voice faded into a whimper.

"No, Sienna." Leon's voice sounded distant though he was sitting on the floor next to me. "We *all* just assumed he was out there doing his thing. You know how Roman is. Once he has a thought in his mind, he doesn't let it go until he follows it through to the end." He paused. "I should have urged my contact to track down his phone when you asked. I didn't realize . . ." His voice faded like mine.

Everyone was starting to crowd around me, and though I appreciated the prayers and concern, I wanted to be left alone to try to make sense of what was going on with my son.

Croix?

Who the heck was that?

I felt the extremities of my body growing numb. A fresh wave of stomach-sickening worry began sweeping through me.

"Excuse me." I jumped up. "I . . . I have to go. Just for a moment. Get myself together so I can think, be of some help. I have to get myself together." How on earth was I going to do that?

I could feel arms, hands holding me back, making me all the more determined to get out of there.

"Don't lose your faith, Sienna." Mother Spriggs was a blur of white through my tears. "We already touched and agreed and prayed for Roman's safety. We are going to trust God wholeheartedly that things do not seem as they appear and Roman will return without so much as a scratch on his head, in Jesus' name. Amen?"

I heard her words, though I did not have the strength to acknowledge her.

I had to get out of there. Breathe.

It was dark as midnight when I stepped out of her house. A chill in the air crept up my shirt sleeves and I realized I had not put on my coat. I hugged myself as I wandered down the steps, no idea of a destination, purpose, or point.

Was there even one?

"Here, use my coat."

I had not seen Laz leaning against the house, but there he was, outside alone, the news crew long gone, the cameras put away.

"You're still here."

"Yeah. I keep trying to figure out what I can do to help, what else I can look up, who to call, you know?"

"Thanks for caring," I murmured.

"Of course. Though I've seen him around church, I haven't had the pleasure of meeting your son yet;

but knowing his mother, I'm sure he's a great kid. I'm hoping and expecting the best here." He was smiling, a warm gesture, but something behind the way he was studying me irritated me. "Tell me, Sienna," he continued, smiling, "what kind of activities does Roman like to do in his spare time? I'm only trying to get a better sense of who he is since I never talked with him."

I blinked at the man, my irritation growing. "Um, do you need to take out your notepad to remember all your questions and write down all your notes?"

"Sienna, what are you talking about?"

"I guess you finally have your big breaking story."

"Sienna—"

"Brother Tyson, you are going to have to go. I can't deal with you right now. My son is missing. I do not know where he is, and you are out here asking me some dumb questions about him so that you can have more to say during your next report. I am sorry that your segment was not long enough to warrant more attention on you, but I really don't care, and I really don't want you here right now." I threw his coat back at him and turned away.

"No, Sienna, no." Laz tried to grab my hand, but I immediately recoiled.

The nerve of this man!

"No, no, you have me all wrong," he pleaded. "I'm sorry for upsetting you. That was not my intent."

"Go away, Laz." I marched toward my car, thankful that although I had not grabbed my coat, I did have my car keys. If people could not leave me alone, I would go away myself.

"Sienna, listen please. You've got me all wrong. Was I trying to get more information about your son to help with my next report about him? Yes. Am I doing that for my own benefit? Absolutely not!"

"Get away from me, Laz!" I pried his fingers off my wrist, heard my voice getting louder as I continued trying to push toward my car. Laz did not let go.

"Sienna, Roman is your son, your pride and joy. You know him. You know his innocence. However, to the rest of the country, to the rest of the world, he is just a black teenage boy from Baltimore. Do you think his missing is going to send shockwaves across the country? Do you think floods of volunteers are going to start combing through deserts and fields, and inner-city neighborhoods to find him?

"I'm not trying to be mean, but I know the media world, Sienna. I know the reality. How much air time do you think his disappearance will get on the news networks tonight? He's not a female, he's not blond, and he's not eight years old. I am out here, Sienna, right here with you and the people who care about him most. Where are the national news vans? Where are even the other local news stations?

"You want me to help find him? I can do that with the power I have using a camera and a microphone, but you need to help me. Other networks—especially national networks—are only going to pick up his story if people care. And people are only going to care if they don't get stuck looking at him as a young black man who they secretly fear or outwardly hate or just don't understand. They need to see Roman as their *own* son who plays video games too much, who . . . who keeps his room a mess, who eats up all the food out of the refrigerator, whose biggest mission in life right now is making the varsity team or making out with a pretty girl.

"Sienna, let me help you by telling the world exactly *who* is missing. I need to know if he tried out for the football team, if he likes peanut butter on his burgers. I need more than his picture. I need his story. "

My hands were over my mouth and every limb of me shook as the truth of his words absorbed into me. "His room . . . is not messy right now," I whispered. "He cleaned it right before he left." Of all the things I thought and felt, that was the only sentence I could get out. "I'll be back. Please, let me go. I need . . . I . . . I'll be back." I stared up into his eyes. He let go of my arm, and took a step back away from me. I took two steps toward my car before turning back to him.

"Officer Sanderson has a key to my house. Get him. You two can go there. You can see Roman's room. Take shots of his trophies, his mola quilt that his father . . ." My hands went back over my mouth as if covering it would somehow shut back the tears. "You two go. Leon can tell you more about Roman. You can see his room for yourself. You go. There is no way that I can go back into my house if he is not there yet." I turned back toward my car, opened the door, got in. I watched as Laz stared after me a moment more, and then he jogged up Mother Sprigg's steps, and disappeared into her home.

I drove away. No destination, no plan, no peace.

"God, I am so afraid. Please help. Jesus, please."

My family, my church community had been offering prayers up all evening, and yet that was the first prayer I'd said out loud that night, the only words I could voice without feeling my stomach churning again.

For God has not given us the spirit of fear, but of power, love, and a sound mind.

Power.

The word comforted me. Emboldened me.

Laz said his power to help my son was with his microphone and camera. What was my power? I refused to feel helpless. I'd been immobilized all evening. Passing out. Lying on couches. Weeping. Whining. Trembling like a leaf on a tree withstanding wind.

But I had not fallen.

My son needed me, and he needed me to walk in power.

I decided that I would not stop driving until I figured out exactly what power *I* had to save my son.

Chapter 38

"Don't mess with momma cheetah."

In the brief time I was with RiChard, in our many constant travels, there was only one trip that we made together that could be counted as an actual vacation. In the midst of village hopping on his quest for revolutionary social justice, we paused one day to go on a safari through the massive African bush and wild lands. We saw elephants, herds of zebras, giraffes. However, there was one animal that struck me the most, simply because it was the single one about which RiChard commented.

The cheetah.

Specifically, we saw a mother cheetah and her cubs, which made RiChard lean in close to me and say, "Don't mess with momma cheetah. She is one feline who stays with her cubs until they are a year and a half, parenting by herself, teaching her young ones how to survive and protecting them from predators. Mess with her and she will go from zero to sixty in three seconds and, believe me, you are not outrunning her."

In retrospect, perhaps RiChard did talk about the other animals. More than likely, knowing how much he seemed to enjoy flaunting his knowledge about nearly any and everything, he'd probably shared facts and tidbits about the other wildlife that appeared oblivious to our passing vehicle.

But it was his comments about the cheetah that stuck with me, implanted somewhere in my consciousness, and made an imprint in my brain.

In recent years, I'd forgotten about the cheetah, her inability to roar, her exhaustion after a high-speed chase. Now, her maternal mission was front and center and reflective of my resolve.

To protect.

To survive.

To run down threats and attack and defend like life and death depended on it.

My drive had taken me to Charles Street, to the historic Mount Vernon area where the nation's first architectural monument to George Washington stood tall and lit in the darkness on a large, park-like island in the center of the road. As I circled the monument, the cobblestone street rumbled under the wheels of my car, startling me, waking me up from the daze of a distant memory, a faded daydream.

"Where am I going?" I shook my head, determined to fight back tears, tiredness, and despair as I contemplated what power I had in finding my son. "I guess I first need to go get some gas." I was nearly on 'E,' Leon's generosity from earlier that day almost depleted. I pulled up to a small gas station hidden in a narrow, unkempt space between two old, tall office buildings. Not my first choice to stop at nearly twelve-thirty in the morning, but I decided it made more sense to stop there than to run out of gas again in the empty darkness.

I parked at a pump and got out of the car before realizing my mistake.

I had not been home all day to get my purse, which had my money, credit cards, and phone charger. Without any coat on, I had no pockets to check for loose change. I searched through my car for any stray coins, pulling out the ashtray, sticking my hand between the seat cushions, turning over the floor mats, checking everywhere that I could fit my hands. Even as I did so, I knew my search was pointless. The gas station did not appear to have any attendants at the window to accept cash payments.

A part of me wanted to laugh, another part wanted to scream. I settled for an anguished cry as I debated how to get myself out of this new predicament. I was not sure that I had enough gas to get back to Mother Sprigg's home, and I had no phone access to call for assistance. The seventy-nine cents I scrounged up in change offered no help.

For the first time in a long time, I wished phone booths were still around. At least I could have made a collect call.

"This is hands-down the absolute worst week of my life," I spoke aloud. "God, I don't know what you are doing, but there is nothing else I can do right now but ask for your help and trust you." I thought of Mother Sprigg's last words to me before I'd pushed myself out of her house. "I won't lose my faith, Jesus," I whispered, shutting my eyes as I leaned against my car door. I was so intent, so focused on praying, that I did not notice the screeching set of wheels that pulled into the station. As a car door opened and sharp footsteps punched the ground, I was forced to open my eyes to see what had pulled up beside me.

A red Lexus.

"Jenellis!" I gasped. My confusion deepened as a second door opened and a man got out of the passenger side. Not Brayden, but David, the young man who had escorted me to Silver's hideout two days before.

"What are you doing here?" I demanded as both marched toward me. Jenellis's hands were thrust deep in her coat pockets and her expression remained blank as she approached.

I didn't have time for any of this foolishness, whatever it was they were up to.

And she knew it. She could see it in my eyes. She came prepared.

"Now," she commanded David, and before I could protest, protect myself, or prevent it from happening, a sharp needle pricked my shoulder, piercing right through my blouse. I remember wondering if wearing a coat would have helped my situation as blackness began to envelope me and my legs began to give way. I was being led, guided, forced to her car, and felt myself being thrown into the back seat, powerless to stop the attack.

As a groggy darkness finished taking hold of me, drawing me deeper into a blacked-out state, I heard Jenellis say, "Get rid of her car."

I heard my own voice whimper, "My son . . ." Felt my last bit of power being sucked away from me.

No.

I still have power. My last thoughts before succumbing completely to the darkness.

The power of faith.

God could work even when I couldn't.

Chapter 39

Basketball trophies . . . Butterflies . . . Mbali . . . Cheetahs . . . The smell of rain when it first hits the pavement . . . Power . . . Smoke . . .

Smoke?

I forced my eyes open, willing myself to come out of the darkened, trance-like state I had been in.

Years ago, when I needed a minor outpatient surgical procedure, my doctor had administered some type of anesthesia that put me in what she called a "twilight sleep": not completely unconscious, but sedated enough that I had no awareness or memory during the operation. I remembered coming to and feeling woozy—and also feeling like only seconds had passed and not the full hour that the doctor said she'd worked on me.

I was having the same sensation at that moment.

Smoke.

My senses were awakening and the smell of something burning overpowered my nostrils. Still feeling flighty from whatever had been jabbed into my shoulder, I willed myself to focus, to concentrate.

To try to figure out what in the world was going on.

A kitchen.

I was in some type of industrial kitchen, I concluded, as my eyes came into better focus. Large stainless-steel vats with stirring mechanisms, multiple ranges with burners, and warehouse-sized refrigerators filled the large room. One of the burners was lit with a high flame and a large pot sat on top of it. Thick, smoke-like steam rolled out of it and I concluded that was what I was smelling.

Burning food.

I was looking up at everything. The burners, the refrigerators, the vats were all taller than me. *I must be on the floor,* I decided, becoming aware that the entire left side of my body, from the side of my face, to my arms, to my legs felt cold.

I was lying left side down on a cement floor.

I tried to move my arms, my feet, but realized every part of me was tied up, and whatever had me bound also had me attached to a four-inch-thick pipe that ran along the length of the kitchen floor.

"Oh, God," I tried to pray, but my tongue, my teeth, were tangled up in what felt like a steel wool scouring pad stuffed into my mouth.

Pieces of memories—the gas station, the red Lexus that had pulled up beside me, Jenellis, David—started infiltrating my consciousness. But none of the pieces fit together, made sense. And honestly, I did not care that they did not. Only one thought, one recent memory mattered most to me in that minute.

Roman.

I was on a mission to somehow rescue my son, and this woman and whatever foolishness she had going on with her had interrupted me. Tears filled my eyes as my sense of helplessness turned to horror. Nobody would know where I was, or that I was even in any danger. I had left Mother Spriggs's house, demanding to be alone, so who knew when anyone would even think to begin looking for *me?*

What time was it? Was it even still the same day? As my senses and consciousness continued to register, a thousand and one questions began filling my mind. I tried to move, but whatever had me bound had no give.

I shut my eyes as the tears continued to streak down my cheeks, stinging, pooling on the cement floor next to my face. My nose started to get congested and I gagged for breath, my mouth a blocked airway.

Survive, Sienna!

A calm, still voice somewhere in the inside of me spoke out and my eyes opened again. I did not have time to sit there and cry. Falling apart was not an option. I had to get out of there. I had to at least try.

The pot on the top of the burner seemed to be rattling, as if whatever inside it that was boiling and slowly burning had a life of its own, and was seeking its own escape.

Someone would be back to check on this food, I realized. I did not know who that someone was or when they would be coming.

I could not wait to find out.

First, I tried to spit the scouring pad out of my mouth. Try as I might, it did not budge. I looked at what was binding me.

Thick, green, industrial-strength garbage bags, rolled up into tight ropes, crisscrossed over my arms, legs, ankles, and midsection, knotted to the pipe. The heavy green plastic looked like a rope of convenience, what had been on hand.

This had been an impromptu undertaking, not a carefully planned attack. That gave me an advantage as I just needed to outwit a hastily formed strategy. It also warned me of imminent danger. Having me here bound up was seen as an immediate necessity and spoke to desperation. Though I did not have a clue as to why, I knew that such desperation could very easily turn deadly for me.

What do I do, Lord?

I studied my wrists, tied up tightly with the rolled-up bags. They reminded me of plastic wristbands at a state fair. *That's it,* I decided, thinking of how Roman would always refuse to let me cut wristbands off of him following carnival or ER visits. He would always pretend to be an escape artist and manage to wriggle them off. Most of the time he succeeded. It was thick, heavy plastic that bound my hands, but plastic nonetheless. Using the bottom corner of a cabinet nearby, I willed myself to imagine my hands being smaller, to believe that I could somehow roll the tight bands off my wrists. The pain was torture as my hands turned red and my fingers turned white from the blockage in circulation, but millimeter by millimeter, I worked that plastic until it was over my thumb knuckles, past my palms.

Then free.

Working quickly, I took the scouring pad out of my mouth. The rest of my body was still entangled in tied knots, still attached to the metal pipe. I used the steel wool to begin scraping the knots down and within seconds I was free from the pipe, though my legs and ankles were still tied. The knots down there were bigger, thicker, tighter, as if whoever had bound me had more time to work on them and had sped through the knots that had tied down my upper body. I pulled myself up, attempting to hop and half slide through the kitchen. I got to the end of the aisle where I had been hidden, seeing that the massive kitchen was made up of several rows separated by racks and cabinets, workspaces, ranges, and storage areas. The pot that was burning, boiling away, was at the end of my aisle. I noted a chopping board on a counter near the range. Quartered potatoes and celery stalks spilled off of it.

There has to be a knife nearby, I decided, and quickened my hops and slides to the counter where the cutting board lay. *Almost there!* I put my all into one last hop to round the corner, but instead of landing back on the concrete floor, I tripped, stumbling forward, began falling forward, but I caught myself, grabbing on to a metal drawer handle, and holding on to the side of a refrigerator.

"Oh, Jesus!" I screamed as I realized what had tripped me.

A white tennis shoe attached to a foot attached to a man who lay lifeless on the floor. He had been out of my view on the other side of a large refrigerator, which was on the other side of the still-burning pot. He had a slight olive hue to his otherwise pale skin, which, together with his dark curly hair, spoke to a possible Mediterranean ethnicity. He lay on his back, his eyes and mouth open as if frozen forever in a look of utter surprise and horror.

A tall white chef's hat was off to the side of him and I saw the knife for which I was looking. It was covered with blood, and the bright red stain trailed from the silver blade to several brutal wounds in the man's chest. A pile of unpeeled potatoes lay scattered between his hat and the knife.

I was dealing with a straight-up, cold-hearted killer.

The air went out of my lungs and the room began turning black as my body threatened to pass out again. *No!* I told myself as I reached out to grab what I could to maintain my balance and stay alert.

I grabbed the wrong thing, and a stack of plates, and utensils, and glasses began crashing to the floor in a loud clatter.

With all that noise, it would just be a matter of time before someone came running in there, I was sure of it. There was no point in trying to stay quiet as I began tearing open drawers, opening and slamming doors to find something to cut the rest of the knotted bags off of me. Finally, I came across a pair of kitchen shears, scissors that had five blades on it that probably were usually used to cut through fresh herbs, but were now being used to trim off the rest of my knotted garbage bag binds. Within seconds I was free.

Common sense told me to hold on to the ultra-sharp blades as I took off running toward a green exit sign. I could not tell if my imagination or my ears were hearing footsteps coming from the opposite direction.

I was not going to wait to find out.

I pushed through the swinging door and gasped. After leaving such a scene of pure evil and violent brutality, I had not expected to walk into the total opposite: awe-inspiring beauty and breath-taking opulence.

I was standing in an atrium filled with all manner of flowers, luxurious draperies, candles, and chandeliers, most of which were in varying shades of red. Round tables were set up with elaborate centerpieces, real linens, covered chairs. The floor-to-ceiling windows that surrounded the expansive room showcased gardens and manicured courtyards as far as the eye could see.

I was clearly at some type of estate, a scenic mansion or lavish banquet hall suited for weddings, receptions, romantic dinners, or the like.

La Chambre Rouge.

Of course. Had to be. Though I had never followed up with my plan to research the name of the place where Jenellis and Brayden were to wed and Brayden/Kwan was to go on his fantasy date with Silver courtesy of *The Soul Mate Show,* my high school French class memories told me the name translated to "the Red Room." Almost everything in that room was red.

A loud crash coming from somewhere in the kitchen reminded me that this was not the time to figure out the connection. I needed to survive.

So I could get back to finding my son.

The windows of the atrium made it hard to figure out where any doors were, as the entire room was surrounded with glass. I began running down one side of the room, pressing constantly on the clear glass until one of the panels finally gave way. I dashed out into the courtyard, knowing that I was still too exposed in this venue of glass and open space. There was a stone pathway that led away from the courtyard and I had no choice but to follow it around the side of the atrium toward a red brick building that sat behind it. The area that looked like it was probably the kitchen from where I escaped connected the two buildings, and I recognized this red brick building as the restaurant that had been in the still shots of the grand prize of the dating show.

Were Silver and "Kwan" supposed to have their fantasy date this weekend? I wondered, still trying to make sense of my circumstances.

I pushed open a door, and was not sure whether to be comforted or alarmed that the restaurant was empty. Continuing with the theme of red, the restaurant was darker, more intimate, smelled of older wood and history than the grander atrium. A black marble fireplace was the focal point of the romantic space and dark cherry wood paneling covered the walls. Red velvet drapes, fringes, and feathers made the place feel more like a burlesque establishment than a restaurant of fine dining. I imagined a ragtime piano and an exotic beauty singing and dancing on the small stage I spotted near the back of the room. I thought about Silver and her line of work. *How is all of this connected?*

My eyes adjusted to the dimness as I stayed along the walls, trying to figure out where to go, what to do, hoping to at least find a phone somewhere to call for help. I found a hallway instead that took me to a set of doors. The wood in the hallway was even darker, older, nearly black, compared to the dining area. The stairs led me to what looked like an administrative wing, I guessed. My hopes rose as I considered that a phone would definitely be in one of the offices. I entered the first one and did a double take at what I saw.

Portraits on the wall told the story of African American management. That wasn't what shocked me; rather, the pictures themselves. A group of men posed in large portraits, obvious business partners who must have taken over the property, in what looked like—I squinted to read the placard beneath—the year 2000. The man in the middle of the group had a square head, an uneasy smile, and the name Sheldon Long.

Jenellis's first husband.

Her *dead* first husband.

I looked at the picture and studied the four other men who surrounded him. Their names and faces meant nothing to me, but I figured that even split five ways, the value of the La Chambre Rouge and its continuing income was still a pretty penny for each of the investors.

And, of course when considering a dead businessman's monetary value, there were always life insurance policies in addition to other liquid assets. As I thought about the article I'd read about Sheldon Long's death, how he had been found lying next to trash cans, stabbed repeatedly, my imagination ran wild. Throw in the abuse both Jenellis and Silver acknowledged occurred, there was plenty of reason to believe that there was more to Sheldon's death than what was showcased on that short news clip I'd found on the Internet.

And then there was that sword showcased in a display box in Jenellis's living room . . .

My mind was working as fast as a calculator, adding two and two, subtracting the excess. I recalled my first conversation alone with Jenellis. She had said her first husband died of natural causes. Why would the widow of a victim of such a violent crime claim his death to be natural?

If I was on the right train of thought, and I had every reason to believe that I was, then it would make sense that Jenellis would be reluctant to tell Brayden how she obtained her wealth. It had been Sheldon's, a man who was murdered. A man *she* had murdered.

And Sheldon had been her first husband, I remembered. *"We've had five marriages and three children between the two of us. That's why this time, we need to make it work":* her words to me when we first met.

Now I wondered about her other marriages—and Brayden's for that matter. What skeletons were hiding in his closet? *And how did they even meet?* A million and one questions filled my mind, but none as great as the one about my son—where was he? I had to get out of there so I could help find him.

I looked at the pictures again, realizing I had been too distracted by them. I scanned the office for a phone and saw one underneath a stack of files on the edge of a desk. The only light in the office came from a large window right next to the desk. I had to avoid the window. I did not know if I could be seen.

The sun was up and its rays seemed to be pouring directly into the room like a high-powered flashlight. Though I could not see anyone out there, I was not making any assumptions with a killer on the loose. I got down on the floor and crawled over to the desk. Using one hand, I reached for the receiver, and the stack of folders that had been sitting on top if it fell to the floor.

"Darn it!" I whispered, first because of the noise and secondly because I realized that the phone was one of those types of office phones where you needed to select a line to get a dial tone. I was still low on the floor and could not see the phone's keys or dial pad. I started to stand, but caught myself, too afraid to stand up right next to the window. Holding my breath, and not hearing any other noises, I reached up my hand again, ran my fingers over the many buttons, said a quick prayer, and pressed one, hoping, praying, desperate for a dial tone.

I heard voices instead.

I'd selected a line in use.

Two men were talking.

"She's still on the property," a deep voice whispered.

"And the other one?"

"On her way."

There was a pause, and I kept holding my breath, afraid that even a simple inhale would be heard over the receiver.

"Stop worrying," the second man spoke up again. "I got this."

"You need to cut the power. Cut the power and all the phone lines."

"Okay, although there's no way she's getting away, even if she broke free. There ain't nothing but woods around here. The main road is over two miles away. Stop worrying so much."

"Cut the lines and all the power just the same. I don't want to take any chances."

"All right, whatever."

The phone went dead. All the way dead. I ran my fingers over the buttons that were still out of my sight, pressing them to no avail.

Don't panic, don't panic, don't panic.
Too afraid to even stand, I crawled back over the floor to the entrance of the office. The hallway, which I realized had previously been lit, was now dark. I listened for any sound, any movement.

Nothing.

I went back into the office, noticing that from the open doorway, the files I'd knocked over were visible on the floor. If someone happened to walk by, the disorder would not be missed. I crawled back to the desk, gathered the files into a pile. Still on my knees, I lifted them up toward their original place, but as I did so, a few papers fell out.

Newspaper clippings.

INVESTMENT BANKER KILLED IN HIT-AND-RUN.

RESTAURATEUR FOUND DEAD IN HOME DUE TO CARBON MONOXIDE POISONING.

ATTORNEY SHOT TO DEATH DURING BOTCHED HOME INVASION.

LEADING REAL ESTATE AGENT DEAD FROM APPARENT PRESCRIPTION OVERDOSE.

LOCAL PLASTIC SURGEON ACCIDENTALLY DIES FROM SESAME SEED ALLERGY.

DENTIST STABBED TO DEATH IN AN UNSOLVED MURDER.

They were headlines from newspapers from cities and towns throughout Maryland, Virginia, Pennsylvania, and Delaware. The deceased were black, white, Asian, Latino, and even a Greek man, from what I could tell from the accompanying photographs. Outside of being men of great wealth, there were no other obvious connecting threads. I reached for the files again, opened up a new one.

Life insurance policies. Bank account information. Estate valuations. All from the men identified in the articles, and a few more whose names I had not seen.

Now this set of papers did have a common denominator.

In each case, the beneficiary was the same. At least the first name was.

Jenellis.

The last name was different on most of the forms as she was identified as either the wife or girlfriend or partner or whatever role she had managed to get in their lives.

I stared at the documents, blinking, wondering if Brayden knew the danger he was in. Though most of the deaths reported in the newspaper clippings appeared to be accidental, there was no accident that Jenellis was involved, I was certain.

Ain't that many coincidences in the world.

I was flipping through more of the files when a sound at the door startled me. I jumped to my feet.

"Oh, there you are," she spoke casually, as if we were bumping into each other at the grocery store. "I was wondering where you went."

Chapter 40

"I'm sure you *were* looking for me, Ms. Walker." I glared at her. "Or whatever name it is you're going by now."

My bravery surprised me, but I had to get finished with this woman so I could get to my son.

Mother cheetah. Staring down danger for the sake of her cubs.

Jenellis glared back at me. "Not sure what you are talking about, but I need you to come with me."

"Oh, so you can stab me with another needle, tie me up, and kill me?" I still had the scissors, I remembered. I could see the five-bladed shears on the floor under the desk where I had been kneeling.

"Kill you?" Jenellis looked taken aback. "Look, Ms. St. James, I'm not going to deny that you have every reason to believe I mean you harm, the way I've treated you." She actually smiled apologetically, like she was trying to be my friend. "But consider this: if I was really trying to kill you, wouldn't you already be dead?"

I looked in her eyes, wondering how I missed so much with her. Then it occurred to me, she had no idea that I'd seen those files, found out her game. She did not know I had the upper hand of knowing who, or what, she really was.

A "black widow."

She was right. She could have killed me, but she still needed me alive for some reason.

I needed to survive to get out of there. The police, justice for those poor men, would come eventually. I just needed to get out of there. I bent down as if to fix my shoe, but reached for the scissors instead, tucked them in my waistband.

"Where are we going?" I walked toward her.

She smiled and motioned for me to follow her, completely ignoring my question. *What the heck am I doing?* I asked myself as I fell in line right beside her. *Surviving.* I patted the scissors on my hip for reassurance.

"I'm so sorry about what I had to do to you, but I need you to help me find my daughter."

And I need to find my son! I could not even get the words out, only wanted to figure out what I had to do to get out of there.

"So, what do you think of our venue for our upcoming wedding?" she asked as smoothly as she'd just apologized for kidnapping me. We were heading down the hallway toward what looked like the main entry of the restaurant.

I decided to keep playing along until I had a better idea of what was going on. "It's a beautiful place. Where is everyone?"

"Oh, they closed it down for the morning. The fantasy date for that dating show, you know? But Brayden and I have talked about it, smoothed out the misunderstanding, and wanted to use this time as a private walk-through to finalize the arrangements and clarify some other concerns."

"I thought you said this place stayed booked?"

"Oh, it does." She nodded. "But the next event wasn't scheduled until later this evening, and when you can offer the right price, you can get almost anything done."

*I'm sure you can, missy, and I'm sure it doesn't hurt
that you have some stake in this establishment as well,
courtesy of your first dead husband's investments. . . .*

"I really was hoping that Silver would show for the
date, though." She glanced at me as she spoke. I stayed
quiet.

Jenellis had no idea how much I knew. My confidence strengthened.

"Where are we going?" I tried again as we entered a
small parlor.

"Oh, Brayden should be here now. It's time for our
final session. Couples therapy, right?" Jenellis flicked a
light switch on and off to no avail. "Why isn't this light
working?" She looked genuinely confused.

Jenellis did not know the power had been cut?

"Hello, ladies," a voice, smooth as butter, sounded
from behind us. Both Jenellis and I jumped, but she
recovered immediately.

"Hi, Brayden, you startled me." She chuckled. David
entered the room behind him. Jenellis's smile dropped.

"David, what are you . . . doing with Brayden?"

All three of them stared at each other, a silent conversation I was not privy to. Jenellis looked nervous,
something I'd never seen before.

Whatever confidence I'd felt began deflating from
me like a pinpricked balloon.

"First things first," Brayden spoke, turning his attention to me. "Where is she?"

"Huh?" I was so scared my thoughts had stopped
connecting.

"Where is she?" Brayden asked again.

"Where is who?" My heart was beating wildly. Jenellis smiled at me.

"You know exactly who I'm talking about." Brayden's
voice held a threat.

David pulled out a silver chain, a broken butterfly charm dangling on the end.

"Silver?" I tried to keep myself from shaking. "I don't know where she is."

"Of course you do. That's why Jenellis bought you here, am I right?" Brayden spoke like a man who was very much in control. I wondered if he knew Jenellis's ultimate plans for him.

"What are you talking about, Brayden?" Jenellis blurted. Now I was thoroughly confused. I did not know who knew what anymore.

Brayden ignored her interruption. "I'm going to tell you a secret, Ms. St. James." He mockingly lowered his voice as he stepped closer to me, but it was clear that everyone in the room could still hear him. "I'm a struggling man. That's right, I am poor. Ain't got but seven dollars and thirteen cents in my bank account. These suits I wear, the cars I drive? They're not mine. I wash the cars and run the errands of a very wealthy businessman in Shepherd Hills. Reggie doesn't even know I've been borrowing his things, but I had to. It was the only way I knew Jenellis would ever notice me. And I needed her to notice me."

"Okay, stop it," Jenellis outright yelled. "I don't know what you are doing, what you are talking about, but we need to stay on topic and finish what we came out here for. Brayden, we don't have time for some silly game. Sienna, where is my daughter?" She blinked at me innocently.

"Wait." Brayden held up his hand. "We'll get to that, but I need to finish my story, because I *am* finishing what *I* came out here for." I didn't miss the hardening in his eyes. "As I was saying, I'm a struggling man, but I needed Jenellis to notice me. I met this woman here a long time ago and was wowed, and I knew that to ever have a chance with her I needed to up my game. But I've learned that beauty and money mean nothing. See, I do my research." He turned to look Jenellis straight in the eye. "And I dig all through the past. There's been a stream of men with money you've met, married, and murdered. Fortunately, I'm not going to be one of them. I know who you are, Jenellis. Exactly who you are."

The files I'd found in the office must have been his, I realized.

Jenellis chuckled. "You're so smart, huh?" She kept smiling. "You think all I've been after is money? Let me explain something to you. The first man I married terrorized me. He beat me and I suffered every single day I was with him. I decided that I wasn't going to take it from him or anyone else and that changed the whole purpose of my life. As far as me having his money—he owed me for what he did to me and my girls. And as far as murder? That's something you're going to have to prove."

"I don't have to prove anything. From what I understand, your own daughter is ready to rat you out. It's a shame she has to be hidden from you, her own mother."

I was taking notes as their conversation bounced back and forth. I also was creeping unnoticed closer to the door. David was in my way, but he appeared to be too engrossed in the heated dialogue to really pay me any mind.

"There is absolutely no way that I would ever hurt either of my daughters." Jenellis spoke evenly, pointedly to Brayden.

"And yet, one is already dead. Shot to death two months ago, burned beyond recognition. And the other has been in hiding, staging her own kidnapping just to stay out of your view."

"If that is what you want to believe, I can't help you. I'm sorry it's come to this. I really liked you, but I can't let you hurt me or my daughters. And I liked you too, David." She smiled sadly at the younger man.

She'd said "daughters." I did not miss that. *Impossible*. The other one was dead, right? I wanted something to make sense. I wanted to get out of there.

Before anyone could say another word or move, both men suddenly dropped lifeless to the floor and I screamed.

"What . . . what happened?" I ducked, I ran, I kept screaming.

"Oh, hush, Ms. St. James." Jenellis rolled her eyes. "They'll be okay. Just a little tranquilized until we decide what to do with them."

"We?" I gasped, still trying to understand how Jenellis had even shot them. Her hands were empty.

"Don't be silly. You would never last as my partner. Would she?"

"Never." A voice came from behind me.

Silver.

A sophisticated-looking tranquilizer gun hung from her right hand.

"I . . . I don't understand." I tried to speak quickly because I didn't think a pair of scissors was any match for that thing in Silver's hand, and I didn't know if they had yet decided on a plan for me.

"That fool thought I was an idiot. I figured out his game a long time ago. I only wanted to see how much he *thought* he knew, and he just told me. I do actually like him, but, unfortunately, he is messing with my mission."

"Mission?"

"Ms. St. James, you and I really are on the same side. We just go about getting results in two very different ways. See, all Brayden saw was that the men I've been with are wealthy; what he did not realize is that they all—all of them—had a history of abusing women. After my experience with Sheldon, I decided to do something about it. Whereas you advocate talking it through and 'therapitizing' these creatures, if that's even a word, I just get straight to the point. I make sure these dirt bags know what it means to suffer, that they know what it means to be at the painful mercy of someone bigger and stronger than them."

"But only rich dirt bags, right?"

"Hey, teaching these bastards a lesson isn't free. And the way I see it, those pigs didn't deserve their wealth. For what I've been through, I deserve every last penny they have."

"You and you alone. You have become the representative and the sole compensated victim of abused women everywhere."

"If I'm the one brave enough to step up, why shouldn't I be the one to live it up? Come on, sister, I'm sure that, as a therapist, you see firsthand the hurt, the pain, the suffering that so many women endure because of domestic abuse. Am I really wrong for what I do?"

"Yes, I do see the hurt, the pain, and the suffering and I recognize the devastation abuse of any nature can cause." I glanced over at Silver, who quickly looked away. "But there are ways to address it that bring healing and real help, and not simply revenge. Think about it, Ms. Walker, we're standing here with two men down—two innocent men, mind you—and a trail of other bodies over the past, what, ten years? And are you really healed and whole?"

"I'm winning."

"So, basically, you're admitting to murder and calling yourself righteous?" Even as I asked her, RiChard flashed through my mind. The social revolutionary who accepted any cost for the sake of freedom as he defined it.

Roman.

He was still out there and I was still here.

God, don't let my son be the ultimate cost for RiChard's self-directed quest for justice and my willingness not to question him. There were principles, spiritual and otherwise, that were surfacing in my well of thoughts and feelings, but I did not have time to draw them up, to examine them.

I just needed to get out of there.

Alive.

As if reading my mind, Jenellis gave me a large smile. "You really are a nice person. I am so sorry that you had to get in the middle of this. I must admit, I guess there is some value in therapy. Now that I've gotten all this out, I do feel better about myself. Silver, can you please see Ms. St. James out while I tend to these two? The tranquilizer should be wearing off soon, and I'm still deciding how to end this painlessly for both of them after I find out the last thing I need to know."

Silver immediately pointed the tranquilizer gun at me. "Let's go." When I didn't immediately move, she added, "You can walk out or I can drag you out. Your choice. Let's go."

The scissors in my waistband would do me no good if I was sedated, I decided. I needed the right moment to move, and this wasn't it; though I was not sure what that moment would be—or even what I would do if and when the moment came.

Survive, I reminded myself. *For the sake of my son,* I convinced myself, trying to brace for possible action that would involve stepping out way beyond anything I'd ever come close to doing.

Chapter 41

I shook as I walked ahead of her, the tranquilizer gun brushing my ear.

"What else does your mother need to know? I might be able to help." I was reaching for anything at this point that could prolong my survival.

"To the car," she demanded, nudging me toward an old, battered Buick.

"Whose car is this?" I asked.

"Detective Fields," she answered as we both crunched through the gravel lot.

"Detective Fields?" I felt hope rise. "Where is he?" And then everything in me collapsed. The window. The back seat. I could see his lifeless body.

"He's sedated?" I asked, hopeful.

"I don't know." Silver's voice was barely above a whisper. "I shot him twice with the tranquilizer gun and it was too much. He hasn't woken up yet and I haven't touched him."

I realized in that moment that she was shaking as much as I was.

But her nerves weren't stopping her from action.

"Hands," she demanded. When I hesitated, she pushed the tip of the tranquilizer gun to my neck. There was nothing I would be able to do unconscious— or worse. I looked over at the detective crumpled in the back seat, hoping, praying that the man was okay. I held out my hands and she put handcuffs around them, led me to the back seat, pushed me down next to the unmoving detective. The scissors fell to the floor of the car. She picked them up, looked at me, and threw them as far away as she could.

No! I wanted to scream, watching the shears, my sole escape plan, go sailing through the wind. She then got out a second pair of cuffs and wrapped them around my ankles.

"You don't have to do this, Silver. I need to get to my son, please! He's missing and I cannot be any later in my search to find him!"

"It's too late for me." She used the seat belts to secure me. "I tried to get away from her, my mother, but she found me anyway. She was the one who had Ms. Mona's house firebombed to get me out of there. Paid off one of the dope boys on her street to do it. Could have killed that poor, sweet old lady. And David, too, even though he apparently was helping my mother this whole time. See what I'm working with here?"

She shook her head, quivering all over. "And that office building where I was hiding? She came up to the security camera late last night and smiled in it. Smiled in it, 'cause she knew I was watching those monitors in the janitor's closet. Smiled and then walked away. I can't hide from her, so I've got no choice but to join her once again."

I made a quick decision to go into therapy mode. Maybe if I encouraged her to talk and showed her compassion, she would have compassion on me. "How did she find you?"

"By following you." She started the car and slammed down on the accelerator. We began moving down a long driveway.

"I am so sorry." So much for showing compassion. The girl probably hated my presence in her life.

"It's not your fault. If it wasn't you, she would have found another way. But you're good at what you do. You're brave. You get answers. That's why they picked you."

I raised an eyebrow and she noticed.

"I thought it was a random Google search that brought us all together?" Google was how I'd been getting my directions lately, so why wouldn't I have believed otherwise?

"After what you did a couple of years ago, not giving up until you found out whether there really was a little girl named Hope? You're a legend in your field. You came recommended to them, my mother and Brayden, though they had different reasons for coming to you."

I had no idea that people knew about my adventures from two years ago and were talking about it now—enough that Jenellis and Brayden landed on my doorstep. I was not sure whether to feel honored or petrified, scared that other people would start coming to me for help beyond what I was really there to do—assuming I even survived this horror.

Survive!

It wasn't an option.

It made sense in a way now, that Jenellis had privately approached me about finding out Brayden's relationship background. She thought I would be willing to dig.

But I only dug for answers when I really needed them.

I'd been doing my best not to look at the man crumpled over next to me. It was all too disturbing. I had no idea what I was supposed to do. I did not know what Silver's intents for me were, if she was even telling a lick of truth. I was surprised that I even had sane thoughts still floating in my head, questions that were keeping me going; but I knew that survival instincts will kick in when needed. When this entire nightmare was over and both my son and I were back home, I'd have time to address the trauma of the past few days. Shoot, I was going to need a therapist myself.

"Silver, how do you know all this?"

She looked at me through the rearview mirror, and lowered her voice even more. "Brayden. He was trying to help me—me and my sister. He was the one who got the detective involved. He agreed to hide us, help us get new identities eventually if we helped bring down my mom. It's a hard thing to do, but she needs to be stopped for what she is doing to everyone, for how she is trying to control us, what she was making my sister and me do to help her, and we both obeyed out of fear for our own lives. You haven't seen my mom in action." She looked at me in the rearview mirror. "She's ruthless."

"Your sister, Contessa." I spoke quickly, a revelation coming to me. "Also known as Gold. She was killed a couple of months ago, supposedly, but it was a front, right? She really wasn't murdered, but your mom needed to think she was dead. And you were supposed to be kidnapped earlier this week so you could have an exit, and escape from her, but the plan fell apart when Gold, and not you, was accidentally targeted for the fake kidnapping."

Silver slammed on the brakes. All that was around us were trees and more trees. *Where in the world are we?*

"How did you know my sister was still alive?" She turned to face me. Anger, sorrow, and fear were all peeking through in her skillfully crafted facial features.

"The butterfly tattoo," I asserted. "I pulled up the surveillance video that the news was showing of her being pushed into a car. I saw the tattoo on her neck when I zoomed in on a still shot."

Silver closed her eyes and shook her head. "My sister and that tattoo. I told her when she got it right after her fake killing that it would do more harm than good, but she insisted on doing it anyway to celebrate her transformation."

"Transforming to a new life away from your mom?"

"Not only in that way. My sister was like you, talking about faith and God and how she believed that despite our pasts and our mother and her men, that she could have a new life and be free just by believing. To her, the butterfly was a symbol of her personal change. She called herself a new creation in Christ and was trying to get me to buy into it. She gave me that necklace I gave you, and then she held on to the other half of the broken butterfly on her own chain, saying that once I was on the other side of freedom with her, we would be whole together, like the charm. But I told you how I feel about God and all that, and look at what's happened now. What's changed? Ain't nothing new."

"Faith is believing even when you can't see it, otherwise it wouldn't be called faith." I exhaled, trying to absorb my own words. "Where is Contessa now?"

"That's the million dollar question. The police and the media put it out there that it was me who was being looked for to try to keep my mother off her trail, but nobody really seems to know where Contessa is."

"Who arranged everything?"

"Brayden and David, but they claim that they don't know what happened."

"You think your mother was a step ahead of everyone and did something to her?"

"No. That's why you're still alive. She thinks you can somehow help find her."

Things make more sense now, I considered. Brayden came here looking for Silver and Jenellis came here looking for Gold. David had been working as a secret bridge between both of them, for some reason, and everyone thought I had answers to everything. And Silver, for her part, was just doing what she thought she needed to do to survive it all.

Survive!

I thought about what Silver had said. I thought about Brayden, David, Jenellis, the events of the past few days . . .

"Wait a minute, that house that was firebombed, Ms. Mona's, she was David's grandmother, right?"

"Yes, why?"

"Is Ms. Mona's name really Ramona?"

"I . . . I think so, why are you asking?"

I remembered the death notice of Sheldon Long; his parents were listed as Ramona K. M. Gilbert and Sydney Long. Perhaps the M in Ramona's name was an abbreviation for her maiden name or a previously married name of . . . Moore, which was Brayden's last name. It was a long shot, I knew, but I was desperate. I needed something to add up.

I shared my observations about the death notice with Silver. "Also," I continued, "when I first met your mother, she said that she and Brayden had three children between the two of them. You and Contessa account for two; do you know who Brayden's child is?"

"We never met him. Brayden said his son was a freshman at Yale, studying pre-med."

"But now we know he was lying about himself, so he probably was lying about his son too. What is David's last name?" My brain was trying to calculate all this information, trying to figure out what it all equaled.

"Forbes? Fordham? Something like that," Silver responded. "He told me once he was named after his mother, but, apparently, there's a lot he didn't tell me. Wait a minute, are you thinking that—"

"When did David start hanging around the club where you and your sister were working?"

"Just in the past few months. He said he'd recently moved from his father's house in Shepherd Hills to help take care of his grandmother. "

Shepherd Hills! She had not been in the room when Brayden said that was where he was from.

"Right before your mom met Brayden."

Maybe what I was thinking really wasn't a long shot. It would definitely offer an explanation as to why Brayden had such a high interest in Jenellis's past. If what I was thinking was correct, that meant David was Brayden's son. And that would make Sheldon, Jenellis's first husband, Brayden's half brother.

"I see where you're going with this, and I guess it could be true." Silver was quickly coming to the same conclusion. "We'd never met Sheldon's family back when my mom was married to him. In fact, I remember she only knew his parents' names to put in the obituary from some legal documents she'd found back then. Apparently, there were clashes over him having money and not sharing."

"More reason why Brayden would want to track down and research who had his late brother's wealth. Plus, it would make sense for him to become a contestant on *The Soul Mate Show* if he knew that the grand prize was a date to La Chambre Rouge, the place his late brother had invested in and Jenellis had ties to it. He must have wanted to have a reason to do his own snooping here."

"And my mother knew that he was going to be a contestant because of the deal they have with this place, and she got me on the show to choose Brayden, not knowing that I had already been talking to him." She paused for a moment. "What you're saying explains why he would want to marry her. He was probably planning to do the same thing to her that she's done to all the men she married. Get the ring on her finger, and then get her six feet under. Only this time, he would be the beneficiary."

"But you and Contessa? Wouldn't you be the beneficiaries if something happened to your mom?"

"I've thought about that. I think that's why Brayden reached out to us and wanted us under the care of that detective, so that if and when my mom was out the picture, he would still have tabs on our whereabouts to finish carrying out his plans, and look like he was on the right side of the law so he would never be suspected of wrong-doing."

"But it seems like no one even knows where your sister is."

She fell quiet and began driving again. We were turning off the main driveway, but the street we were on didn't look much different. More trees. No other cars.

"My mother realized what Brayden was up to. She called me an hour ago to say she found files of newspaper articles he'd been collecting. She knows and he knows and now everybody knows. I don't think there was any intent for anyone to leave that room today. That's why I need to find my sister with nobody on my tail. I don't trust anyone. Not even my mother. Especially my mother. I need to find my sister before she does; that's why I need to hurry up with you so I can get back there quickly. Nobody can protect us from our mother. Not the detective, not Brayden, not you."

Hurry up with me? What is she planning? My mind was working at full speed.

"Silver, I need you to trust me. I need you to *help* me. I need to get back to finding my son." I had to tell her. I had to hope that I could appeal to her caring side, despite her life of no one truly caring for her. "My son . . . he might be with a pr . . . pre . . ." *Predator*. I could not even get out the evil word. "Please." I had no idea what time it was, where I was. All I knew was that I had nothing to do with any of Jenellis's and Brayden's dysfunction or foolishness. It was unfair, and I wanted out. "Where are we going?" I managed to get out.

Silver paused a long moment before answering. "My mother is expecting me to return without you. And you know too much. I'm so sorry, Ms. St. James. Like I said, it's too late for me and nobody can protect me and my sister from our mother. She's so intent on covering her tracks, my sister and I know she would be done with us in a second if we didn't go along with her plans. That's why I don't have a choice. Like I said, I'm sorry." She made a sudden right turn onto a dirt road and the car began bumping and jostling as she increased the speed.

"You always have choices. Everyone has choices." I thought about my situation and thought about hers. "Look, you asked me last time I saw you why God let so many bad things happen to you over your life. I don't have the answers, but I do know that God lets people have choices, and too many people choose wrongly. Sin is the issue, and God loves us so much, that's why he sent His Son to address sin, because He knows how much sin hurts us. He gave us freewill, and provided a solution for when our wills don't match His."

The car continued bumping along the dirt road and Silver said nothing.

"God gave us all choices," I continued, desperately praying for the right words to say, "and I imagine that it hurts His heart to see us hurt each other. But when we choose to seek Him, to love, to forgive, to do good—and it takes faith to do all these things—then all of us have a chance to live whole lives. Maybe the situations that hurt us the most are the perfect situations that make us seek God the most. Sometimes things happen that *force* us to seek Him, that force us to learn a new fact or dimension about Him, about His ability to love and care for us, that we would not have known otherwise."

I didn't know if Silver was listening to a word I was saying, but I needed my own sermon right now.

Jesus, I am seeking you, your protection, your help. I am not afraid because I trust you. Mother Spriggs said not to lose my faith. A little bit of faith can move mountains. This here is a mountain with a valley of the shadow of death beside it. I will not be afraid because you are with me and you love me and perfect love casts out fear. The opposite of fear is power, love, and a sound mind. Power. Love. Sound mind.

"You're saying that I need to help you?" Silver sounded irritated, seeming to ignore everything else I had said. "I need help finding my sister!"

Peace. Love. Sound mind. I took a deep breath, letting those words fill me, calm me. *Sound mind. Think, Sienna.*

She was pulling to a stop. We were deep in the woods. There were overgrown trees and shrubs, tall grasses.

And what looked like a deep, bubbling creek.

"I'm sorry, Ms. St. James." Silver cut the motor, got out of the car, and opened my door. She looked at the detective, still slumped over in the space and floor next to me. Then her attention turned back to me. "This will be painless, like you're going to sleep. You won't even feel yourself drowning." She looked over at the creek, then down at the tranquilizer gun, which was back in her hand.

Sound mind, Sienna, think.

"It's not too late for you, Silver."

She closed her eyes, raised the tranquilizer, aimed.

Sound mind, Sienna, think.

"Wait!" I shouted as a thought came to mind, clear as day. "I can help you! I think I know where your sister is! The necklace, Silver!"

The tranquilizer gun was still raised, but her hands were shaking. "What are you talking about?"

"Back there, when I was with your mother and them, David held up a necklace with a broken butterfly. I had assumed that it was the one you gave me and that he had gotten it out of my car when he took it, but that's impossible," I spoke quickly, in one breath. "I put the necklace you gave me in my purse, dropped it down right next to the lion's head ring, which means nothing to you, but your necklace is in my purse, and my purse is at home! I left my purse in the foyer at my house yesterday morning." I recalled how I had not been able to charge my phone, get gas, or do anything else because my purse was home. "You said your sister gave you the necklace and kept the other half of the butterfly on a chain of her own, so the one David has—"

"Is hers," she interrupted, the gun slowly going down. "But that doesn't tell me where she is." She stared at me intensely, raising the gun again.

"I overheard a phone conversation between them." I recalled the two men talking on the phone. *She's still on the property. There's no way she's getting away, even if she broke free.* I'd assumed they were talking about me, but what if . . . "Silver," I spoke quickly, "I honestly believe that your sister is somewhere at La Chambre Rouge. Find my car. David had it last and he was the one with her necklace. Maybe she's in there. Maybe she broke free like me. We need to go back up the hill to find her. Find my car! We have to hurry though, and *get back up that hill!"*

Silver looked at me, looked at the tranquilizer still in her hands, the detective, the creek. Then she ran around the car, jumped back in, and pressed the gas like her sister's life depended on it.

It probably did—if it wasn't already too late.

I exhaled, grateful for at least a few more moments of living. I had no idea what was happening at the top of the hill. I thought of the chef lying dead on the kitchen floor and the other two men who Jenellis was deciding on how to finish off.

But going up that hill was the only way both Silver and I could literally continue with our lives. Without a hill, without a mountain to move, faith would not have a chance to shine. I thought about being afraid, but I decided that wasn't an option. At that moment, fear didn't stand a chance against me; my faith was ready to move mountains.

We were back at the main property in less than three minutes. Silver sped up the driveway, skidded on the gravel, and jumped out the car before it fully came to a stop, running back toward the restaurant, the tranquilizer still in her hand. The motor was still running, the keys in the ignition; a groan sounded from the floor.

A groan sounded from the floor!

"Detective Fields!" I yelled. "Detective Fields, wake up, wake up!" I remembered how woozy and off-centered I'd felt when I came out of sedation. It was going to take awhile for him to come fully to his senses.

But we did not have that kind of time.

"Please, it's Sienna St. James. We're in danger. Please, please wake up," I hollered and carried on.

Agonizing seconds passed by, but within moments the older gentleman slowly came to attention, sat up, stared at me, confused.

"The key, the keys to the cuffs," I shouted, shaking the links that had my feet and hands bound. I hoped the cuffs had been his, that Silver had taken them off his person once he was unconscious.

I was right.

With much and continued coaxing, the detective slowly pulled some keys out of the inside of his coat pocket and rattled them, as if trying to still wake himself up. He finally freed my hands. I snatched the key from him and freed my ankles and let loose the seat belts.

"Everyone in there is trying to kill each other," I gave as an explanation as I opened the car door, ran to the driver's seat. "I've got to get back to finding my son." I put the car in drive, readied myself to slam down on the accelerator, much harder than Silver had done.

"Wait!" Detective Fields yelled clearly. He got out of the car. "Pop the trunk."

I obeyed and grew wide-eyed at the assortment of rifles, shotguns, and other weaponry he pulled out of it, strapped on, and clicked together.

He was a one-man SWAT team.

Good thing Silver hadn't rummaged through his trunk or nobody would have ever had a chance to make it out alive, I was sure of it.

Last thing he did was pull out an earpiece, an old-fashioned walkie-talkie, and a cigarette. "Get out of here," he shouted. "I'll be in touch to get the background details, but for now, go somewhere safe. I've got it from here."

Didn't have to tell me twice and I didn't have time to stay for any debriefing.

I was halfway down the hill when I heard the first siren, and was turning back onto the main road when an army of flashing lights, emergency vehicles, and helicopters whizzed by me.

I had no idea where I was, but saw a sign indicating that Interstate 95 was five miles ahead.

I had done all I could for Silver, Jenellis, Brayden, and their disasters. Now I was heading home to mine.

Chapter 42

The car dashboard said 12:11 p.m. It had been nearly twelve hours since I'd left Mother Sprigg's home—the longest morning of my life. I followed I-95 to 695 to Route 40 to Rossville Boulevard, a total of an hour-and-fifteen-minute trip. Though I had said I would not go back into my house without my son, I needed my charger. I needed my purse. My purse held the lifelines to the rest of my world.

When I pulled onto my street, all manner of television trucks and cameras were flowing out of my cul-de-sac. I had to park Detective Fields's car a block away and start walking. I remembered that I had told Laz to get Leon to let him in so that he could tell Roman's story.

I guessed he had been successful. I hurried my pace. Anxious, desperate, yearning for an update, for good news.

I was three houses away when a shout rang out. "There she is!"

The prayer party had moved to my residence, I realized, as my mother, Yvette, Skee-Gee, and several church members came bursting out of my front door.

"Oh, my God, girl!" Yvette marched up to me. "Where on earth have you been? This ain't the time for you to go rogue, trying to do your own thing without telling us a single word of where you are!" She looked ready to slap me right across the face.

I looked at her, too tired, exhausted, and traumatized to even begin explaining to her the horror I'd survived. Where would I even begin or end?

Besides, only one thought, one name, one question filled my mind.

"Roman." I needed to know something, anything. No, not just anything. I needed to know that he was okay, that he was at home or on his way home right now!

Yvette took my hand, rubbed it with both of hers, sighed, and shook her head. "There is some news."

"What is it? Tell me now!" I tried to read her face, but before she could open her mouth again, Leon came jogging down the steps.

"Sienna." He smiled, an encouraging sign, as he wrapped long, warm arms around me. "I can only imagine where you've been, how you've felt over the past twenty-four hours. I'm just glad to see you."

And then he stepped back, the smile gone. "Look, I don't know how much Yvette has told you—"

"Nothing," I said, breathless.

"Well, we found out who this Croix is."

My chest suddenly felt like a thousand horses were stampeding across it. He paused again and both he and Yvette looked at each other. She nodded her head, encouraging him to continue.

"His last name is St. James."

Chapter 43

I was glad that my mother forced me to eat before I left for the airport. She'd prepared a simple meal—chili, cornbread, garden salad—and had not left me alone until I had cleared my bowl, finished my plate, sopped up every crumb. Good thing I listened to her. I had no idea when I'd be able to eat again.

My nerves.

"We'll be landing soon." Laz spoke in a hushed voice, as if a single wrong word would make me crumble. I almost laughed. All I had been through this week? All that I had faced? In the past few hours alone, I had been bound up, tied down, threatened, seen a dead man, nearly tranquilized and thrown in a creek to drown. If I could go through all that and not go crazy, then surely I could get off this plane and keep my composure.

I realized that I was laughing out loud.

Maybe I was a little off.

"Ladies and gentlemen, we are beginning our final descent into the San Diego area." The pilot came on the loud speaker, making this journey, this destination real. I was on another red-eye flight to California; the last one I'd taken had been when Roman was an infant and I was trying to track down RiChard.

Same story. Different year. Had I really been on the same hamster's wheel? Bubbles began filling my stomach and I was afraid of what might come out of me.

"It's seventy degrees and sunny. Please keep off all electrical devices until we have arrived at the gate. We will be at the gate in twenty minutes."

I'd turned my cell phone off for the entire flight, but I did not need it on to remember the single text that had been waiting for me the moment I'd plugged it up back home.

Roman.

> I know you're mad at me, Mom. I'm sorry for hurting you. I love you, and I am ready to come home.

He'd apparently sent it after seeing himself on TV, around the same time that Jenellis had snatched me from the gas station. That boy didn't realize he'd almost lost his mother while I was worried about losing him.

Croix St. James.

I shut my eyes, willed my nerves to calm down, prayed that God would help me in time to forgive.

That would be another story.

For today, I was reuniting with my son, who had plenty of reasons to be ready to come home.

Taking no chances, I was flying out to meet him, to escort him myself from San Diego back to Baltimore. Laz, wanting to have the exclusive report of our reunion to air on TV, flew with me. He was giddy with excitement, buzzed about his extended report about Roman's disappearance getting airtime on national cable networks. With access to Roman's room, he'd been able to offer a compelling portrait of a young man on a quest to find his father—complete with a photo of the lion's head ring—and then give information about teens and Internet safety.

This was a career-changing moment for him.

And a life-changing moment for me.

I braced myself for the landing, still not believing the secrets my self-proclaimed "warrior prince" son had uncovered.

They were waiting at the gate, specially escorted by TSA officers through the terminal to meet us as we got off the plane. I had no intentions of going anywhere but back on a plane to home.

Laz stuck to his part of the deal, making sure that only Roman and I made it in his camera shot. The others I would address only after I held my son.

"Mom." Roman stood still as I approached him, braced himself as I reached up to hug him.

I guess he was expecting to be choked instead of embraced. I didn't blame him for his initial hesitation.

There were a million and one things I wanted to say to my son, and I would say them eventually; but for the moment, I just wanted to hold him, praise God that he was okay.

I looked up into his face, saw the tears in his eyes, understood why he was crying.

Devastation.

We both felt it.

"Okay, cut the camera." I turned to Laz. He immediately complied. He would have to get his exclusive later.

I turned to the small crowd of people who had accompanied Roman to the airport, and immediately identified Croix.

He was nearly sixteen himself, a few months younger than Roman. Same height, same build.

Same look of hurt, betrayal, in his eyes.

He could have been Roman's twin, except that he was several shades darker, a beautiful, rich and clear shade of pure cocoa. Plus, he wore glasses.

"Hello, Sienna." Croix's mother stepped forward to greet me, her beauty, poise, and grace the same as it was when I first met her over a decade and a half ago.

"Hi, Mbali." I tried to smile and nod at her, at Croix, at the twelve-year-old girl and twin five-year-old boys standing beside her. All four children were beautiful blends of Zulu, the Caribbean, and Italy—the cultures and countries that made up their DNAs.

The twelve-year-old had RiChard's green eyes.

I turned away, grabbed Roman's hand, deciding that I did not want to hear her story after all. But she followed me.

"Sienna." Her accent made my name sound exotic. "Please let me explain." She touched my shoulder. I tightened under her touch, but turned around to face her. "I never loved Kisu." Her eyes brimmed with tears. "My father only wanted me to marry him because it would have helped my family. RiChard told me that it was unjust the way I was being treated, and he promised he would help me. I did not know until years later that he had faked Kisu's death. He had convinced Kisu to go along with his plot, telling him our village would be more willing to fight for the causes in which he and Kisu believed if they had a martyr. Kisu did not know until years later that RiChard and I had wed."

"You married him?" *But he was married to me!* I wanted to scream, but I knew there was no big database somewhere that flagged marriage license requests.

"We married in my village," she explained.

There definitely wasn't an international database to keep track of polygamy, I knew. I tried to breathe.

Roman squeezed my hand.

"When you left KwaZulu-Natal back then," she continued, "he told me that you had left him permanently. I believed him. He said he would return to the States and build a home for me to come to and I could resume my studies. Against my father's wishes, I left my home, and I came here. I did not know you were still married. I did not know he had given you a son. I am so sorry." She glanced at Roman. "RiChard lied to all of us."

"So his trips over all these years?" My voice stumbled.

"What trips?" Mbali looked confused. "I do not know of what trips you are talking."

"The gifts?" I whispered.

She shook her head. "I don't know what gifts you are talking about."

"RiChard used to send Roman and me gifts, hand-made crafts from all over the world. He said he got them during his travels . . ." I let go of Roman's hand, collapsed into an airport seat next to me, winded.

Mbali shrugged her shoulders. "I do not know of these travels. He opened an art and gift shop right here in San Diego featuring imports from all over the globe. He obtained his doctorate in world history and culture, and used to give lectures on the most unique of his merchandise. He probably was sending you the overstock."

I was shaking. Roman wrapped his arm around me.

"The lion's head ring." I could not stop shivering. "That was not overstock. That was real. I was there when Kisu's father gave it to him."

"Yes, the ring." Mbali's face darkened. "I'd forgotten all about it until I found it while cleaning one day. That was the cause of our divorce. I came across the ring wrapped up with all these letters to RiChard from Kisu. I could tell from the content of his letters that RiChard was giving him stories about our progress in our village to make it seem as though Kisu's sacrifice had not been in vain. I approached RiChard about it, and he finally told me the truth about Kisu—but not about you."

"Divorce?" The only word I heard.

"Yes, that was three years ago. He promised that he would still take care of me and the children, but he left on the morning of March third that year with nothing but his wallet and his bag lunch and we never heard from or saw him again."

"That was my thirteenth birthday," Roman said softly, "the last time he contacted us, when he called me a warrior."

"I waited a year to see if he would return," Mbali continued, "if he would keep his promise of still helping to provide for our four children, and when he didn't I sold all he had left behind, including the ring, in a divorce estate sale to settle all our debts and bills."

"So . . ." I shook my head, still trying to find a way to absorb the shock. "RiChard's not dead?"

"Maybe he is, maybe he isn't. I don't know where he is, and I don't care." Mbali spoke flatly. "I have no room or time in my life or my heart for a liar."

The five-year-olds were getting restless. Our flight back to Baltimore was boarding. She saw me check the time.

"We must stay in touch, Sienna. Our sons are brothers. All my children are Roman's blood, and therefore yours as well."

Red is the color of love and blood. I thought of the Chinese sword that had been framed in Jenellis's living room, understood why she would want to use it, keep it.

Love and blood.

I don't remember how the conversation with Mbali ended. I don't remember getting on the plane. I can't recall the flight back home. Laz may have said something. Roman may have grabbed hold of my hand again. I don't remember landing or how I got back to my townhome.

What I do remember is waking up in my own bed, walking to my kitchen, and seeing my son chomping down an entire box of cold cereal poured into a mixing bowl.

It was a dream come true and a nightmare from hell all at once.

Chapter 44

Sunday dinner.

My mother insisted that we have a good old-fashioned soul food spread. Barbecued ribs. Fried chicken. Collard greens with smoked turkey. Corn on the cob. Red potato salad. Brown sugar baked beans.

I sat on a loveseat in front of a muted television, watching my mother and sister work together in my kitchen, listened to them argue over my late grandmother's yeast rolls recipe. Roman and Skee-Gee were in my son's bedroom heavily debating video game scores, my other nieces and nephews engaged in a pillow fight in the guest room. My father was stretched out in my recliner, struggling to sleep, throwing out random threats to everyone who was keeping him up.

So much fighting and so much love in my full little home.

"Ah, here it comes now." Laz was sitting next to me, the remote in his hand as he unmuted the follow-up story he'd taped of Roman and me walking into our front door and into the arms and kisses of our family and friends. Laz's smile stretched farther as he pulled up the YouTube Web site on my laptop.

"Over 123,000 hits and counting." He grinned at me as he watched the segment again on the Internet video site.

I'd had enough of the news. Had already watched it earlier when the incident at La Chambre Rouge was detailed. Only one fatality—an unfortunate chef who came early to prepare for a "fantasy date that didn't happen" and was in the wrong place at the wrong time. I closed my eyes, and winced at the horrid memory of the man lying there on the kitchen floor . . .

The news had gone on to detail that a Jenellis Walker, Brayden Moore, and David King all received minor injuries while resisting arrest. Apparently, and fortunately, Jenellis had not completed her plan with the men who regained consciousness sooner than expected and had closed in on her. The detective had come just in time. Jenellis, for her part, was being investigated for the mysterious trail of abuse, money, and death littered with the bodies of her former husbands and lovers.

Noticeably missing from the news reports were any mention of the twins, Anastasia and Contessa Simmons, or as they were better known, Silver and Gold. I figured it was safe to assume that they had probably accepted a deal to witness against the woman who had only added to their life of terror and they were now both living a hidden life of obscurity for their protection.

"You are a strong, amazing woman."

I did not realize that Laz was watching me as I sat on the sofa, dazed, numb, waiting for a sense of normalcy to return to my life.

"You are going to get through this, and you will be an even better, stronger person because of it. You and Roman will recover from RiChard."

RiChard.

The mere thought of that man's name had always brought a sting of pain. Now, a new sensation was trying to take root in me.

Bitterness.

Bitterness so sour, so strong I could taste it in my mouth, feel it in my breath, feel it snaking through my veins with every beat of my broken heart.

Not broken over him. Broken over the years of my life I had wasted believing him, believing in him.

A knock at the door forced me to move.

"I can get it," Laz offered.

I shook my head no as I stood and headed for the front door. I needed to get up, feel myself move. Begin steps toward healing.

Leon was at the door.

And he was not alone.

I looked at him, the young woman standing next to him, the baby in her arms. Up close and personal, she was more stunning than when I'd seen her in the diner booth with Leon. Hair, long and smooth like golden corn silk; a smile that looked like it belonged on a toothpaste commercial. I guess the baby carrier had been on the other side of her seat at the diner, out of my view.

Breathe, I told myself

It didn't work.

"Sienna." Leon gave a shaky smile. "I wanted to . . . There hasn't been a good time to talk."

I tried to speak, but could only sit down on the carpeted stairs beside me.

"This is, uh, Sha'mya. My niece."

"Your . . . what?"

"My niece," he repeated. "My little brother, you know the one who was gunned down years ago? The one I told you about who inspired me to start working for the PAL center? Well, this is his daughter. I lost contact with her when she was only, like, three months old, when her mother moved away to Houston. She found me just last month."

I tried to stand, felt my feet stumble, sat back down.

"Sha'mya, this is Sienna, my . . . well, a good friend of mine," he continued.

"Hi, Ms. St. James." She grinned. "I've heard so much about you, been watching your son's story on TV. I'm so glad he's okay."

"Thank you." I smiled, weakly, trying to figure out what else I had left in me to say. "Um, we're having dinner."

"Oh, look, a baby!" My mother screamed over me. I had not heard her come down the steps behind me. "Come here, young lady. Let me hold that beautiful child."

I had to stand up to get out of my mother's way. My mother embraced Sha'mya and the two began a spirited discussion of all things baby.

"We can't stay, Sienna," Leon said after smiling at them.

"You're leaving? Where are you off to?" I gave a light laugh, though my heart told me there was more to what he was saying.

"I've been trying to tell you, but too much has been going on." He smiled a warm smile. "You know my grandmother raised me. She and my brother were the only family I had and knew. Sha'mya, she has no one. Her mother passed away last year. No sisters, no brothers. I'm the only family *she* has." He bit his lip, looked down, then continued. "Sienna, you and your son have helped heal me, prepared me, over the past two years; gave me a place to be a man. I love you, both of you."

"I know. Thank you. I love you too."

My mother and Sha'mya were still laughing, talking, and sharing. The baby gurgled and cooed and reached out to touch the collage that hung in my foyer. The collage Laz had complimented me on during his first visit to my home, I recalled.

Leon and I stared at each other.

"I wanted to be so much more for you, to you," he whispered.

"You've been more than I even knew I needed. And, now I . . . We . . ." I tried to smile.

"My niece just enrolled in school. Houston Community College."

I nodded.

"She's had a rough life. This is major for her. She's got college and a new part-time job that took her despite her record." He nodded. "I want her to succeed. She's the only family I have left." There was a long pause. "I'm going back to Houston with her. For support. Help. 'Til she gets on her feet. Sha'mya is only nineteen, has a baby, and another child, a three-year-old she's trying to get out of foster care. I have to be there for my family, Sienna. My grandmother would expect that of me. My grandmother was there for me, and my brother."

"Yeah." I couldn't stop nodding. "I understand. We . . . I . . ."

"Of course Roman can call me anytime."

"Yes, yes. Of course."

I could hear my mother inviting Sha'mya to come upstairs, to eat, to at least fix a plate to take with her. They disappeared and I heard Yvette squealing over the baby.

"It's been good," Leon whispered. "It's been a good season for both of us."

"A season?" I took in a deep breath. "A season." I nodded, trying to be strong, feel strong.

He looked at me a few seconds more, and brushed away the single tear that I didn't realize was coming down my face. He cupped my cheek with his hand. Pulled me close to him.

His lips touched mine. Soft. Then certain. I held his hand against my cheek, not wanting him to go, to let go.

But he did.

He was on his way up the steps to grab a plate behind Sha'mya before I could even open my eyes.

Gone.

I could hear Laz laughing loudly at some sitcom rerun Roman had turned on. My mother joined in the laughter and Skee-Gee said something I could not make out. Everyone was laughing.

I was alone in the foyer.

Season. I let the word sink in.

We had grown, tremendously grown, over the past couple of years. All of us. My son was taller. My mother and sister were closer.

I had my answers.

And that was just the beginning.

I opened the front door, looked up at the sky where the sun was beginning another descent, the day coming to an end. A chilly breeze blew over me, sending goose bumps up and down my bare arms.

Season. Though the air was cool, I knew spring was right around the corner, a new time of planting.

I could not let seeds of hurt, pain, or bitterness find fertile soil in my soul.

I did not want that. I wanted to believe that I could fight it, that I could stand my ground against the numbing sorrow that threatened to overtake me. I felt it—anger—trying to burrow a home deep in me. I did not know if or how I could fight it.

"Jesus, help me."

The way I felt, I did not know if it was possible to ever fully let go of the hurt, to feel anything again.

To forgive.

The breeze outside my door grew stronger. I heard a flapping sound, looked down at one of the evergreen bushes that framed my entry.

An envelope peeked out.

I picked it up, flipped it over, wondered where it came from. There was no address, no words written across it. I opened it anyway.

Inside were two silver necklaces. They were joined by their charms, two butterfly halves that were each broken down the center. I put the two halves together, turned them over, read the back.

WITH FAITH ALL THINGS ARE POSSIBLE.

"Sienna!" my mother blasted from upstairs. I could tell from my father's heavy, plodding footsteps toward the dining room that grace was about to be said.

I looked at the chains in my hand, looked at the one empty corner of my collage, the corner that was supposed to represent me, the one place I'd never filled. I grabbed a push pin from a nearby drawer, centered it in the empty spot of my collage, and hung the chains off of it. I watched the broken butterfly flutter in the breeze that still wafted through my open door and I smiled.

"Mom?" Roman was standing on the steps.

"I'm coming."

He returned a smile before running back up the steps, trying to beat Skee-Gee to the buffet table.

I had not missed the sadness in his eyes.

We would be okay. I had to believe that. *With faith all things are possible,* I struggled to remember the inscription; struggled to believe it was true.

I exhaled and took one last look outside, examining the edges of some clouds that lingered in the now purple and blue evening sky. I closed my eyes, felt the chill of the mounting wind; inhaled it, the scent of both honeysuckle blossoms and dead leaves filling my nostrils.

Barren winter, the promise of spring. Intersecting. Competing.

Then I shut the door.

Reading Group Guide

Many themes emerge in Sienna St. James's story as she searches for her son, digs up answers about her estranged husband, and manages new clients whose interpersonal problems threaten her life and well-being. Consider some of these themes as you work through the following questions individually or with other readers.

1. **Trials and Tribulations:** When disclosing the abuse inflicted by her stepfather, Anastasia "Silver" Simmons asks, "If there really is a God, why did He let that monster destroy our lives?" "Why do bad things happen?" is a question that is often raised when disaster and hardship strike. What were Sienna's thoughts on this matter? What are yours? What role, if any, does God play in tragedy? What does God's Word (the Bible) say about suffering? Reflect on Romans 5:3–5 and search the scriptures for other passages that address suffering.

2. **Relationships:** Leon has been patiently giving Sienna time to seek closure from her past. How much time is needed to establish a relationship with someone who is recovering from emotional wounds and scars? Is an ultimatum ever justified? Laz appears to be a potential new love interest for Sienna. Of the two men, who would be a better match for her needs? Why? What qualities should a woman look for in a man? Does God's Word weigh in on this issue at all?

3. **Family:** Sienna describes her family as "screwed up." Describe her relationship with her mother,

father, sister, nephew, and son. How do these relationships impact her? Consider her emotions, decisions, and connections with others and how her family relationships impact these areas. What words would you use to describe your family relationships? How did your relationships get to where they are now? How have these relationships affected your emotions, decisions, and connections with others outside of your family circle?

4. **Church Members:** Sienna interacts with several members from her church throughout the story. Were these interactions largely positive or negative and how so? What role, if any, should church members play when someone is facing a crisis? What are your thoughts about Mother Spriggs's approach?

5. **Parenting:** Sienna often reflects on the sacrifices she has made to raise her son as a single mother. She has especially struggled to find a balance between her pain as an abandoned wife and the "worship" her son has for his father. What does she do well as a mother? What areas of parenting could she improve in, if any? How can she best address the absence of RiChard from Roman's life?

6. **Faith:** While talking to Silver, Sienna acknowledges within herself that she has been having her own "crises of faith." What does she mean by this? How can these "crises" be addressed? Faith is mentioned frequently throughout the story as the opposite of fear, and as a basis of love, power, and a strong mind. What are your thoughts about faith, what it means, and what it can do?

7. **Social Justice:** As a therapist and a social worker, Sienna has been trained to be an advocate for the vulnerable. RiChard appeared to be on a mission for those who were not enjoying full equal rights. Jenellis seeks revenge on abusers. What are your thoughts about their respective points of view, as well as their methods to address social ills? Is there such a thing as a just mission with unjust tactics and/or an unjust mission with just tactics? Explain.

8. **Fear:** What does Sienna fear most? Why? Does she overcome her fears? If so, how? If not, why not? What are your fears? Are you addressing them? How? Find and reflect on verses in the Bible that discuss the causes of and solutions to fear.

9. **Forgiveness:** What characters in the story are in need of forgiveness? Why and from whom? Are there any people in your life who are in need of forgiveness? Why and from whom? Is there anyone in your life whom you cannot forgive? Should you? Why or why not? What are the consequences of not forgiving and who does it affect? Is forgiveness always possible? Is revenge ever justified? Reflect on Psalms 37, Psalms 73, and Hebrews 12:12–15.

10. **Moving Forward:** What's next for Sienna? What should be her personal goals and why? What do you think her response would be to whatever future events you imagine for her? What do you see as the next major goals in your own life? What challenges do you face in meeting them? What is your timeline to achieve these goals? Are there verses in the Bible that inspire you as you think about your future?

Author Bio

Leslie J. Sherrod, a native of Baltimore, Maryland, is a wife, mother of three, and a licensed social worker. Her novels include *Losing Hope, Secret Place,* and *Like Sheep Gone Astray.* She has also contributed to the bestselling *A Cup of Comfort* devotional series and has a short story, "The Jericho Band" available exclusively on Amazon Kindle. Leslie received the SORMAG Readers Choice Award as Christian Author of the Year (2012).

UC HIS GLORY BOOK CLUB!
www.uchisglorybookclub.net

UC His Glory Book Club is the spirit-inspired brain-child of Joylynn Jossel-Ross, author and acquisitions Editor of Urban Christian, and Kendra Norman-Bellamy, author for Urban Christian. This is an online book club that hosts authors of Urban Christian. We welcome as members all men and women who have a passion for reading Christian-based fiction.

UC HIS GLORY BOOK CLUB pledges our commitment to provide support, positive feedback, encouragement, and a forum whereby members can openly discuss and review the literary works of Urban Christian authors.

There is no membership fee associated with UC His Glory Book Club; however, we do ask that you support the authors through purchasing, encouraging, providing book reviews, and of course, your prayers. We also ask that you respect our beliefs and follow the guidelines of the book club. We hope to receive your valuable input, opinions, and reviews that build up, rather than tear down our authors.

WHAT WE BELIEVE:

—We believe that Jesus is the Christ, Son of the Living God

—We believe the Bible is the true, living Word of God

—We believe all Urban Christian authors should use their God-given writing abilities to honor God and share the message of the written word God has given to each of them uniquely.

—We believe in supporting Urban Christian authors in their literary endeavors by reading, purchasing, and sharing their titles with our online community.

Urban Christian His Glory Book Club

—We believe that everything we do in our literary arena should be done in a manner that will lead to God being glorified and honored.

We look forward to the online fellowship with you. Please visit us often at www.uchisglorybookclub.net.

Many Blessing to You!
Shelia E. Lipsey,
President, UC His Glory Book Club

Notes

Notes

Notes